RAVEN

RAVEN

Charles Grant

TOR®

A TOM DOHERTY ASSOCIATES BOOK
NEW YORK

F
GRA

RAVEN

Copyright © 1993 by Charles Grant

This book is printed on acid-free paper.

A Tor Book
Published by Tom Doherty Associates, Inc.
175 Fifth Avenue
New York, N.Y. 10010

Tor® is a registered trademark of Tom Doherty Associates, Inc.

Library of Congress Cataloging-in-Publication Data

Grant, Charles L.
      Raven / Charles Grant.
          p.   cm.
      "A Tom Doherty Associates book."
      ISBN 0-312-85364-5
      I. Title.
PS3557.R265R38   1993
813'.54—dc20   92-43656
                                                  CIP

First edition: March 1993

Printed in the United States of America

0 9 8 7 6 5 4 3 2 1

For David, who knows bark, berries, and garrottes;
And Donna, who knows David;
But especially for Matt . . . sleep well.

RAVEN

Past sunset in early February, the worst time of the year. Too far from Christmas and too far from spring. Too cold. Too quiet. The light, never strong, too soon gone. Trees without leaves, scarred bark, empty nests, fading into the dark; weeds along the roadside, trembling stiffly, shedding burrs, flaring in passing headlights, and fading into the dark; house lights and streetlamps and traffic signals growing brighter, growing brittle, trying desperately, and failing, not to fade into the dark.

No snow.

No wind.

The landscape grey and dead.

While the county road from the interstate, two lanes and narrow, climbed the hills and crawled pocket valleys, skirted pastures and frozen ponds, barely straightening at each town several miles from its neighbor, barely lighted when the woodland became a mottled wall on either shoulder reflecting the headlamps in grey bars and splotches, or not at all; throwing shadows, pulling them back.

Throwing shadows.

Every so often, eyes gleaming above a branch, on a rock, in a ditch; every so often something dashing across the blacktop, too far away for a name.

Climbing higher, leveling off, to a stretch without a curve for nearly half a mile. In its center, on the north side, a streetlamp little more than a hooded bulb on a tall pole, woods behind it, blacktop below. There were other poles, three of them, but they were useless and dark.

One light, and no stars bright enough to do more than

prick weak holes in the night. Directly opposite, on the south side, a crescent cleared and sloping downward from the verge to a creek. A large painted sign on chains between two tall logs cemented into the ground; hooded bulbs again, three, and MACLAREN'S FOOD AND LODGING, facing east. In the middle of the crescent, a fine-gravel parking lot between the road and a log building one story high on a raised stone foundation, low peaked roof, four large and long windows, its entrance in the center off a two-step concrete stoop.

A light over the door.

Spotlights at the corners.

A man inside, looking out. From the road he was a shadow, he wasn't real, he wasn't there.

He grunted softly, shifted slightly, hands loose in his pockets, thumbs hanging out, head slightly bowed. Tall, but without the weight that would have made strangers nervous. Fair-haired and lots of it, some of it combed, most of it going its own way over his forehead and ears. His face marked the time he spent outdoors all year round, though the lines there and the shading weren't part of a betrayal— he was handsome now with the lines; when he was young he had been pretty. Hooded eyes, like the bulbs outside, seldom showing all their light.

Checkered flannel shirt, dark chinos, dark shoes that should have been boots, hiking or Western.

A slow inhalation, and a touch of a finger to the door's ripple-glass upper half. It nearly burned. He kept it there, just to be sure, then pulled his hand away and rubbed the finger thoughtfully against his side.

It was odd out there tonight. He didn't know why. Nothing was out of place that he could see, no one lurking with evil intent or otherwise, no strange cars drifting past. The round-rail fence that fronted the road hadn't changed, hadn't fallen; the faint lights he had put in the corners of the eaves hadn't burned out; no slavering, virgin-hunting monsters lurched out of the woods across the way. It was just . . . odd. Slightly uncomfortable, but without a warning. He raised an eyebrow at his imagination and grunted quietly to himself, mocking. This was a reaction people from the city usually had. He had been here over a decade and ought to know better.

The night was just the night.

A half smile and he put his back to the door, counted the customers in the room. Grunted again; there weren't many. Three high-back booths on either side of the entrance, eight square tables set for four and large enough for half a dozen; beyond the tables, broad wood railings extending chest-high from either wall, transformed into walls themselves by tall and spreading potted plants stretching upward, meeting closely spaced spider plants in clay pots hanging down from the ceiling. Bare hardwood floors comfortably chipped and worn. Lights hidden in the exposed rafters. In one of the booths, a couple holding hands, not eating very much; at one table, a family of four, and at another, a family of three. They smiled, they spoke softly.

He pulled at his nose, scratched a cheek. A curious thing—when there were people in here, the rough-pine walls and airy ceiling made the place seem much larger; when it was empty, it didn't look much bigger than a closet.

He walked around the display counter, set perpendicular to the entrance, and opened the cash drawer of the register atop it. The afternoon had been fair, the dinner hour not half bad. A handful of boisterous skiers escaping the city a day early, the usual late lunchers from Hunter Lake and Deerfield, a few tourists passing through on their way to Pennsylvania needing directions and a cup of coffee; nothing spectacular, nothing disastrous. Early February had always been a dead time here. The worst of winter's storms—if they came at all; not much in the way of casual weekend sightseers, and the locals hadn't quite been struck yet with cabin fever. Fair. What the hell. He would survive until spring the way he always did, making a decent profit, banking some, spending some, making sure the small restaurant didn't look as if it were on its last legs while, at the same time, keeping up repairs on the seven one-room cabins tucked in the trees and invisible from the road.

so what more do you want

He yawned, blinked rapidly in surprise and rubbed his eyes, told himself things would probably liven up later in the evening; after all, it was Friday night. A roll of his eyes to prove he didn't much believe it. The most he could reasonably expect this time of year would be a handful of people returning from the movies down in Sparta or Newton who might drop in for coffee or a drink; a few more late getting home from the city might drop in for a quick bite. And a drink.

February.

The dead time.

But it was the territory; it all goes with the territory. And it sure beat getting his face shot off by some drug dealer or crazy. Or lousy cigarette smuggler. A nod to himself, another yawn, and he made his way through the tables to the gap in the middle of the foliage wall. Beyond it, two wide steps down, was the lounge: curved leather-and-brass-stud booths along the left-hand wall, a handful of smaller tables in the center, the bar itself on the right.

The back wall was virtually all glass above darkwood wainscoting waist-high, the ground below and beyond cleared and carefully sloped some sixty feet down to the wide, shallow creek. A few years ago, tired of looking at his reflection in the glass, he had set a handful of low-wattage bulbs into the trees along the bank, three more into the base of the foundation, so that drinkers and diners could see the water, could see the woodland and hill, could once in a while see deer or possum, raccoons or just shadows. He had once considered building a deck off the lounge, a pleasant way to spend a spring or summer evening, filtered through the leaves and setting sun; then he considered the mosquitoes, the flies, the bees, the gnats, and changed his mind. Besides, with people out there, the animals wouldn't come; it had taken them forever to get used to the light.

A scraping of chairs behind him.

He turned and saw that the families were ready to leave. He gave them their checks, took their payment, held the door open and wished them a warm night. No waitress today. He could handle it himself and preferred it that way.

"Hey, Neil, got a minute?"

He looked to the occupied booth to the immediate left of the door. A young man, ruddy cheeks, freckled nose, a mass of dark hair and a suit not quite large enough for his shoulders, beckoned with a grin. The woman seated opposite him could have been his twin, except she wore a well-fitted ski sweater and jeans and her hair wasn't quite as long.

"He lied," she complained lightly as Neil walked over. A high voice. Not childlike, but child-soft. "He said I didn't have to get fancy or anything, then he went and wore his good clothes."

Neil stood there, waiting, patiently smiling. Ken Havvick and Trish Avery had been going together, off and on, for what he figured from the gossip had been most of their lives. He wondered how they stood it. The gossip also mentioned that Trish had been seeing other men as well, on the sly.

Havvick released his hold on her hand, exposing a small diamond ring on her finger. "We're gonna get married." A wider grin pulled thick lips away from his teeth.

Trish giggled.

Neil made a show of scanning the empty room before looking back and shaking his hand. "You know, Ken, I have always admired your dramatic sense of the romantic." He leaned over the table. "You mean to tell me you asked this gorgeous woman here—who could certainly do a hell of a lot better, if I do say so myself, but it's her life, I suppose—you asked her to marry you . . . in here?"

Havvick nodded, still grinning.

Neil sighed loudly toward the ceiling, leaned over, and kissed the young woman's cheek, smelled the peach scent of her hairspray, and wondered if the gossip was true. "Congratulations, Trish," he said warmly. "I'll bring some champagne over in a minute, but don't you dare give this creep any. He doesn't deserve it."

She kissed him back, giggling, covering her mouth with both hands.

Oh brother, he thought, shook his head and left them, reached the bar steps and glanced back.

They were holding hands again, beaming at each other, trying to climb into each other's eyes, and they cast no reflection in the drapery-framed window. There was nothing there but the night, and the faint glow of the blacktop road beyond the fence at the top of the gentle slope.

Startled, somewhat unnerved, he leaned sideways a little, a spider plant's tendril caressing his cheek before he brushed it away.

There it was.

It had been the angle.

Lustful ghosts set in ebony, a ghost room behind them.

The angle.

A silent suggestion that he'd been working too hard, and he hurried over to the bar. Behind it, the bartender, in ruffled white shirt and snug black trousers, leaned back against the bottle shelf, reading a book. She glanced up as he approached, staring at him as if he were a stranger, and an unwelcome one at that.

"Champagne," he said, dropping onto a leather stool, its curved back just high enough to keep him from toppling to the floor. "Havvick finally popped the question."

"You're kidding."

"Kissed the bride-to-be myself."

"Hell," she muttered, "you wouldn't be the first." The book dropped to the bar. "Jackass. All he wants to do is get laid for free."

"Hey, give the kid a break, Julia."

Her expression was doubtful, but she shrugged, *it's his stupid funeral,* blew a stray hair out of her eyes.

He acknowledged the unspoken apology with a wink, and allowed himself to watch her shirt, her trousers, stretch and tighten as she reached under the bar for a chilled bottle and glasses. Maybe the cabins hadn't been such a great idea since they were seldom ever occupied, and maybe he really ought to add the deck and the hell with the damn animals cute or not if it brought in some extra profit, but hiring Julia Sanders to tend the drunks and the wine crowd and the bourbon or scotch-forget-the-damn-water guys had been, even if he did say so himself, a touch of unaccustomed brilliance. Dark flame for hair and dark emeralds for eyes, she was attractive enough to keep the men around for one drink more than they'd planned on, but not threatening enough to drive the ladies away.

And one night, during her second weekend, Nester Brandt had tried to pinch her, and Julia had decked him without even looking away from the cocktail she'd been making. The subsequent applause from the assembled patrons had startled, and obviously pleased, her; what pleased Neil more had been the way she had leapt effortlessly onto the bar, taken a bow, and leapt down again without a word.

No one tried to pinch her, or pick her up again, either.

Except Ken Havvick.

A silver tray, bottle nestled in a silver ice bucket, tulip glasses with pressed white linen napkins folded just so. She handed it to him, said, "Maybe she'll drown," and picked up her book.

He tried not to laugh as he delivered the gift, tried not

to look at the window as he left. He did anyway. The reflections were there.

Vacation, Maclaren, he told himself then; take a few days off and . . . do what? Find someone to buy this place, that's what. Get out from under. Hard work, nice people, a great bartender in Julia and a fine cook in Willie Ennin, and none of it added up to a penny more for the pension. A few hours short of forty and not much to show for it but Maclaren's and callused hands.

Not terrible.

Not terrific.

So what do you want then? he asked as he decided to get some fresh air, told Julia he was going to get something from the house; aside from winning the lottery, hitting it big in Atlantic City, tearing Julia's clothes off and making love to her on the bar, what the hell more do you want? You're not starving, for god's sake, so what else is there?

He put on his denim jacket, and stood on the stoop, huffing at the cold bitter and dry, watching the road.

He didn't know.

A wink shy of forty, and he goddamn didn't know.

He couldn't leave, though.

He couldn't.

There was no place else to go.

He squeezed his eyes shut, opened them quickly. This wasn't the way to think, what in hell was the matter with him tonight? He liked it here. Hell, he loved it here. People left him alone. He left them alone. His regular customers were all the company he required, with the infrequent women who shared his bed for a while and moved on, it's pretty damn boring here, Maclaren, no offense, and none was ever taken.

He liked it here.

He did.

what more do you want?

Headlights to the east, winking through the bare

branches, flaring as they rounded the sharp curve, steadying, slowing as they reached the sign. The car didn't stop. The driver couldn't see him, could only see that Maclaren's wasn't exactly lit up with fireworks and huge crowds, and sped up, dragging the dark after him, leaving him alone.

No, he realized; no.

Not alone.

He frowned puzzlement and looked left toward the flagstone path that led to the cabins.

Not alone, but nothing there.

Quietly he stepped down to the gravel and waited, listening, hearing nothing and knowing that any sound, any sound at all, would carry easily when the air was as brittle as it was tonight, as cold and as still. His vision soon adjusted to the outline of the restaurant, the outlines of the trees in the glow of the feeble streetlamp, and there was still nothing out of place. The parking lot was empty except for Havvick's long gray van, not a flicker of traffic on the road, nothing moving in the woods, not even a breeze.

Not alone.

He stiffened suddenly and pulled his hands from his pockets, flexed his fingers.

The Holgates.

His chin lifted and his head turned slowly as if he were sniffing the air, searching for a spoor. He wouldn't put it past those idiots to try something again. They were trouble, Curt and Bally, seeming to have nothing to do with their lives but give him grief and grin inanely about it. Just out of their teens and time on their hands, waiting until spring, when their army enlistments began. Most days he didn't even see them and never gave them a thought. But at least once a week they came by, their chrome-burdened pickup belching oil-smoke exhaust, perforated muffler sounding like something belonging on a dirt track. They'd give Ennin and Julia a hard time, all the while smiling and nodding and flashing their money to prove they were genuine, that they had rights just like everyone else, that it was all just good-old-boy fun and games, nothing to get all bent out of shape over. They would leave just before Neil lost his temper in front of the others. Perfect timing every time.

They hated him.

Twice, one of his front windows had been smashed with bricks; once, someone had taken a shotgun to his sign, blowing a hole through his name, blowing out all the lights and perforating the shields. By the time he had reached the road from his house, the vandals were gone.

But he knew the sound of the pickup.

It hadn't been enough for the police, however, despite their sympathy. What he thought he had heard, at night, in the middle of nowhere, had no credence in any court.

He forced himself to breathe easily, flexed his fingers again, and stepped down to the ground, easing his weight to minimize the crunch of gravel beneath his soles. If they were out there, they could see him, and all they had to do was wait. And if he stood here much longer, he'd freeze solid.

They hated him for no other reason than that they thought him a coward.

That much he had figured a long time ago.

They hated him for what he was, because what he was now was a result of what he had once been.

A long while ago, not quite a lifetime and perhaps more than that, he had been a New Jersey State Trooper, seven years right out of college, eventually and primarily patrolling the Turnpike and the Parkway. He hadn't been great; he hadn't bagged millions in drugs or any of the FBI's most wanted; he had been okay, he had been competent. And when, at the end of those seven years, he had been passed over for promotion for the third time in a row, he made an appointment with his commander to complain and find out why. It hadn't taken very long. The senior officer, who

liked him well enough and knew his family, told him
bluntly he was wasting his time, and the state's time and
money, trying to turn himself into something he didn't
really want to be. Neil had been furious at the implied
insult, then deeply hurt, then filled with self-pity until the
commander had said, gently, "Maclaren, face it, you're just
not your father."

And he wasn't.

The bitch of it was . . . he wasn't.

Mac Maclaren was dead, shot to death on the Jersey side
of the Delaware Memorial Bridge. Smugglers. Two-bit
smugglers in an eighteen-wheeler, bringing untaxed cigarettes from Carolina for distribution in New York. Not
guns. Not drugs. Not white slavers. Lousy cigarette ban-
dits, who shot Mac down when he tried to check their
papers, while Neil was still in school.

Until then, he hadn't known what he wanted to do with
his life; eight months to the day after graduation he had his
first uniform on.

But the commander had been right—when the passion
had subsided, there was nothing left but the job.

Two weeks after the meeting, Neil was packed and
gone, feeling like a miner just back in the sun after being
lost in the tunnels, not knowing what to do, not knowing
which turn to take, terrified without admitting it that he'd
die there, in the dark.

Although his former profession was no secret in town,
he didn't think he owed anyone a detailed explanation. A
few knew, like Nester and Julia, and Willie in his way. As
far as the others were concerned, he had been a cop once;
now he wasn't anymore.

Simple as that.

Curt and Bally Holgate, however, decided there was a
secret, decided he'd run away, deserted under fire, some
damn nonsense like that.

Stupid bastards.

His shoes were loud on the gravel, his balance not quite even, as he walked to the corner of the building and down the easy slope toward the worn hard-dirt path that led to his home, thirty yards back, huddling against the trees at the back of an oblong. Cautiously. Checking the shadows. Finally concluding, almost reluctantly, that the Holgates weren't around.

By the time he reached the house, a clapboard cottage with wraparound porch, five rooms, an unfinished stone cellar, his temper had grown foul, his footsteps more like stomping. At the front door he stopped and checked over his shoulder one more time. Lights from the bar turned the dead grass grey, and there were no mysterious figures waiting in ambush between the trees' twisted boles.

Nothing there.

Damnit, nothing there.

An owl called softly from across the creek.

He could hear water running over a tiny waterfall he'd fashioned himself two springs ago.

He knew what it was then, and was surprised he'd been so spooked.

Storm coming.

Visitors thought it almost magic, the way he and the others who lived here all the time could tell by the feel, the scent of the air that rain, or snow, was on the way. But the sky had been clear all day, not a cloud, not a wisp, and the last forecast he had heard had declared good weather until Monday.

But it was still there—the feeling, if not the smell.

Curious.

He stepped back off the porch and looked up, trying to locate the moon, found it glaring without haze or halo, and frowned again.

Okay, so if it isn't a storm, but it feels like a storm, what are we talking about here?

"Male menopause," he muttered, chuckling, and

climbed the stairs, unlocked the door and reached around the frame to turn the living-room light on. Now that he was here, he would have to find something to bring back to keep Julia from ragging him for the rest of the night. But what? The account books, or a clean shirt, or what the hell did it matter? He'd gotten his air, cleaned out his lungs, spooked himself royally, and decided that the Holgates were too stupid to care about and too stupid to live. Julia's razor tongue he could live with, for a while.

A car pulled into the lot.

He turned the light back off and closed the door, feeling like a jerk.

The owl called as he started back.

Deep in the woods, something squealed, screamed, and died.

The moon died a few seconds later.

He saw it happen.

Standing on the stoop, hand ready to open the door, he looked up and saw the smoke. Cloud smoke. Drifting across the face of the moon.

A gust of wind rattled the trees across the road.

A band of dead leaves slipped under the fence and scrabbled toward him, vanishing under the chassis of a large, unfamiliar automobile parked beside Kenny's van.

The moon died, slipping into the black slowly, crater by crater, star by star.

Something flew over the restaurant, the single flap of its wings like a sheet snapped in the wind.

They sat in the back corner booth, two women and a man, Julia taking their order, one hip cocked. She glared at him as he came down the steps from the restaurant; he shrugged and moved around the bar's corner where it made a rounded right turn to let the customers there look outside without having to leave their stools. Eight feet later it ended, the rest rooms back there, a trapdoor leading down to the storeroom, and a door marked EMPLOYEES ONLY. He pushed in and sighed at the warmth, the feel of steam.

"Willie?"

The small kitchen was mostly stainless steel and tile, a huge freezer, three ovens, a cozy alcove in the far corner where Willie had a shelf he used as a desk when he needed to study and had some free time, a marked calendar on the wall, a schedule of meals, a list of things Neil needed to order. Fluorescent lights embedded in the acoustical ceiling. A center island of cabinets overhung with pots and pans and utensils he'd never been sure were any use, and topped by a six-foot-long butcher's block scarred with blade marks and faintly stained with juice and blood.

"Hey, Willie."

A door looked out toward the cabins hidden by the fence and a wandering stand of black oak. Along the flagstones, marking the way, he and Willie had set electric lamps on three-foot black posts. They were out now as he peered through the pane, shading his eyes against the room's glare. It didn't take him long; Willie was on one knee by the gateless opening in the fence. In one hand he had a shoe box, in the other a trowel he used to scoop something up from a patch of dead weeds.

Oh lord, he thought, and stepped away, waited, and

when Willie walked back in, cheeks red and lips trembling, he said, "What is it now?"

Ennin gasped in surprise, sputtered, hunched and hurried to his alcove where he dropped the box onto the desk. He muttered something, shrugged, pushed past Neil to a sink where he began to wash his hands.

"Willie, what was it?"

"Mouse."

A glance toward the shoe box. Another customer for the graveyard his cook kept across the creek. The little man never let a dead creature rot or become a scavenger's meal; if he saw it, no matter what state it was in, it was buried.

Ennin turned, his lips parted slightly in what passed for his smile. Not much taller than five feet, barely wider than a shadow. His face too long for his height and always three days without a shave. Tiny eyes. Tiny feet. Dressed in white that somehow, despite the cooking, the cleaning, the digging, the work, was never stained.

"Damn cold, Mr. Maclaren," he said, briskly drying his hands on his apron. "Damn cold."

"Willie—" He stopped; it was no use. Willie Ennin would leave a banquet for the president if an animal needed a grave. "Never mind."

The cook grinned and pointed to the island, bread and lunch meat, lettuce and chopped onions. "Going to be crowded tonight," he announced. "Gotta be ready."

"You think so, huh?"

Ennin frowned as if Neil ought to know better than to ask. "Sure. Can feel it in the air, Mr. Maclaren. Folks are going to be cold, they're going to be hungry, they're going to want one of my famous sandwiches before going home." He spread his hands. "Ain't that right?"

"If you say so."

"I'm always right, Mr. Maclaren." He eased Neil away from the work space without actually touching him. "If I wasn't right, we wouldn't have this place anymore, people wouldn't come, they wouldn't eat, I'd have to buy my own meals, you'd have to go back chasing the bad guys."

"Speeders, Willie, speeders," he corrected with a laugh, a hand on the man's shoulder before heading for the door. "The worst guy I ever caught was some idiot from Virginia doing a hundred and thirty on the Turnpike."

"He could've killed somebody," Ennin said simply.

Neil didn't answer.

There was never an argument with Willie Ennin. For him, life was divided into things that were eaten, things that got eaten unless he buried them first, and the Lone Ranger. It was sometimes frustrating as hell, but just as often, he wondered if that wasn't the way to go. Simplify the hell out of things and let the world leave you alone.

And why not?

He sat two stools from the corner, so he could watch the room, be the host if he had to, and at the same time see movement through the plants in case someone came in for a meal, or if Havvick was ready to leave.

Why not? There were worse ways to live.

"Philosophy with Willie," Julia guessed, drifting toward him, slipping an empty glass into soapy water. The book was gone; she was back on duty.

He smiled. "How can you tell?"

"It's that look." She blew hair out of her eye. "The one that reminds you that there's a death penalty in this state." A glass of water with a lemon twist placed on a cork mat. "Drink up, boss. It's good for what ails you."

One of the women stood up, and he said, "Oh my."

"Sexist," Julia whispered.

Although the lights were kept deliberately dim and aimed away from the booths toward the bar, it was still sufficient for him to see that what she wore, and what there was of it, wasn't designed for the season—a knit dress that almost made it to her knees, short sleeves, a neckline that, on a woman with a smaller bust, would have been just about right. She hurried past toward the ladies' room, nodding once to him, hair bobbed several decades out of style.

Neil drank quickly and fanned himself with one hand. Julia scowled.

He grinned, drank again, and glanced outside. Shivered. The glass looked too thin, the air too damn cold.

A burst of muffled laughter from over in the corner. When he looked, the man was trying mightily to get out from around the booth's table, his companion convulsing each time he failed and fell back.

"They were smashed when they came in," Julia said. "Swear to God."

He didn't think they were drunk, and the more he watched, the more he was convinced. The man was acting, playing the fool, and playing now to him as he tried to wave him over and nearly toppled his glass of beer.

"Oh my, don't you know I just live for days like this," he said as he stood and handed her his empty glass.

"I'll bet."

A barely heard chime from high behind the bar; someone else had come in.

With apologies to Willie, Neil made his way over, forcing himself not to stare when he realized that the woman was wearing the same dress as her friend, and the man was in a dark velvet tuxedo. This time he stood easily enough, gracefully, and held out his hand.

"Hugh," he said, his voice professionally deep. "Hugh Davies. You, I take it, are the owner?"

Gleaming black hair combed straight back and tight from a high brow, Roman nose, cleft chin. Neil wondered how much all that work had cost him.

"Neil Maclaren. Yes. This is mine."

Davies nodded to the woman—*told you so, my dear, I'm never wrong about things like that*—and took Neil's arm, carefully guided him several steps toward the glass wall, so carefully, so skillfully, Neil found it difficult to take offense.

"It's obvious I'm not from around here," the man said, slipping a cigarette from his inside jacket pocket, setting it with a gold monogrammed lighter. "But I want you to know that what you have here, Mr. Maclaren, is a gold mine."

Neil waited.

"Potentially, of course."

Of course, Neil thought. And waited.

"I mean, it's just rustic enough to feel homey, you know what I mean? But it's not phony, either, it's not made of clever plastic. People like me, we drive all the way out here, we see a place like this, we know we're going to have a great meal, some good laughs, and we'll tell all our friends, you know what I mean?"

Neil watched the creek glint silver, shift to ink, shift to silver again. He didn't look at the man; he couldn't; he'd drop to the floor, laughing. "New York," he said instead, "is almost two hours away the way the roads are. Nearly seventy-five miles." He did look this time. "Nobody in their right mind is going to come all the way out here just for a drink, a meal, and the hope of good times."

"And you're absolutely right," Davies agreed readily. Smoke blown at the ceiling. Hand brushing across his tie, keeping it in line. "But they do come out every summer for the lakes and fishing, every winter for the skiing, am I right?" He examined the room, watched a man come down the steps and head directly for the bar. "Aside from the locals—Deerfield's what, a mile west, something like that?—seems to me you're not getting your fair share of the trade." He turned to the woman for confirmation. "Am I right, Ceil? Don't you think I'm right?"

"Don't listen to him, Mr. Maclaren," she said with a trace of amusement, a shade of boredom, her face deep in shadow, her bare arms pale as they rested on the table. "He's sweet, but he's a little dumb."

Davies laughed and shook his head.

Neil wasn't sure how to react. The man wasn't pushy or condescending, and he wasn't glib enough to be insulting. Friendly enough to be serious; aloof enough to be teasing for no other reason than it was fun.

"Five million," he finally answered.

"What?"

The woman laughed. Deep in shadow.

"Five million and it's yours, lock, stock, and barrel." This time it was his hand that did the guiding. "Five million dollars for ten prime acres, a fishing creek, seven cabins, this restaurant, the liquor license that goes with it. Out here, that's a steal." He brought Davies to the bar, pointed to the newcomer busily emptying a snifter as if it were a shot glass. "I'll throw in Nester here, too. See that pay phone on the wall beside the coatrack? Direct line to Nester's bookie in Newark. Soon as he hits the big one, he'll buy you out and you'll double your investment, guaranteed."

"Screw off, Maclaren," Brandt said, glaring, and grinning falsely.

Neil blew him a kiss and brought Davies home. "Think about it, okay? The next round's on the house."

"Thank you," the woman said. Face not quite clear. Pale arms. Chest not nearly as obvious as the other woman's. A flare of something white near her throat. Pearl. Opal. "Ceil Davies. You've met my brother." She paused, leaned back. "You've seen my sister. God help her, her name is Mandy."

Neil mumbled something he hoped sounded appropriate in whatever the hell kind of situation this was, shook Davies's hand again, and retreated to the steps. He could see that Brandt was in no mood for company just yet, didn't want to listen to Julia's sarcasm anymore, and wasn't at all sure what to make of Davies and his sisters.

Nuts; all of them.

And he snapped his fingers without moving them.

Be damned, maybe that's what was bothering him—it was going to be one of those nights.

They happened.

God, did they happen.

As if, on a single somehow hallowed occasion, all the loons were let out of their cages and given a map to his place. Wives fought husbands with words and brandished forks, fathers argued red-faced with red-faced sons, drunks tried to climb the spider plants, girlfriends found new boy-friends with their old boyfriends simmering in the next booth, things not known to modern science were stuffed down the toilets. Every so often. It made no difference if the moon was full or not. They came out, they came to Maclaren's, they made his life hell and they sometimes made him laugh.

Brandt, for example and by his current mood, had probably had a battle royal with his wife of fifteen years. There was a small rip on one sleeve above the elbow, his cheek was enflamed as if slapped or punched, what was left of his hair hadn't seen a comb in several days. She had probably caught him with another woman. It didn't matter who; the gambler wasn't fussy. And he seldom took precautions to prevent her from finding out. He bragged to his buddies. She heard. They fought. He came here to scream at his bookie and snarl at Julia and drink the best whiskey and brandy Neil had to offer. Sometimes, before midnight, he passed out; sometimes, after midnight, he'd take a bath in the creek, with everyone in the bar looking on.

"So what?" he had once demanded, standing in the water, naked, skin like a mangy bear's pelt. He stabbed a branch toward the lounge windows. "They ain't never seen a man before?"

"Not like you, pal," Neil had answered.

"Tough shit."

"C'mon, get out."

"Ain't done my armpits yet."

He sat down, knees up, and Neil had walked away.

There had been no talking to him then; there was no talking to him now.

On the top step he paused when music, loud enough to hear but not loud enough to distract, came over the audio system he had installed last year, the speakers invisibly tucked into the rafters. Big Band music. Always. Benny Goodman, Gene Krupa, easy on the tempo. He looked at Julia, standing by the receiver and the multidisc CD player, which were beside the old-fashioned popcorn machine he'd rescued from a dying theater. She waggled a finger at him. He saw Davies and one of his sisters dancing near the window, both her hands around his neck, his hand low on her waist.

Sister, he thought, my ass; if they got any closer, it'd be incest.

Havvick and Trish were still in their booth, on the same side now, facing him and not seeing him.

He didn't look any closer.

One of those nights.

So look," Brandt said to Julia, elbows on the bar, leaning partway over to watch her clean glasses, bend down, stand up, cock her head when the fruit in the tux danced by and gave her an order, some kind of fancy bourbon. "The damn horse comes in, right? Long shot five lengths across the wire ahead of the favorite. The stupid son of a bitch sends me my money instead of calling me to come get it.

Sends it! Can you believe it? The old crone opens the mail, sees the check . . ." He shrugged sadly, elaborately, sipped dry a Chivas Regal, set the snifter down for a refill. "She says she's going to divorce me." He rubbed his teeth with the side of a finger. "She won't, though. She loves me too much." Striped button-down shirt, jeans tucked into wading boots. "Besides, she's too fat and too old to find anyone else this stage of the game. She's stuck with me. Lived in Deerfield all her life, she wouldn't know how to find her way out of the county. She cashed the check, too, would you believe it? Bought one of them recliner things for in front of the television and won't let me use it. Tells me I have to get another horse." He chuckled, and fumbled through his pockets. "Damn, where's all that change I had this morning? She probably took that, too. She does that, you know. When I'm sleeping, she goes through all my pockets just to make sure I'm not holding out on her. How the hell can I? She's always going through my pockets." A sigh of discovery. He dropped a fifty-dollar bill on the bar. "I got my ways, though. Look at me, you wouldn't think I'm a rich man, right? Not really rich. Better than some, though, you can bet on it." He looked in the silver-edged mirror behind the neatly tiered bottles, patted a palm over his scalp. "You think them places in New York that does the movie stars, they know how to make a fifty-five-year-old man with no hair to speak of look good?" He patted his scalp again, scratched at it a little. "Cost a fortune, right?" A thin mustache that curled down past the corners of his mouth; he stroked it with his thumbs. "I ain't got a fortune, Julia, don't get me wrong. Better than some, though. You'd think the old crone would know that, live with it, roll with the punches. Makes sense, right? It's gotta make sense. Stupid bitch. One of these days I'm going to leave her, let her empty her own pockets for a change. Jesus

Christ, who *are* those guys over there? Hookers and pimp? What the hell's this place coming to? Where the hell's Neil, I'm gonna complain."

Julia returned with empties on her tray, dumped the glasses into the sink, wiped the tray down. Brandt prattled on. She moved around the corner to a large open rectangle in the wall where she could get Willie's attention.

"Plate of sandwiches, Willie," she called.

He looked up, saluted.

She returned the salute and, when he wasn't watching, threw him a kiss. Then she went back to Brandt and said, "Do me a favor and shut the hell up."

"Nice talk," he said.

She pointed at her ass.

Willie knew the bar lady had thrown him a kiss. She did it every night when she thought he hadn't seen.

His hands flew over the sandwiches, over the arrangement on their plates, paused over a cleaver and thought about Nester Brandt. Even in here, with the music going and conversations, he could hear the man talking.

The cleaver waited for him.

Not now, he told it with one eye closed.

Not now.

Later.

Ken eased himself into the corner of the booth, the pane
not quite touching his shoulder but feeling the cold just the
same. Trish was so close she was nearly in his lap, sitting
slightly sideways, right arm resting on the table.

Her legs were crossed.

Her left hand was in his lap.

"It'll be easy," he said, swallowing, feeling his gaze
wander though he wanted to be sure he could see anyone
who came close. "I'll talk to Dad in the morning, okay?
He's gonna flip when he finds out, Trish, really. He loves
you. He really does." His voice hardened just a bit. "People around here, I know they make fun of him sometimes
just because of the farm. But hell, somebody's got to make
the milk. If my dad didn't do it, somebody else would and
feed them babies, make all the money. I guess they're
jealous. If you look at the TV all the time, you'd think
every farmer in the country was going down the tubes."
He shifted, spread his legs a little more. Trish's eyes were
half closed; he didn't know if she was really listening. He
didn't care. Listening wasn't why they were going to get
married. "If you really want to know the truth, if you want
to know what you're really getting into, I'd guess, and it's
just a guess, that my dad could buy and sell just about
anyone in the county. That's not bragging. Watch it, hon,
Maclaren's prowling around. I'm really not bragging. It's
not just the farm." He straightened, waved to Maclaren
without invitation, and watched Trish's left breast press
against the seat's back. Jesus. He swallowed again. "Investments, you know? Not like that shithead Nester. Real
investments. He knew things weren't always going to be
great. I don't know all he owns, but you should see the
damn checks that come in every quarter. Christ, they could

choke a horse." He laughed. "Choke a cow." He laughed again. Trish sighed. He recognized the sound and knew they wouldn't be staying here very long. "So look, all you have to do is make sure that your folks don't blow it. You know what I mean. They already figure they own half of me just because we're going out. They come on too strong when Dad's around, he'll shitcan the whole thing, and that'll kill him, it really will because he likes you so damn much." He held her wrist for a moment, just long enough for her to look at him, look him in the eye. "Patricia, do you know what I mean?"

Slowly, very slowly, she licked her lips. And winked.

He relaxed.

Her hand moved again.

"Son of a bitch," he whispered hoarsely, "but I'm the luckiest bastard in the world."

Neil checked his watch. Just a sweep hand away from nine. He glanced over at the booth and saw the dreamy look on Havvick's face, the awkward way Trish was sitting, and felt something hard land in his stomach. Maybe it would be one of those nights, but he'd be damned if it was going to be one of *those* nights, not if he could help it. The little prick had gone too far. Somebody walks in now, they'll think it's a massage parlor, for crying out loud.

He started over.

Brandt stepped up from the bar. "Hey, Maclaren, wait up."

And Trish leaned forward suddenly, her right palm pressed against the window. "Hey, look, an eagle!"

Disgusted, Ken shoved her away. "Jesus, Trish, watch it, huh?"

"No, I mean it. Look." She searched the room until she saw Neil. "Mr. Maclaren, come here, quick." Then, as if fearing she'd be overheard, her voice dropped to a loud whisper. "Hurry up, wait'll you see this."

"Maclaren!"

Neil hushed Brandt with an impatient wave, collided with a chair and snarled it back into place. At the booth, both Trish and Havvick beckoned now, commanding urgently, and when he reached it, he looked out, and felt his mouth freeze open. He leaned on the table, palms down, head forward.

Brandt came up beside him, huffing, indignant. "You got hookers back there, damnit, Maclaren, did you know you—holy shit, will you look at that!"

Through the window, past the reflections floating on fragile black ice, Neil saw a bird perched on the roadside fence's top rail. Because of the upward slope, and the height of the foundation, the creature was nearly at eye level, and the biggest thing he'd ever seen outside a zoo.

But it sure wasn't an eagle.

"Crow," Havvick said quietly.

Neil shook his head; he didn't think so. Crows were large around here, but not that large. It had to be a raven. Its size, the shape of its beak, the bulk and arrogance of it. It stood in profile, as if staring up the road, waiting for someone. Streetlight lost in its feathers. Unmoving. Watching. Its visible eye almost lost in the black of its head. Shifting backward a step when a gust of wind spat out of the trees.

Brandt said it aloud: "Raven, I'll be damned. I didn't know we had them things in Jersey anymore." He glanced sideways at Neil. "Do we?"

Neil only nodded at the bird. If they didn't before, they sure did now.

Trish tried to squirm closer to the window and Ken shoved her back again, rudely. She glared at him, slapped his arm. "Don't they go south or something for the win-ter?"

Neil guessed not, not with the evidence out there on the fence.

It spread its wings slowly.

Ken eased backward, pushing his fiancée with him.

The wings folded, shuddered, fluffed, spread again and settled.

Neil wished he had his camera. " 'Once upon a mid-night dreary,' " he said then, deepening his voice melo-dramatically, narrowing his eyes, " 'while I pondered, weak and weary, over many a quaint and curious volume of forgotten lore.' "

" 'While I nodded, nearly napping, suddenly there came a tapping,' " Trish whispered at the window, " 'as of some-one gently rapping, rapping at my chamber door.' " She grinned proudly. "Poe, right?"

I'll be damned, Neil thought; surprise me again, young lady.

"How the hell'd you know that?" Ken asked, not amused.

"I went to school," she answered bluntly, "and paid attention."

Another burst of wind that shook the pane briefly, shim-mered the reflections. Neil shortened his vision, looked at the faces, wondered why Ken didn't seem to care, admired Trish's open admiration, didn't much like the way Brandt had cocked his head, closed one eye.

They said nothing.

Cold spilled from the wide sill, across the table, over his hands. He flexed them without lifting them, pressing fin-gertips to the wood.

The raven fluffed its feathers again, and strutted along the rail to the next post, hopped onto it, and turned, strutted back. Stiff-legged. Slow.

Standing guard, he thought.

"Night," said Trish then.

"What?" He and Ken together.

She nodded toward the bird. "It's night. It's late. What's it doing out there now?"

A brush against his hip, and Brandt hurried away before he could respond. He heard the gambler mutter something about finding a gun, and, gesturing to the couple to keep watch, call out if the bird left or did something different, he followed the older man into the lounge. Just as he reached the steps, he heard Trish say, "Snow."

Brandt lurched past the metal coatrack as he announced the sighting to the room, and moved to raise the bar flap so he could get behind. Julia blocked him.

"Forget it, Nester," Neil told him.

"But damnit, Neil, that thing's a trophy. A goddamn trophy!"

Davies and his sisters headed to the front.

"You're not going to shoot it."

Brandt turned on him. "You got a gun back there, I know it, I've seen it. You pop that sucker out there just right, you'll have the biggest goddamn trophy in the whole goddamn state. It'll be worth a goddamn fortune." He turned to a distinctly unimpressed Julia. "It's big as a dog, I swear it." He spread his hands apart to indicate the size. "Beak to tail, I swear to God."

Low voices up in the restaurant.

When Julia noted them with a curious glance, Neil told her to go ahead and have a look; Nester, for once, wasn't exaggerating. They exchanged places without letting the gambler slip past them, and Brandt swore he'd use a slingshot if he had to. Something like that was too good to pass up.

Neil took his arm. "Leave it," he said evenly. "Just leave it, Nester, all right?"

Brandt glared at him, dared him, lowered his gaze and angrily shrugged off the grip. "Once a fucking cop."

Neil stared, disbelieving, felt his left hand curl into a loose fist while his right hand fluttered sharply, a cat's tail trying to whip energy away. He and Brandt had known each other for over ten years, and while they weren't exactly close friends, not once had the man ever mentioned his police background unless it was in teasing. This wasn't. This was sullen. This was anger. And he could only watch, baffled, as Brandt stomped in frustration across the floor and up the steps, watch the empty space he left behind and take several deep breaths to calm himself down. He looked at his fist and waited until it opened. He glanced at the backyard and saw a few darts of white vanish into the dark.

Why the hell don't they just leave it alone?

A sad cry from the front.

A moment later, Julia returned, followed by the others.

"It's gone," she said simply.

The tone was meant to tell him she didn't much care, but he couldn't help noticing how, once back behind the bar, she immediately immersed her hands in the sink's soapy water, agitating it, pulling out a glass and nearly dropping it. She gripped the stainless steel rim and smiled at him wanly.

"I don't like birds," she explained.

He allowed as how ravens were kind of spooky, especially in the middle of winter, especially one that size.

"Bad omen," she answered.

"Sure." He didn't believe it, and couldn't believe she did.

"It looked at me, Neil," she said. Hands back into the water. "Right at me."

Brandt had joined Davies and his sisters in their booth. Loud. Boastful. Regaling them with stories of the wild animals that roamed the hills around them.

Ken and Trish came down, took a table in the center.

"Right at me," Julia repeated, talking to the water.

"Hey, it's only a bird, for pete's sake," Neil said, not understanding. "C'mon, Julia, it's just a bird."

"You didn't see it."

"Of course I saw it."

"It didn't look at you."

Davies called for another round, and something for his new friend. For a moment, Neil didn't think she would answer. Then she slapped the water, hard, with her palms, and dried her hands brusquely. An apologetic smile. "I hate birds. Sorry."

No problem, he told her silently, felt someone take the stool beside him.

Mandy Davies.

"Pretty neat," she said, not looking at him but at the mirror.

She was older than he'd first guessed, certainly older than her sister, close to his own age, fine lines at the corners of her eyes, which were almost almond-shaped. Her hair, like Ceil's, was short and flipped under to appear even shorter. Not the fashion, as far as he could tell, but it suited her. The proper frame for her face. Attractive, not beautiful. Her left hand tugging absently at her neckline, pulling it up and failing, smoothing the skin across the flat of her chest. Keeping the hand there as if trying to hide the exposure of her breasts, the hand sliding away and returning to start the dance again.

He wondered what she was so nervous about.

Her head turned toward the creek. "You get a lot of animals out there?"

"Sometimes. In winter, usually only deer, if I leave something out, and a couple of raccoons."

"You feed them?" She sounded genuinely pleased. A faint accent. Not quite English, definitely not homegrown. Lilting, but not Irish.

"Sure."

"That's nice."

He shrugged. He didn't think of it as nice, or anything very special. It was just something he did.

When she finally looked at him, he was startled, and she smiled. "Scared you, huh."

He didn't answer.

Her hand drifted away; he willed himself not to look.

"I thought . . ." A glance without moving her head. "That girl, she said birds don't go out at night."

"Some do, some don't."

"Do ravens?"

"Owls, mostly. Some hawks, things like that." A shrug, one shoulder. "Not ravens. Not usually."

Ken snapped something harsh and touched with acid, the words lost as the music, muted horns and saxophones, filled the room for a moment.

"You have any pets?"

"Not like a dog or cat, no." He pulled a darkglass ashtray to him, began rotating it slowly between his palms, staring at a crystal star embedded in its bottom. "Just some buddies that come around once in a while."

"Buddies?"

The star revolved, catching the light without flaring.

"Yeah," he said without thinking. "Like Rusty."

"Rusty?"

He laughed. "Do you always ask questions?"

"Me?"

He laughed again.

Her thumb tucked some hair behind her right ear. "So who's Rusty? A mountain lion or something?"

"No, not quite." And he could only watch as she gently freed the ashtray from his hands and pushed it away, patted his wrist to tell him it was all right, don't worry, she wasn't going to bite.

For the second time that night he felt like a jerk.

"Rusty," she prompted.

"She's a squirrel."

A laugh brief and friendly.

"No kidding." He crossed his heart and explained how, soon after he had bought this place, a squirrel with a rust belly and matching scrawny tail had come up to him while he'd been sitting on the steps, wondering what in god's name he'd gotten himself into. By the five little ones trailing skittishly behind, chattering loudly, tumbling over each other in explosions of playtime, he assumed it was a she. Impressed by her boldness, he fed her peanuts and grapes and a few acorns he had picked up around the cabins. She was back the next day. And the day after that. Every year for six years, every morning and every sunset, she and her latest brood came to feed, to play, and to listen to his problems. Along the way, he also managed to pick up a pair of overweight raccoons, a family of skunks, some solitary deer, and, last year, a black bear that had sent him wheeling and gasping inside, out of breath and terrified until the bear found the garbage cans, found them dull, and waddled off.

"A bear?" Her eyes widened, but only slightly. "In New Jersey?" She laid a hand on his arm and examined his face, searching for the gag. "You're not kidding, are you. I'll be. A bear." A look back to the creek. He couldn't help the temptation to trace a finger down her spine, pulled his hand away just in time, and swiveled around to face the room, to catch his breath, to wonder where his mind was, reacting like that. A customer. A woman. "There's someone out there."

He blinked as she slipped off the stool and tapped his side.

"Someone's out there," she said again.

Brandt bellowed laughter, not much louder than Davies.

Ken held Trish's hand, but she wasn't paying attention. "Is the raven back?" she asked excitedly as they passed.

Neil shook his head.

Mandy pointed, tapping the window. "Back there."

The trees bordering the far side of the creek were closely

spaced, birch and pine, oak and hickory, the gaps filled
with shadow that swallowed the woods only a few yards
beyond, hid the hill that turned invisible every night. It was
snowing. Small, hard flakes that had already begun to shade
the grass, but not rapidly enough to be alarming.

No wind.

They fell straight, dodging now and then on their way
to the ground.

"It's pretty," Trish said.

"By that one there with the white bark," Mandy told
him, touching the window again. "Next to that big rock
in the water, see it? See over there?"

He nodded.

There was no one there.

Unless, he thought suddenly, it was one of the Holgates
out for mischief.

Alerted, he watched carefully, not looking directly at the
places he wanted to check; to do that would invite seeing
things that didn't exist, especially with the light so artificial,
especially in the snow.

"What did he look like?"

"Who?" Davies asked. "A prowler? Peeping Tom?"

"Keep it down, Hugh," Ceil scolded without bite.

Mandy settled an arm across her stomach. "I didn't see
him, not that clearly. He could have been Jack the Ripper
for all I know."

One of the bulbs in the trees snapped out.

Another.

"Damn," he said.

A third one, and a fourth, a fluttering shower of sparks.

Nothing now but the three diffused bulbs down at the
foundation, creating a disconcerting haze that softened the
cold's edges and made the woods seem as if they were
drifting back into fog. In the distance all was black and
grey.

"Hey, Nester," he said, still looking around the birch, "I think maybe Curt and Bally have come to party."

The woman beside him tensed; he could feel it, saw it in the way she shifted her weight uneasily from foot to foot. He assured her the Holgates weren't worth her concern. Local jerks, experts in pinhead harassment, and like all bullies they were cowards when it came to confrontations they didn't expect. He touched her shoulder and walked away, grabbed his jacket from the rack and headed into the restaurant, Brandt right behind.

"Gun?"

Neil looked at him.

"Just thought I'd check."

They crossed the floor, slipping into their coats, snapping up their collars.

Muttering behind them, inquisitive but not excited.

"What's eating you tonight, Nester?"

"Nothing much. The usual."

He swung the door open, held his breath when the cold wrapped him and pulled.

"She's gonna leave me, you know. She really means it this time."

He looked over his shoulder; Brandt wasn't kidding.

One of those nights, he reminded himself; just one of those nights.

They swung to the left, passing the automobile and the van, and Brandt's bicycle leaning against the front of the building. Around the corner, where Julia and Willie parked their cars. A look up the path. A look into the branches. Brandt puffing steam, his boots nearly silent. Past the kitchen door, Willie standing there, peering out, a knife in one hand.

At the back corner Neil held Brandt back with a cautioning hand. Listening. Shaking his head slowly, blinking the snow from his lashes. This was a waste of time. If the Holgates were there and didn't want to be found, he could chase them all night and not see them once. There wasn't enough snow yet to allow decent tracks, too many leaves and fallen needles back there across the creek. A flake settled on his neck, melted instantly and made him shiver. On the grass, on the weeds, on the stones by the water, the flakes were frostlike gems, like the gem at Ceil's throat. Sparkling. Hissing softly as they fell through the branches, the needles. Almost, but not quite sleet.

He looked at Brandt, who looked back and shrugged.

Waste of time.

Besides, he decided as he started back, it didn't have to be them anyway. It could have been the snow, even though they were supposed to be outdoor bulbs, sudden wet cold against their heat; it could have been a coon or a possum exploring; he hadn't heard any shots, it didn't have to be the Holgates.

"I think—"

Brandt stopped him at the corner, and pointed.

The raven was back; on the fence, and watching.

He could hear muffled voices and knew the others had seen it, too, stepped away and looked up, Mandy and Trish in one window, Ken and Hugh in the center.

The raven opened its beak and closed it.

Not a sound.

Snow caught on its back.

Glinted.

For no reason at all, Neil thought *fairy dust* and almost laughed.

Larger flakes mixed in with the others, and a slight wind began to push them around.

The front door opened and Ken stepped out, suit jacket only, pulling on a pair of gloves.

"Hey, guys," he said cheerfully, "you see that thing?"

At the noise, the raven spread its wings, flapped them once, squatted, leapt and lifted off the rail.

Not a sound.

The wings flapped again, and the bird glided in a lazy arc across the road, into the trees.

"That kid," Brandt whispered behind him, "is richer than God and dumber than shit."

Neil nodded his agreement, laughing, as Havvick jumped to the ground and ran up to the fence, vaulted it with a one-hand brace and trotted carefully to the opposite shoulder, where he stopped and put his hands on his hips. He was under the streetlamp, a sparkling pale veil.

"I can't see it," he called.

Brandt groaned.

And Neil said, "Traffic."

"What?"

He slipped his hands into his pockets and swerved around the back of the van, heading for the road. "Traffic," he said again.

"What about it?"

"There isn't any."

And as far as he knew, there hadn't been all night, except for the one car he had seen earlier, before the Davies clan arrived. It was Friday. Deerfield proper, such as it was, was only a mile up the road, Hunter not that much farther on, and between here and the several miles to the county seat in the other direction there were at least four bars that did a decent weekend business. Two other restaurants. The highway was never bumper-to-bumper, but there should have been something. He stopped at the fence, looked east and west. Delivery trucks. Big rigs. Kids out for a joyride. Unless there'd been an accident someplace, there should have been something. The blacktop glittered. Damn, there should at least have been a sander, the roads were going to be hell in an hour.

"Still can't see it," Havvick yelled, edging closer to the trees.

"Because it's black, you dumb shit," Brandt yelled back.

"Kenneth, get in here!" Trish called from the door.

"You're going to catch pneumonia, and I want to go home!"

"Bet you five hundred they're divorced by summer," Brandt said as Havvick surrendered with a wave to the trees, ran back, vaulted the fence, slid and fell and skidded down to the steps on his rump. "Maybe even by spring."

Neil turned to look at the restaurant, at the people moving around inside. He could see Mandy by the door, hugging herself, looking out.

Brandt slapped his arm, *let's get going, okay?,* and trotted away.

Small, Neil thought; in the dark, in the snow, it all looks so damn small.

He pushed away from the fence, suddenly hunched his shoulders and looked up.

The snow falling out of the night, the wind in the woods finally finding its voice, and the inexplicable feeling that the raven was up there too, just out of sight. Circling. Or watching. It didn't make any difference. It was going on ten o'clock, and the bird should have been nesting.

In the bar, one of the tables was laden with sandwiches and fruit.

"I heard about the wedding," Willie said nervously, and nervously dried his hands on his apron. "We should have a party."

Ken applauded his approval.

Trish grabbed his arm, said in a stage whisper, "I don't want a party, Kenny, I want to go home. It's snowing." She whispered something in his ear that made him blush and the others laugh.

Davies took her hand then, bowed over, kissed it, pulled her away and said, "May I have this dance?"

She looked apprehensive.

"I won't eat you," the man said.

Trish said, "Hey, I know you!"

"Then we're friends and we'll have to dance, won't we?"

She giggled and let him lead her around the floor in time to a violin waltz. "He's on the radio!" she exclaimed as they spun past Havvick's table. "Every night. I listen to him every night."

Ceil took the chair beside Havvick and rested her forearms on the table. "I'd watch him if I were you." She picked up a sandwich wedge and popped it into her mouth, wiped a crumb from her lower lip with the side of a finger. "He eats little girls like that for breakfast."

Havvick frowned skeptically. "Is he really on the radio?"

She nodded.

"No shit." He smiled at her. "Famous, huh?"

"In his way." She was bored.

"Does he know the guy who sells the ads?"

She slid her chair closer, her knee brushing against his. "He may dress like Cary Grant, but he's got the morals of George Raft."

Havvick frowned. "Who?"

Ceil laughed and handed him a sandwich. "Never mind. You'll find out."

Julia watched them dance—Valentino and Shirley Temple—and wondered if Neil would let her use one of the cabins if the snow got too bad. Sometimes he did, sometimes he didn't. He was moody. Very moody. These past three weeks he'd been walking his temper through mud. As she opened another bottle of champagne, she watched him, trying to gauge him, failing, swearing when the cork slipped through her grip and bounced off the ceiling. Brandt applauded her from the end of the bar. She glared until he looked away, stood abruptly and went to the pay phone. From the way he cupped the mouthpiece in one hand, she knew he wasn't calling his wife. He dressed like a half-witted hick, talked like someone who's never seen the inside of a school, and seemed to take down more money in a week than she made in six months. He spent it, too. But not on his wife.

He hung up and returned to his stool, ordered a brandy and gave her another fifty-dollar bill. "Keep the change," he said grandly.

Dream on, she told him with a look and a sour smile; my bed's not for sale, not for the likes of you.

He sent her a two-finger salute—*no hard feelings*—which made her turn away before she hit him. Like the first time. A lucky punch, his astonishment, and a legend was born. But damn the man, he hadn't stopped trying. Not overtly, not like that night. Little ways—huge tips, tips on horses, polite innuendo, the occasional leer when he thought Neil wasn't looking. Persistent. A slimy old creep, almost pathetic in his way, but she had to give him his persistence because he wasn't nasty about it, wasn't ugly.

Not like Kenny Havvick, who seemed to think he was

God's gift to the unwedded, which in his mind meant unbedded.

The little prick.

The music played on.

Something about a bird.

She suppressed a shudder, didn't want to but looked out the window anyway.

The raven wasn't there.

But it had been.

And it had looked right at her.

Another shudder too quick to cover, and she turned away to watch Trish Avery press closer to Davies. She changed her mind—Shirley Temple that girl's not. And him . . . she wondered why it had taken the others so long to recognize him. Hugh Davies. The East Coast's top-rated evening talk-show host, soon to go national if the papers were to be believed. She had recognized the voice the second he'd opened his mouth. He spoke almost exclusively to women. Women alone. All ages. Advice and readings and suggestions for good times; sly humor, intimate, the perfect man in a darkened room.

She listened to him often, and imagined he was Willie.

M y turn," said Havvick, suddenly pushing to his feet.

"Of course," Davies replied gallantly, and released Trish to her fiancé.

Ken took her in his arms, put his head next to hers: "Thought you wanted to go home."

"He's famous, Kenny, did you know that?"

With half-closed eyes he watched the radio man stroll over to the bar; watched Ceil leave the table and walk over to the window; watched the one with the tits talking quietly to Maclaren; watched Davies pick up a glass and toast the bartender grandly; watched Maclaren shrug at something the tits said; watched Ceil watching the snow.

"Ken, you're squeezing too hard, I can't breathe."

Horns and saxophones again; Glenn Miller.

In the mood.

Neil moved a step down and leaned a hip against the blunt end of the iron rail. He'd thrown his jacket over the top of the rack and watched, dumbly, as the weight of it pulled it slowly off the ledge. When it fell, he made no move to catch it, no move to retrieve it and hang it up.

Mandy stood below him, still hugging herself.

"Chilly?" he asked.

She half-turned, and he wished she hadn't. "A little."

"Got just the thing." He stepped down beside her. "Follow me."

Behind the bar flap was an unmarked swinging door. On the other side, a small unlighted hallway, not much bigger than a vestibule, a door on the left leading into the kitchen, one on the right leading into a room barely larger than the vestibule itself. A rolltop desk and swivel chair, two filing cabinets, on the wall over the desk an oil of Deerfield in the 1800s. A black rotary telephone. A narrow closet door that seldom caught on its latch. Three brass hooks on the wall. From one he took down an elbow-worn cardigan and handed it to her.

"Keep you warm."

He checked the desk, the chair, the painting until she'd slipped into it, leaving the buttons undone.

"Thanks."

He shrugged. "I'll turn the heat up, too."

"Don't bother, it's all right. No one else seems to be complaining."

He smiled. "Next time you're out this way, do me a favor and wear something a little warmer." He indicated her short and short-sleeve dress with a quick hand. "That's not exactly February wear. At least, not out here."

She checked herself, slowly, looked at him without raising her head. The corner of her mouth curled upward. "You didn't seem to mind."

Before he could answer, though he had no idea what he'd say, she cupped a hand to his jaw and kissed him lightly on the cheek, leaned away, judged his reaction, kissed him again. "That," she said, "is because you seem so gloomy."

Startled, he could only sputter, open the door, and follow her out. Then, amazing himself, he said, "I'm forty tomorrow."

Her palm was up to push into the lounge. It dropped, and she faced him, less than a hand between her chest and his. "It's not so bad, you know. You either push middle age up to fifty and still count yourself fairly young, or you cut your throat and leave a note." An eyebrow up and down. "Fifty looks pretty good."

She left.

The door swung shut.

The door opened again, her head poked in and she said, "By the way, I'm not his sister."

Left again.

He stood there, one hand brushing through his hair, the other moving from his cheek where she had kissed him, to the kitchen door, to the lounge door, to the door to his office. When he realized what he was doing, he froze, cast about for his composure and, when he found it, yanked it on so hard he shuddered. This was nuts. He had wrestled drunks, once worn a gun that would blow a barn door in a man, driven a vehicle that damn near flew, had a couple of fights with drunks who wouldn't be wrestled, had seen dozens, maybe hundreds of women with low-cut dresses and figures to match. Had been kissed. Hadn't been a virgin for over twenty years. Had seen a king-size raven in the middle of the night. It was nuts.

He hurried out and ignored the smirk on Brandt's face, dropped the flap behind him and hesitated, not sure what to do next. Julia and Davies were talking, Ken danced with Ceil while Trish ate standing up, and a glance through the spider plants showed him no one else had come in. It was still snowing.

Friday night.

Six customers.

A grumbling outside.

A spiraling reflection in the glass wall.

He hurried up to the entrance and looked out, just in time to see a county sander growl its way west, covering the blacktop, caution lights whirling, its cab dimly lighted.

Thank you, he called to it; thank you.

The sander passed, and passed on, swirls of dry snow in its wake, lifting in a haze and settling again despite the wind.

He waited to see a car, just to be sure.

Instead, he saw a man.

He stood just behind the reach of the streetlamp, directly across from the restaurant door. In the trees. Impossible to say how tall or heavy he was. He just stood there in shallow shadow, vaguely defined, seeming almost transparent. Neil couldn't tell if he was wearing a hat, but it looked like it; he couldn't tell if he was wearing an overcoat, but it looked like it, or a duster, and it was black, ruffling like a sail when the wind blew, the hem slapping low around his shins. The snow on his shoulders and arms glittered.

Not fairy dust.

A dream.

He didn't move.

He just stood there.

Neil couldn't see his face.

Curt, he decided; Bally Holgate was squat and bearded. This one, just standing there, was built more like Curt.

He made to open the door, and changed his mind. By the time he got over there, the kid would be long gone, nothing left but mocking laughter or some idiot trick, a booby trap, maybe a diversion while his brother set some havoc in motion somewhere else. The question is, then, whether to give him the satisfaction, or ignore him. Make him stand there like a jackass, freeze his balls off.

He grinned and turned away.

No contest.

An afterthought took him behind the display counter, where he dialed down the restaurant lights, reached in and snatched out a chocolate bar he stripped as he headed for the lounge. Ate in large bites. Tossed the wrapper into an ashtray and barely noticed that Davies was dancing with Trish again.

Violins again.

Ken sat in the corner with Ceil and Mandy, a large glass in his hand.

Trouble, he wondered, or not.

He stood by Brandt, who was finishing off another snifter. "Curt's playing games."

"Who cares?"

Brandt swiveled the stool around too fast and nearly slipped off. Neil caught him, pulled back his hands when the gambler angrily twisted away. A look to Julia, *don't serve him anymore,* before he said, loudly enough for the others to hear, "The sander's just gone by. I think it's probably all right to hit the road if you want to, before it ices up again."

Davies and Trish danced on.

"Who cares?" Brandt muttered. "She ain't gonna be there anyway, who gives a shit?" He thumped the bar with a fist. "Where the hell's my whiskey?"

Julia ignored him.

"Goddamnit, where's my drink?"

"Hey," Ken called, "shut up, okay?"

Brandt squirmed off the stool, swayed, and would have charged across the room if Neil hadn't grabbed his shoulder and yanked him back down. The gambler grumbled but didn't move again, not even when Havvick laughed shrilly, suggested to Trish that she not get any closer or else he'd have to sue the ass off the radio man before she got into his pants.

Trish, without moving her cheek from Davies's chest, took her hand from his neck and gave Ken a slow waggling finger.

Havvick laughed, and forced a belch.

so what more do you want

Sure as hell not this.

"Back in a minute," he said to Julia, and walked into the kitchen.

A little sanity. A little simplicity. Willie standing at the butcher's block with a cleaver, working on some meat. Watery blood running in thin streaks into the gutter that ran around the counter's edge, the cleaver streaked with it, not a drop on the cook's apron or shirt.

The blade rose and fell.

From a speaker over the service window, Benny Goodman.

Rose and fell.

And Neil realized that Willie was chopping the meat to shreds, not steaks or strips.

"Willie."

Rose and fell.

The fluorescent lights made everything too bright. Everything bleached. The little man's skin had no color, the meat had no color, or the floor, the ceiling. Only the blood, and it was pale.

"Willie."

Ennin stared at the meat.

Too cold.

A draft that made Neil roll his shoulders and frown.

"Prick," Ennin whispered.

Neil saw the side door wide open and hurried to close it, peered out at the snow and sighed resignation when he also saw that the ground was at last fully covered. In a while he'd have to go down into the cellar storeroom, drag out the blower and decide when he would start clearing the lot and the flagstone path—now, to keep up with the weather, or later, when the storm ended. Most of the time he waited. Tonight he wasn't sure he wanted to stay inside.

The cleaver rose and fell.

"Willie."

The floor trembled as the furnace bellowed on.

"Willie!"

Ennin froze, the cleaver level with his shoulder. He turned his head, slow enough for Neil to imagine he could hear each bone and tendon creak. Mannequin. Sideshow dummy. The man breathed deeply once, and smiled, looked down and said, "I think maybe they're going to want some real food in a while, Mr. Maclaren. Those little sandwiches don't fill nobody, not for long."

He chopped.

Neil forced a laugh. "Willie, you're killing the damn thing."

"Has to be dead, Mr. Maclaren. Has to be dead before you eat it. The prick."

Neil moved closer. He had no idea what was wrong, but whoever had set the cook off, whatever was on his mind, it had to stop. Despite the gibes and concerns of some who had met him, Willie Ennin was not retarded; but there were infrequent moments when he temporarily lost his current connection with the world. The cook called them temporary vacations, with a sheepish grin. A flicker. A waver. The world was gone and he was alone, all the rules and standards his. Like when he had to bury a mouse. Bury a baby bird. And one other time, when Bally Holgate had clipped him with a rock and he'd started to cry and suck his thumb. But not like this; never while he was cooking.

The cleaver caught in the butcher's block, and Neil took gentle hold of the wrist before the blade was freed.

"Enough, Willie, that's enough, it looks fine."

The man resisted weakly; Neil tightened his grip.

"Forget it. It's a good idea, but most of them will be gone in a few minutes. They're going to want to beat the storm."

He looked up then and saw Julia peering anxiously through the service window. A reassuring smile.

"Company, Willie," he said in a low voice.

Ennin saw her. The cleaver toppled sideways. "You want a steak?" he asked.

Julia saw the mess and shook her head. "Not tonight, okay?" She smiled apologetically. "It gives me gas if I eat too late."

Neil backed away, reaching around the cook to pick up the cleaver and drop it into the sink. There was blood on the floor.

Willie saw it and wrung his hands. "Lord, what a mess!" Quickly he grabbed a metal bucket from a stacked pile by one of the ovens and scooped the meat into it with his hands. "I'll get my mop, Mr. Maclaren. Clean in no time."

"No problem, Willie."

"Snow looks bad. You think I can leave early?"

Neil hoped his relief didn't show. "Whenever you want. The sander's been by, but if the road's not right by the time you're ready, you can use one of the cabins. Nester's going to have to, I think, he's half in the bag already."

Willie didn't answer.

A drum solo from the speaker.

Thumping slow.

Like the cleaver.

I am making too much of this, Neil decided as he left the kitchen; Willie's not dangerous, Curt's being his usual asshole self, Brandt's getting stinking, nothing more, nothing less.

One of those nights, that's all.

One of those goddamn nights.

He stepped into the bar just as the solo ended, Davies dropped Trish in an old-fashioned dip, grinned wolfishly and kissed her. On the lips.

"Hey!" Havvick struggled to his feet. "Hey, damnit!"

The couple straightened, Trish flushed and fussing with her hair, Davies smoothing his cummerbund with a palm.

"My apologies, Mr. Havvick," he said in his best, late-night voice. "Carried away by the music. Swing does that to me."

"Yeah, right," Havvick muttered, grabbed Trish's arm and said, "C'mon, let's go before we get damn snowed in here."

"But it's my party!" she whined, dug in and refused to move. "I don't want to go."

"Ten minutes ago you were ready."

She pouted and adjusted her sweater.

Havvick looked around the room, smiling gamely. "Women," he said with a slow shake of his head. "Can't live with 'em, you know what I mean?" He took her hands in his, tugged gently until she came to him. "One more glass of champagne, okay? Then we have to go."

She agreed.

They kissed.

Julia opened another bottle.

Benny Goodman.

Neil wandered around to the end of the bar, stared down at the trapdoor, at the inset black ring. What the hell. Do it now, get it over with, you'll thank me in the morning. He flicked a switch on the wall beside the rest-room entrance, then reached down for the ring. The door came up easily, revealing a short flight of stone steps and a stone floor below.

Julia leaned over the bar. "What are we out of?"

"Life," he said, starting down.

"Very funny. God, I'll be glad when your birthday's gone."

"Me, too," he called up, feeling the cold climb his legs as if he were stepping into lake water. Added, "I'm getting the damn snow blower before it's too late."

He couldn't hear her reply, if there was one; he couldn't hear anything down here but the thud and blast of big-band music, especially the bass, feet on the floor above, the wind finding masonry cracks to whisper through, to whistle. Four naked bulbs on four of the squared posts that held the building at bay. On the left was the furnace, fat tentacle pipes reaching across the beams, vanishing into the ceiling; beyond it, the floor canted upward toward the front, following the slope of the ground. As he moved through the huge room, he automatically checked the lock of the old wood door that led out to the lawn. Sidestepped stacks of liquor cartons, soda and food crates, and found what he wanted in the far corner. He sneezed, and swore at the dust; he dragged the machine to the door, knelt beside it, opened the gas tank and peered in. He couldn't see anything and took a dipstick from its place on the handle.

"Son of a bitch."

It was empty.

All goddamn winter he'd used it maybe four or five times, and not once had he thought to check the level of the gas-and-oil mixture.

"Damn."

"My ex-husband used to kick things when they didn't work."

He jumped, lost his balance, fell against the wall and swore when his skull smacked the stone. Firelight. Starlight. A cool hand on his head as he winced and someone whispering, and laughing.

"Sorry."

Mandy stepped away when he waved that he was all right, that he'd live.

"I didn't mean to scare you again."

"You didn't." His voice was hoarse. He glared at the blower and pulled his foot back to kick it. "I scared myself."

"Okay."

Gingerly he probed around the spot of the impact, and decided he would live. But he didn't want to know how bad the headache would be. Then he looked around for the snow shovels and remembered with a groan that he'd left them at the house the last time he used them.

He didn't want to go outside.

Mandy sneezed, rubbed her nose vigorously, gathered

the cardigan over her chest. "What about that?" She nodded toward the furnace.

At first, he didn't know what she meant, then saw the
dust-covered generator squatting in a gap between the
furnace and the outside wall, set to switch on automatically
should the electricity fail. An *I don't get it, what are you
talking about* look until he also saw the two cans of fuel
beside it. "Sorry, wrong stuff," he said glumly. "That's just
gas."

"Oh." Another sneeze. "You live down here or what?"

"No," he snapped, and instantly chided himself for it. "I
have a place over by the creek. This is just where I get
really stupid now and then."

"I see."

He looked from her to the stairs. "What?"

"Mr. Havvick—the boy who owns the dairy thing?—he
sent me down. He thinks there's going to be trouble."

"Oh, Christ, now what?"

"The other man—Nester?—he said something to your
bartender and the cook—"

"Jesus!"

He ran for the steps, taking her arm as he passed her, and
scrambled up, slipped once, nearly fell onto the floor when
he reached the top. He looked around anxiously, but nothing seemed out of place. Davies and the others were still in
their corner booth, Julia was at the register, and Brandt—
where the hell was Nester?

Dry-mouthed, he charged into the kitchen, and Willie
jumped away from the island, wide-eyed, mouth open, a
wood salad fork in one hand.

"Where is he?"

"Who, Mr. Maclaren?"

"Nester. I thought . . ." He put his hands on his hips and
bent forward, took a breath. "I thought there was trouble."

"No trouble, Mr. Maclaren. I'm making a spinach salad

to take home. That's all right, isn't it? You said I could, when I wanted to."

Neil wiped his face with three fingers. "It's okay, Willie, don't worry about it." And hating himself for it, he tried to spot the cleaver, found it on the counter beside the sink, dry, gleaming, and lying on its side.

A look behind him, but Mandy wasn't there.

"You all right, Mr. Maclaren?"

"Old age, Willie, just old age," he said with a self-mocking smile. "I feel like I've run a million miles." He plucked a spinach leaf from its wood bowl and nibbled at it. He would rather have lettuce. "Willie, you don't much like Nester, do you."

Willie sprinkled dressing over his salad. "He swears at Julia all the time. It isn't right. You're never supposed to swear at a lady."

"Amen," he agreed solemnly. "But Nester's a drunk, and you know it as much as anyone. He's also a good six inches taller than you, and outweighs you by a good fifty pounds. If there's any trouble, just tell me about it, all right? Don't . . . never mind. Just tell me first."

Willie said, "Julia hit him, though."

"That was different. She's entitled."

Ennin lifted the fork as if it were a dagger, turned his head, smiled. "I have to clean up before I go. Will you tell them the kitchen is closed?"

Neil nodded. "But before you leave, come out and have some champagne before it's gone. No reason why you shouldn't be part of the party."

Ennin laughed. "Part of the party. That's pretty good, Mr. Maclaren. That's pretty clever." He shooed Neil out with both hands, still laughing. "In a few minutes. I'll be out in a few minutes."

And Neil found himself back by the trapdoor, staring at the steps and wondering what had happened. Mandy sat on the end stool.

"I thought you said—"

"That's what Ken, or Kenny, or whatever he is told me."

He lowered the door carefully, was working on something to tell Havvick when Trish, standing by the wall, said, "That creep's back, I think."

He stood on the far side of the creek.

Black against black.

Snow streaked at angles.

A gust of wind rattled the pane.

A birch partially hid him; a bough of pine bobbed and swayed lazily in front of his face.

He just stood there.

Watching.

They drifted to the glass wall, one by one, not speaking, forming a line in front of the pane, holding glasses, cigarettes, Brandt lurching in place as he tried not to fall.

"Looks like some kind of cowboy or something," Trish said, clearly puzzled. "Doesn't he look like a cowboy, Ken?"

"Ain't Curt," Brandt declared loudly. He blinked as he looked at Neil. "That ain't Curt the sonofabitch." He frowned as he concentrated. "Who the hell is it?"

"A drunk," Davies suggested blandly. "Some poor pathetic slob in his cups, still thinks it's Halloween." He turned away, lips darker, flesh more pale. "A drunk. You're wasting your time."

Julia agreed as she rubbed her arms briskly. "We stand here, he gets his rocks off. This is dumb." She didn't move.

"Maybe," she said to Davies, "you could have him on your show."

Davies looked over his shoulder. "I doubt it. I doubt very seriously the poor wretch can even speak."

"My real name," said Ceil, sipping champagne, "is Llewelyn."

"Spoilsport," Davies scolded.

The wind blew much harder and the glass trembled, the snow thickened.

Large wet flakes slapped against the wall and melted, ran erratically toward the bottom, merging, splitting, vanishing beneath the sill.

Ceil brushed the glass with a palm as if to clear it.

The wind died.

No one moved.

Until Neil said, "I've had enough of this bullshit," and stalked away, realizing before he was halfway across the room that he was probably acting like a jerk, but he didn't care. Nester was wrong. That idiot outside was Curt Holgate, and he wasn't going to take the little shit's nonsense anymore. As he snatched up his jacket from where it had fallen, he looked at the wall phone, half tempted to call the police and have them haul Curt's ass away. But the kid still hadn't done anything yet, and the cops would only laugh and tell him to throw a snowball at the creep. He probably would have done the same. Hell, he had done the same, pretty much, years ago, to more than one exasperated civilian being pestered by someone not exactly breaking the law. It felt lousy being on the other side. It felt worse than lousy.

He took the steps into the restaurant at a jump and kicked out when his left arm caught in its sleeve.

"Hey," Brandt called, "you want the goddamn gun?"

He almost stopped.

And the moment the thought crossed his mind—*sure, why not?*—he banished it with an angry slash of the air with his hand.

Stupid was one thing, which was what he was, taking Holgate's juvenile bait; but really stupid was something else again.

He threw open the door and immediately slipped on the icy stoop, pitching over the two steps and landing on his knees on the gravel, spitting his rage at the snow. On his feet again, he ran as best he could, batting the flakes from his eyes, holding on to the building as he rounded the corner. Slower now so he wouldn't fall, one hand brushing the wall as a potential brace, squinting at the spot where Holgate was last seen.

Into the light suddenly, his shadow swinging ahead of him toward the water.

Wind slapped his back.

His ears began to sting.

He slipped again, to one knee, and took a moment to catch his breath and calm down.

They were watching him, he could feel them, but out

here, the snow in dervishes around him, he couldn't see very far and nearly tumbled into the creek when he reached it.

The man was gone.

Not this time, he thought angrily; not this time.

He shifted left, following the bank to a low walk-bridge of flat-topped stones he had laid down after he'd finished the waterfall. He could hear it now, some twenty yards upstream, and could see the rocks already capped in white. He hesitated. A slip, a slide, and he'd be ankle deep in freezing water. Frostbite. Pneumonia. He didn't care. His arms out for balance, he shuffled across, kicking the snow away as he went, and ran back through the trees, ducking a branch that dumped snow on him anyway, using the boles to keep him on his feet. Wind pelted him with what felt like ice. He shook his head to clear his hair, and most of the snow dribbled down his collar, his neck, sluiced down his spine.

He came to the birch a few minutes later and stood there, one hand on the trunk, shading his eyes with the other arm while he stared into the woods.

Nothing but hissing snow and dancing white.

"Bastard," he said, steam from his mouth temporarily blinding him. "Bastard!" he yelled, shaking a fist, then turning abruptly when he remembered he had an audience. He swallowed. He shrugged at them. He looked down to see if Holgate had left something behind.

He hadn't.

Not even a footprint.

Except for his own tracks, the snow was clear.

Which was, he thought as he headed back to the crossing, clearly impossible. But not so impossible if he considered how heavily the snow had begun to fall, and how long it had taken him to make up his mind to chase the bastard off. With leaves and pine needles on the ground, the snow wouldn't have been very deep in the first place—it was only an inch, not much more—and a few minutes blowing would cover everything up as if it had never been.

No big deal.

Nevertheless, he veered straight into the trees when he crossed the creek again, following a worn trail that led to his house. Thankful that for once he hadn't been conscientious about locking up after he'd left earlier, he stumbled inside and sagged back against the door. His ears burned, his lips felt chapped, and the warmth of the building felt painfully tropical as he waited for the cold to leave his lungs and let him breathe properly again.

Once done, and remembering the others, he opened the coat closet, reached in, and pulled out a rifle carefully wrapped in oilcloth. He tossed the cloth aside. A quick check to be sure the weapon wasn't loaded. A box of ammunition from the shelf behind a hat he never wore. He hoped the damn thing worked. The last time he'd fired it more than once was at a town-sponsored turkey shoot three Thanksgivings ago, the prize a free meal for ten in a Hunter Lake restaurant. He wasn't a hunter; the rifle had been his father's. And the turkeys had been cardboard. He hadn't won the meal.

As a matter of fact, he remembered with a grin, Nester had won that year, claiming he'd need all that food just to feed his wife.

The other times he'd used it were essentially whenever he had thought about it, never more than a half-dozen times a year; a cleaning, a shot or two into the air, a cleaning, a putting away until next time.

He'd look awfully stupid if he had to use it now and it blew up in his face.

After rewrapping the rifle to protect it from the weather, he left, didn't stop until he reached the parking lot, to check one more time to see if Holgate had returned. When he couldn't find him, when the wind practically slammed him against the wall, he hurried inside and gasped aloud as the storm shoved him over the threshold.

Brandt was there, his coat half on, dangling from one shoulder. "What the hell is that for? The goddamn raven's long gone."

Neil shook his head, too cold to answer, and let his own coat fall to the floor, stamped his feet to get the feeling back. Then he reached over the counter and propped the rifle against the wall, picked up the jacket and dropped it into the near booth. "Next time the jackass shows up, I'm going to scare the hell out of him."

Brandt coughed, hard and long.

Voices in the restaurant; the music had stopped.

"Going home," Brandt announced, finishing putting on his coat. Sniffed. Wiped his nose with a sleeve. "She'll kill me, I don't come home."

Neil rubbed his hands for warmth, rubbed his forearms. "On the bike, right?"

"Sure." Brandt licked his lips. "You think I'd walk on a night like this?"

Mandy came up the steps.

Neil put his hands firmly on the gambler's shoulders, looked him in the eye. "You can't."

"Sure I can. I ain't old."

"Never said you were."

"You say *you* are, damnit, that means I'm practically ancient, for Christ's sake." He slapped the hands away. "Leave me alone, I want to go home."

"Nester, c'mon, I can't let you, you know that. You fall in a ditch and freeze to death, the crone'll skin me alive."

Brandt backed away, drew himself up. "Fuck you, cop."

"Hey, c'mon, Nes."

Brandt heard Mandy's approach and stumbled around to face her. "He was a cop, y'know. Fucking disgraced the family, walked right out on his buddies."

"Damnit, Nester."

Brandt spat dryly at the floor. "You fuck him, lady, you'll probably die."

Before Neil could lose the rest of his temper, the gambler shoved him aside and kicked open the door. "I can ride in any kind of damn weather I want to."

Snow blew on the floor, scuttling toward the tables.

Neil grabbed for him.

The wind caught the door and slammed it back against the outside wall. Startled, Brandt half-fell, half-ran down the steps, threw out his hands and yelled wordlessly at the sky.

"Christ," Neil said, "I hope he doesn't want another bath."

Brandt yelled again and began to shamble across the lot toward the road.

"Neil," Mandy said, and pointed.

"Know him!" Brandt yelled, spun around, cupped his mouth. "Sonofabitch, I think I know him!"

Paying no heed to the cold, the snow, Neil stood on the threshold, Mandy right behind him, peering around his shoulder.

The man was back, in fog behind the streetlamp.

Brandt reached the fence and fell against it, grabbed the top rail to keep from sliding to the ground. "Neil, I think I know that bastard!" He lurched around and braced himself on his elbows. "Hear me, cop? I know him! I know who he looks like!"

The man in black reached into his long coat.

"Oh Jesus," Neil said, and plunged out of the room.

Something gleamed in the man's hands.

Brandt waved. "C'mon, Neil, I'll show you, I'll prove it."

Neil fell on his hands and knees, and the wind toppled him against Davies's car. He used it to pull himself up.

"Neil, you sorry bastard. I ain't drunk! He looks like—"

In the snow and wind, an explosion, fire and smoke.

Brandt screamed.

Mandy screamed.

Neil watched the gambler collapse, right arm wrapped around the top rail until his weight pulled it free and it flopped twisted to his side.

"Nester!"

The shotgun fired again, and Brandt jumped, snow in a geyser.

Neil started forward, then ran back to get his rifle, knocking Mandy off her feet, barely hearing the shouts and cries inside, raced back out and stood for a moment before leaping off the steps and running low to the fence.

He knew without looking that Nester Brandt was dead.

The ragged overcoat smoking, steaming, spilling dark onto the snow.

Neil looked up.

The man in black was gone.

For the longest time nothing moved, not the snow, not the wind, not even Neil's hand as it pressed against the back of Brandt's neck.

A cloud of smoke over the road.

Mandy back on her feet in the doorway, hands pressed to her mouth, and someone behind her trying to see what had happened.

Nothing moved.

When sound and sense returned, Neil realized his teeth were chattering and an impulse to leap the fence and chase the murderer into the woods was aborted; he ran-slid back to the door, and Mandy grabbed his arm and pulled him in.

People asked questions.

"Call the police," he ordered, and snatched his coat from the floor. "Ken, come with me."

For the longest time, nothing moved.

He grabbed Havvick's arm and thrust him away. "Get your goddamn coat and come with me." One word at a time. "Will someone for Christ's sake call the damn police? Nester's dead."

He left the rifle and ran out again, heard Havvick following and waited for him by the body.

The young man skidded to a halt against the fence, looked, and doubled over. His coat was short, not a real topcoat at all and buttoned hastily to the neck, his suit jacket poking out below it.

"We have to get him inside," Neil said.

Havvick shook his head; he couldn't do it; he couldn't touch it.

"He's gone, Ken, it's okay. The guy's gone, he's not going to shoot us."

Havvick moaned, stared at the trees.

Neil leaned down and slipped his hands under Nester's arms. "Take his feet."

The young man spat and wiped his mouth, several times with the back of a rigid hand.

"Take. His. Feet."

Havvick obeyed.

They struggled down the slope and around the building. In the storeroom, Neil decided; put him in the storeroom until the ambulance comes. Not exactly procedure, whatever the hell that passed for around here, but he couldn't leave his friend out in the cold. Not with *him* out there. He'd shot Nester in the back, shot him when he was down. No question of the cause of death; the frozen blood would mark the place.

"Why?"

Neil glanced up at Havvick's bloodless face, understood that the question had already been asked several times.

"I don't know. Don't drop him."

Jesus, Nester, how the hell'd you get so heavy?

Havvick was trying desperately not to look at what he held. "Why?"

It didn't occur to Neil to check the creek until they were already around the corner and into the light. The storeroom door was already open.

Mandy skipped aside when they stumbled in, at her feet a crumpled length of tarp. She didn't look; she waited by the staircase as they laid the body against the side wall and covered it. Ken started back outside; Neil took his arm and shook his head. Havvick nodded weakly, moved to the stairs and started up. Head and shoulders disappeared before he leaned down and said, "Don't you feel sick?" And disappeared again.

A knee began to buckle. He sagged against a post and let

the tremors work their way through him. Teeth chattering again. Blinking so fast that when Mandy stepped before him she seemed trapped in a dim strobe light that made him dizzy. Trying to move away when she reached out a hand. Feeling the cold. Swallowing bile. Raising his head helplessly toward the ceiling when she put an arm around his waist and held him, saying nothing, squeezing once in a while, finger-combing the melting snow from his hair.

I'm supposed to be mad now, he thought, watching cobwebs shift lazily in a draft; I'm supposed to go outside with forty guns strapped to my chest and blow the bastard away.

I'm supposed to be mad.

I'm acting like a baby.

Mandy said nothing; she held him and squeezed once more.

It felt like an hour; it was only a few seconds.

"The cops?" he finally asked, voice rasping.

"The phone is dead. Both of them."

"Someone will have to go."

She tugged. "Not now. Upstairs. It's warmer."

He didn't think he could move, and was amazed that his legs didn't splinter when he finally tried to walk. By the time they reached the staircase she had released him, but stayed behind him, guiding fingers lightly on his leg as he climbed the stairs hand over hand as if it were a ladder. Once he was through and out, Davies took his elbow and led him to the nearest table, and as he sat, Julia put a glass beside his hand. The hand jumped. The fingers clutched and opened. He stared at them, commanding them to knock it off. And when they didn't, couldn't, he curled the hand into his lap and stared blindly at the creek.

"Someone has to go."

"On my way," Davies volunteered without hesitation.

"West or east?"

"Deerfield," Julia told him. "West. It's closest. You

can't miss it. A blinking light at a T-intersection. Turn right and it's about a mile up, on the right." She faltered, cleared her throat. "It's a State Police barracks."

"Give him the gun," Neil told her. He cleared his throat, cleared it again. "Give him the gun."

"Oh, now wait a minute," Davies protested, holding up a hand.

"Don't argue. Julia, give him the gun."

Davies moved away to fetch his coat, still refusing. "Wouldn't do any good, believe me, I've never used one. Don't worry, I'll be fine."

"He's crazy."

"I'll be back before you know it."

"The sonofabitch is crazy."

He closed his eyes then and leaned back. The hand in his lap jumped once and steadied. Someone helped him off with his coat, and he moved as little as possible, listening to the building take on the wind, to footsteps moving cautiously around him, whispers, a woman trying not to cry and failing, but softly; rustling cloth, the clink of a bottle against a tumbler, the furnace, the scrape of a chair, the trapdoor being lowered back into place.

i think i know him

Who was it, Nester?

i know who he looks like

It wasn't a Holgate.

He hadn't seen the man's face clearly, but he knew it wasn't one of them.

So who was it, Nes, who was it?

"Hugh?"

"Don't worry, love, I won't take any chances."

A door opened and closed.

He opened his eyes and managed a grateful smile when he saw Mandy seated across the table. She returned the smile, touched her hair, nodded to the drink Julia had poured. He wasn't sure he could lift it, but he was able, with concentration, to bring it to his lips without spilling a drop, sip without choking.

It burned, and he was glad.

"So what do we do?" Havvick asked. He was in the corner booth with Ceil and Trish.

"Wait for the police."

"Don't . . ." Trish had a handkerchief balled up in her hands. "Don't you think we should get away from . . ." A fearful look at the glass wall.

Neil tensed, but the man wasn't out there, and he finally said no, there had been enough opportunities for him to fire again if he had wanted. Besides, he had a shotgun, and at that distance, and through thick glass, unless he was some kind of magician, the damage wouldn't be all that bad, the injuries nonexistent. "But if you want, you can sit up above, close the drapes. If it'll make you feel better."

Trish slid immediately out of the booth and hastened to the front. She didn't look at Kenny once.

"Feeling better, Mr. Maclaren?"

Surprised, he turned around and saw Willie standing behind the bar. His apron was gone. White shirt and white trousers, white tie. He looked as if he was on his way to church in some tropical republic.

"Yeah," he said gratefully. "Much better."

It was true. In spite of the fact that a friend's body lay in the cold beneath his feet, the reaction had passed, his mind had stopped spinning. More than anything, in fact, he felt acutely embarrassed. He was the ex-cop. He was supposed to know arcane cop things and have nerves of steel, be a leader. Be a man. He had done what he'd had to do, but somehow felt it hadn't been enough. But since no one had seemed to notice, he supposed, with guilty relief, it was, for the time being, all spilled milk. And when he heard Trish say something and heard Davies answer, he only shifted his chair instead of standing when the radio man stood in the gap at the head of the stairs and said, "The car won't work."

"That's silly, Hugh," Ceil told him. "It's practically new."

Davies shrugged. "What can I tell you? The motor won't catch. It just makes noise. Actually, it caught once and then died before I could move. And no, dear," he added patiently when her mouth opened to interrupt, "I did not look under the hood. I wouldn't know what to look for." He didn't take his coat off when he took a seat at the bar. "There are other cars, however, and that van."

It didn't take but a few seconds before Julia and Ken had handed him their keys. Willie balked, insisting he could start his own car himself. Neil didn't interfere, and the two men left, giant and child.

"Why?"

It was Ken, and from his voice, recovered.

Neil had no answers and told him so.

"A terrorist," Ceil guessed. "Kidnapper or something, wouldn't that make sense?" The cigarette in her hand wobbled until she brought it to her lips. "He cuts us off, terrifies us, and then, when he's good and ready, he'll make his demands." A wave of a hand. "Money, something like that."

"Then why did he kill Nester?" Julia wanted to know.

"He knew him," Mandy answered before Neil had a chance. "I heard him say so. He kept yelling that the guy looked like someone he knew. Then . . ." She took a breath, a shuddering deep one, and lowered her gaze to the table. "Not very good, is it."

"That he was killed just because he thought he knew who the guy was?" He took another drink and pushed himself to his feet. He couldn't just sit. "No, not very, because we all saw him too. And Nes was pretty drunk; he'd've been lucky to recognize his own wife. Besides, it wouldn't make much sense, even as some kind of graphic example. Except for Mr. Davies, I think Nester probably has more money squirreled away than the rest of us put together."

Havvick laughed scornfully. "Yeah, in your dreams."

Ceil looked at him from a distance without moving an inch. "Do cows make that much money, Mr. Havvick?"

The front door opened as Havvick launched a protest, and the two men entered noisily, stamping their feet, blowing vigorously on their hands, Davies announcing irritably that none of the other damn vehicles worked either and he was getting a bit fed up with all these ridiculous games, didn't they realize he had to be back in New York City by morning, what the hell was going on here?

Neil listened as he crossed the floor, mumbling, clapping his hands, cut himself off and said, "Jesus, this is too much."

Something; he had to do something.

"Damn right it is," Ken declared, and swaggered to the window, posed with hands on his hips, legs apart. "Bastard." He laughed. "Bastard has to shoot drunks, hasn't got the guts to shoot real people." He snorted. "Bastard." Rapped the glass with his knuckles. "Hey, stupid," he yelled. "Hey, you want to stop screwing around and . . . you want to come in . . ."

Silence.

Ken snapped his fingers nervously. Nodding, shaking his head, nodding again. Right foot tapping.

"Ken, honey?" Trish said, a child's voice. "Ken, please don't stand there, please?"

"Sure, sweetheart," he said. Nodded quickly. "Sure."

Neil understood at once what had turned the young man's bravado. Despite what he had said before, all that glass, all that open space, was too much exposure. A shooting gallery. Come and get me, you big bully; only, the bully had a weapon. Suppose the guy had more than a shotgun? Suppose he had a rifle, or some high-powered semiautomatic? He took his time, however, moving over to the switches by the door, calmly announced he was turning off the lights, and did it.

The outside leapt in.

The snow reduced to flurries.

It seemed much colder.

Too cold.

A moment, and his vision adjusted. He could see them all, twilight ghosts drifting toward the restaurant stairs, away from the light, whatever white they wore glowing, everything else simply black.

"What about the cars?" Davies wanted to know. Composed, not demanding.

Neil beckoned to Julia, nudged her gently to join the rest. She didn't protest, didn't look around when he moved over to the register and unlocked the cash drawer, and the false bottom beneath it. He took out the revolver lying below; he didn't have to check because he knew it was loaded.

"The cars," Davies repeated, not two feet away.

Neil jumped, but kept his expression blank as he stuffed the gun into his waistband. The barrel was cold, unyielding, and it didn't feel comforting at all.

"Mr. Ennin claims they weren't tampered with."

"He should know, I guess. He fixes mine all the time. The poor thing's a real clunker."

Davies was surprised. "You have a car?"

Neil's smile was sour. "Oh yeah. It's in a garage now in Deerfield, getting operated on." He laughed shortly as he came around to the floor. "Willie's good, he's not a genius."

There was no response, not even a polite laugh.

So what do you want? he demanded silently; you want me to go out there and find the son of a bitch, hogtie him with my bare hands, bring him to justice?

He paused on the steps, looked up at Davies's back, and nodded.

Yep; that's exactly what they want.

"Mr. Maclaren?"

Willie sat at a table with Julia and Mandy; Davies joining Ceil and Ken at another. Trish stayed by the plants as if they could afford her cover from the nightmare. The drapes were closed, the booths empty. He could barely see the rifle's barrel against the wall behind the counter.

"Mr. Maclaren, I don't think I understand."

Neil remained by the steps, perched on the railing. "You got me too, Willie."

"How can he stop the cars?"

"Well, obviously, he's done something to them," Davies answered.

"He didn't," the cook insisted.

"He's right," Trish said. She pointed to the entrance. "I was closing the drapes, right? He couldn't have done anything, or I would have seen him."

With a sigh Ken shook his head. "Honey, it's dark out there and the guy's wearing black, for Christ's sake. You wouldn't see him until he jumped up and bit you." He laughed—*what can you do, huh? all bed and no brains.* "Brother."

Trish took a step toward him.

Neil wasn't sure he liked the way she moved. The sweet little hysteric had heard one word too many.

Ceil coughed lightly. "So it seems as if we're just going to sit here for the rest of the night? Is that right? Eight of us and two guns, and we're just going to sit here. Have I got that right, Mr. Maclaren?"

"We could always have an orgy," Ken said, poking her with an elbow.

"You'd never live through it," she answered tonelessly, still looking at Neil.

"Tracks," Trish said to Ken, arms stiff at her sides.

"Miss Llewelyn," Neil said.

"Ceil."

"Ceil. Look, I guess I can understand what you're thinking, but whoever that guy is, he's crazy. And we are not stuntmen in the movies, no offense. I can use a gun, can you?"

She only stared at him—*what a stupid question.*

He lifted a hand in a shrug. "And it's dark. We've got woods all around us. He apparently knows his way around pretty well and he *can* shoot." He felt his patience begin to unravel but refused to lose his temper. "Besides, neither you nor Mr. Davies—"

"Hugh. Please."

"—are really dressed for the weather, and I'm not about to try to get to my place just to see if I have clothes to fit."

"But you have a telephone there."

"Ken," Trish said. Another step. "Are you listening to me?"

"If he cut the line here, he cut the line over there."

"You don't know that."

Easy, he thought; easy does it.

He waved to the door. "Okay, go ahead. You just go down the path that starts on the other side of the parking lot. The door's unlocked." He waved again. "Be my guest."

She blew smoke toward him. "As you said, I'm not dressed for it."

He gave up, turned, and collided with Trish, who grabbed his arm and leaned on it while she said, "Kenny, there weren't any fucking tracks!"

Ken gaped at her.

Davies looked confused. "I'm sorry, but I don't—"

Trish looked up at Neil, pleading. "You went out to get . . . him, and the snow's all messed up where you went. There aren't any other tracks, Mr. Maclaren. If that guy out there messed around with the cars, there'd be tracks or something from the road." She glared at Ken. "There aren't any goddamn tracks!"

Ken pushed his chair back and stood. "Christ, what the hell are you talking about?" He stomped over to a booth, knelt on the seat and shoved the drapes aside. "I was out there, remember?"

"Little prick," she muttered.

Neil was inclined to agree, but held his peace. And he wasn't about to say anything about the tracks. She was wrong, but forcing her temper farther along to real explosion wasn't going to do any of them any good.

Then Ken said, "She's right." Looked over his shoulder, wonder on his face. "I'll be damned, she's right."

Ravens," Julia said, watching her fingers twine and twist. "They never come out at night."

Willie covered her hands with his.

She stared at him, and pulled away.

There's been a lot of snow," Neil reminded them. He pushed away from the window, sat on the edge of the seat, hands clasped between his knees. "He had plenty of time to do . . . whatever . . . while Ken and I were taking Nester to the storeroom." He told them about the tracks he hadn't found by the birch. "The wind blows, the tracks are covered pretty quick." A thumb jerked over his shoulder. "If we were out there, we'd be able to see the depressions."

Trish remained by the stairs, backlit by the bar windows. "Do you believe that, Mr. Maclaren?"

He couldn't see her face.

Hell, no, I don't believe it.

"Sure."

He could see her shrug, could tell she wasn't sure about the lie—if it was a lie, if he was humoring her, if he wasn't lying at all.

Suddenly she turned. "My god."

Neil stood, and saw him.

On this side of the creek now, on the bank, standing in a faint mist rising from the snow, from the water. Collar up on a black duster that reached the ground, a flat-crown wide-brimmed black hat that kept his face in shadow in spite of the light shining directly at him, black gloves.

Standing there.

The mist shifting, curling around him and over the water that just for the moment seemed frozen.

His right hand moved into his coat.

"Down!" Neil shouted.

Chairs toppling, tables scraping, the girl not moving.

"Trish!"

Two shots.

Explosions.

Flares of flame.

Two floodlights went out.

The silence almost hurt.

The wind came up again.

A minute, maybe more, before Neil shook his head clear of the gunshot echoes and rose unsteadily to his feet. The revolver was in his hand. He tucked it away quickly, but not before he saw Mandy looking at him oddly.

Trish marched over the table and grabbed Ken to his feet by the front of his shirt. He tried to smack her hands away, but she yanked him, virtually dragged him across the restaurant floor and down the steps to the lounge. When he called her a bitch, she swung him around in front of her and slapped him. Hard. With the back of her hand. Turned him around again and shoved until he collided with the window.

Then she leaned close, grabbed a fistful of hair, and shouted directly into his ear, "See, you shithead? Do you see?"

Neil grabbed her arm before she slammed Ken's face into the glass.

But she was right.

The man was gone.

The snow was clean.

We have got to get out of here," Ceil whispered to Davies.

They were alone at the table, the others joining Ma-claren at the bar window.

"Hugh, are you listening to me?"

He ran a manicured finger down the side of his glass. "What do you suggest we do, darling? Make a run for it?"

She decided to slap his face, decided against it, decided that yes, she did want to run for it, decided that that was just as stupid as it sounded. She coughed. She cleared her throat viciously. She wanted to walk away from him, away from all of them, but there was no place to go and she knew her legs wouldn't hold her up for more than a few steps.

"Ceil, are you all right?"

God, she hated him.

Sometimes in the middle of loving him, she wanted to cut his throat. So smug, so damn knowing, so almighty sure of himself that if he walked on water, he'd probably bitch about his precious shoes getting wet. Nothing surprised him. Nothing. When she had told him she was pregnant, he hadn't blinked, hadn't smiled, hadn't frowned, hadn't yelled. He hadn't done anything. Until she had started to cry with frustration because she was goddamn tired of making all the goddamn decisions, goddamn tired of having to assemble his wardrobe and make his appointments with all the right people and make the reservations at all the right restaurants and sit there practically all night in that goddamn stupid, smelly, smoky radio station booth and decide which people calling in wouldn't make him look like an ass.

"Ceil, darling, would you like a drink?"

Why the hell didn't he know how scared she was? They were going to die! There was a creep out there sneaking around like a goddamn Indian, blowing people away, blowing out the lights, and when they were all frightened enough, he was going to blow away the door and come in and kill them all. Why the hell couldn't he see that? What the hell was the matter with him?

"Here, Ceil, let me put that out for you before you burn your finger."

He took the cigarette and stubbed it out in the ashtray.

He smiled at her.

She didn't want to tell him.

She wanted him to *know*.

Like she had wanted him to *know* that she hadn't wanted the abortion; like she had wanted him to *know* that she truly hated New York, wanted to be back in Chicago; like she had wanted him to *know* goddamnit that she thought it an extraordinarily stupid idea to call Mandy, of all goddamn people, to join them in a drive out here into the middle of nowhere, a stupid idea when they had all of Manhattan to find things to do in, a stupid idea when he had *her,* for god's sake, if he wanted excitement; like she wanted him to know *now* that if she loved him one more minute, she would have to kill him.

"Wine?"

She closed her eyes and felt the tears. "Yes," she surrendered quietly. "That would be nice."

"I thought so."

His hand patted her shoulder, gripped it, squeezed it, caressed her back tenderly before pulling away.

When her eyes opened again, she was alone, and the room looked as if it had been flooded. She grabbed a napkin and dabbed at her eyes. Carefully. Mustn't mess. Mustn't let him see.

Mustn't let him.

Mustn't.

After looking at the snow with everyone else, Willie decided it would be better if he waited in the kitchen. All the people were making him nervous, they were even starting to talk about ghosts and stuff like that which didn't even exist. Next thing he knew, they'd be doing things like he saw in the movies, putting garlic around the doors and finding silver crosses to wear around their necks and saying prayers and beating drums and doing dances, and none of it was going to do them any good. The man outside wanted it that way. He knew that. It was clear as a bell. As the nose on his face. As mud in a stream. The man wanted them all so scared they wouldn't be able to see straight, think straight, find their noses in front of their faces, find their ass with both hands. Then he was going to come inside and kill them all just the way he had killed the drunken prick. He didn't feel bad about that at all, Nester dead and rotting. Julia had hit him, he was bad, he deserved to die, no question about it. Willie would have made sure of that himself if the man outside hadn't done it first. But Julia didn't deserve to die. It wasn't like they were going together or anything, it wasn't like she had let him touch her, but she was a pretty good friend all in all, and she sure didn't deserve to die like the drunken prick. And he was going to try to make sure that it didn't happen. He didn't have a gun. He could use one, he'd used them before, but he didn't have one now. What he had was his kitchen. And everything in it. He knew how to use all that, too, and if the man came in the side door, he'd never leave the kitchen alive.

Willie knew how to use everything.

He knew how to use it well.

She twisted her wrist out of Maclaren's grip and walked away from them, to the bar. She didn't have to look out there a second time. She knew what she saw. The man in the black coat didn't leave any tracks. The wind was screaming quietly across the roof, but the snow wasn't that dry, and even if it had been, it couldn't have covered the tracks all that fast.

He just didn't make them.

She didn't know how, and she didn't care right at the moment. She did care that no one touch her because then she'd have to start screaming, and if she started screaming, Ken would say something nasty and she'd have to scream at him. And then. And then. Then maybe he wouldn't marry her.

She leaned over the bar and flipped open a chrome lid, found a beer down there and pulled it out, twisted the cap off, and drank from the bottle.

She burped.

She saw herself in the mirror and blew a mocking kiss at her reflection.

Married.

Jesus.

He was a cold bastard, a cruel bastard, a sometimes sadistic bastard, and about as stupid as they come. Men, that is. Tight sweaters and tight jeans and bikini panties and black or red bras and a little feel now and again, a long, loud, submissive fuck now and then, and their balls were hers. Sometimes it was so easy, she had to throw up afterward. Sometimes she actually enjoyed herself, and still threw up later.

Ken was something else again.

There were days when he smelled like cowshit, days when he smelled like the damp inside of a barn, days when he smelled like everything that ever came out of the ass end of a chicken, even though he had never worked his old man's farm a day in his life. He, the hero, worked in the office. Counting the money. Helping his old man make the money. Helping himself to the money and spending it on

her. His old man hated her. When Ken was in the kitchen
once, getting coffee after dinner, the old man called her a
slut and told her it would be a cold day in Hell when she
got a single penny of his business.

She didn't want his fucking business.

She wanted the money.

But she wasn't going to get it if they didn't get out of
here, and soon.

She drank.

She watched herself drinking.

Ken called her. Ordered her to get over to his side.

Heel, Trish, good girl.

The man out there, the man with no face . . . she
shuddered and swallowed and emptied the bottle before
taking another breath.

Hugh, still wearing his muffler, sat on the last stool near
the rest rooms, Neil standing beside the window.

"So when are you going to get him?" Davies asked, as
though he were asking when Maine lobster would be back
on the menu.

Neil didn't bother answering. So many films, so much
television, and him the ultimate hero cliché—a former cop
aching to be back on the line. What bullshit. What he
wanted to do was live. What he wanted to do was figure
out how the hell the man in black was doing what he did.
He didn't have to check the thermometer to know that the
temperature had drifted into the low twenties, damn near
zero with the wind. And that creep out there wasn't
dressed warmly enough to be able to stay out there long.
He shouldn't have stayed there this long. Unless he was
really packed under that coat. Unless . . . he looked at the

side wall. The cabins? Could he have been hiding in the cabins? Was that where he went when the cold got too much? Or the house? The house had an oil furnace; the cabins only fireplaces and space heaters. But they were protection from the wind.

So was the house.

So where were his tracks?

"I take it that means no."

Neil turned to him slowly, tried to keep his voice even. "You haven't been paying attention, have you?"

Hugh leaned back. Said nothing.

"Why don't you try it?"

"I checked the cars."

"So check out the guy."

Hugh shook his head. "This is your country, Neil, not mine. I'm a city boy, remember? All I have to worry about is muggers in broad daylight."

"Bullshit." Neil stabbed a thumb at the window. "We got trees, you got buildings, it's all the same, pal. Country boy, city boy don't wash out here."

Hugh brushed at the muffler, pulled at both ends as though drying his neck. "Maybe yes, maybe no, but I'd still like to know who that guy is before I try anything stupid." His smile came and went. "And I think just about anything we try will be awfully stupid, don't you?"

"Patience."

"Patience," the man agreed.

Neil leaned against the wall, gazed out at the creek. The mist had been driven away by the snow falling again, but it seemed foggy all the same. The branches were laden, sagging, dipping, every so often a clump of white tumbling to the ground. A hand to his mouth to touch his lips, then into a loose fist that pressed its knuckles lightly against the pane. He supposed, if he kept the rifle and gave Hugh or Ken the revolver, one could station himself down at the storeroom door, the other outside. If the man came around to the road, the rifleman could take him; if he showed up at the back again, there'd be two chances to get him.

If it happened in the first five or ten minutes, no problem; any longer than that, and they'd be too cold to do anything. Too stiff.

Assuming the man in black didn't spot them first.

Assuming Nester's death had been the result of a lucky shot.

Right, he thought; right.

He heard Davies shift, the leather creaking.

Something clanged, muffled, in the kitchen, and it was a chilling long moment before he remembered Willie was in there.

"Time?" Davies asked.

Neil held his wrist up to the light, squinted. "Eleven, give or take."

"It feels like the dead of the morning." He grunted. "So to speak." He took off the muffler, folded it neatly on his thigh, flapped it open and draped it back around his neck. "Maybe we ought to have a plan."

Neil cocked his head—*go ahead, give me one.*

"I mean," said Hugh, lowering his voice and glancing quickly toward the others, "it'll give them something to think about besides him."

"You know, I've been thinking about a bunch of things along those lines," Neil said, watching his breath fog and fade on the pane. He shook his head. "I don't know if anything would work."

"Doesn't have to, as long as they're busy."

"I've been thinking too that things are awfully calm in here." He looked at Davies. "You know what I mean? A man's been shot—in the back, too—and once that was over, we've just been . . . sitting around."

"Well, whose stupid fucking idea was that?" Ken demanded, moving down the bar, spinning the stools.

"Seems to me you're the one who made it clear we shouldn't do anything but wait for the cavalry."

Neil nodded. "Yeah, I guess I did."

"Seems to me Curt was right."

"Oh?"

Ken looked at Davies, *we're talking man to man here, okay?* "What you got, see, is trouble here. Bad trouble, am I right? So what a guy does—a real guy, that is—what the guy does is, he does something about it. Somebody wants a fight, you fight, am I right? Somebody wants to blow your head off, you make sure he doesn't. Course, you're not a real guy, see, you just kind of stick around, pull your head in, wait for someone else to pull your ass out of the fire. Am I right?"

Davies crossed his legs. "So what do you suggest?"

Ken sniffed, looked around and saw Julia standing at the bar's turn. Trish had taken a stool; Mandy sat beside her. He waggled his fingers at them.

"What we got," he continued, speaking now to Neil, "is two guns and a whole shitload of big knives, right? Okay. So we get as warm as we can, use the tablecloths if we have to under our coats—hell, the radio man's lady got a fur coat, for god's sake, it must be good for something besides tickling her chin. We get ready and start walking to Deerfield. We don't have to get as far as the cops, even. Hell, there's that development—Meadow Heights, Meadow View, something—long before we get to the light. Maybe what, half a mile up, tops? We stick to the middle of the road, guns front and back, and we move it." He grinned proudly. "Even in the snow it isn't going to take all that long."

"What about the killer?" Mandy asked.

"No sweat. You got lanterns, flashlights, shit like that, right?" he asked Neil. "We all carry something, keep it on the woods. Somebody sees him, we pop him."

"What if he sees us first?" she said. "What if he shoots first?"

"Hey," he said, spreading his arms, "it's a chance, okay? You gotta take a chance. If he does shoot first, we'll know where he is and pop him anyway." He shrugged. "Hey, it's a chance."

She looked right at Neil and said, "Okay."

Ken applauded. "Right! Smart lady!"

"But first you have to tell me about the tracks."

"How the hell should I know about the damn tracks?" he snapped, almost shouting. "He's a fucking angel, how the hell should I know, who cares? He's got a gun, he pulls the trigger, he ain't no ghost. Jesus Christ!" He stamped a foot. "Jesus . . . Christ."

"Ken," Trish said.

He looked back at her and rolled his eyes. "Yeah, yeah, so you're scared. So what else is new?" When she refused to meet his gaze, he leaned back, elbows up on the bar, almost smug. "Look, no hard feelings, Mr. Maclaren, but maybe this ain't your kind of thing, you know what I mean?"

When you get old, Neil thought at him, you're still going to look like a teenager. No lines. Big eyes. Your hundred-year-old aunt is still going to want to pinch your cheeks.

And you'll still be a jerk.

He looked down at the yard.

The man hadn't been standing in the snow, he realized then; not in the snow, but at the edge of the creek on the lip of the bank. There are rocks and pebbles there, thick grass. There's a fair distance between us and him. We couldn't see his tracks even if we wanted to.

You're not an angel.

You're not the Devil.

Son of a bitch, how about that.

None of it, however, made him feel any better. As it

was, he didn't dare speak. What the young man had said had stung almost as bad as Nester's drunken accusation, and he would not, dared not let himself be provoked. That way lies not only madness, but sure death. He hadn't been kidding. He wanted to live. And he wasn't about to provide the madman out there with a human shooting gallery.

"If you want to try it," he said to the window, "go ahead. I'm not going to stop you."

Havvick snorted—*as if you could.*

"Ken," Trish said, "that's crazy."

"Perhaps," said Hugh, "but the young man's effort may lead us to something better."

"Like what?" Ken asked, twisting to press his chest against the bar. "You got something in mind?"

Hugh shrugged. "Not at the moment, no. But as I said, what you've suggested might be used as a starting point to another idea. That's what I meant."

"So. None of you want to try it? You're just going to let this guy shit all over us, right?"

Neil frowned. Why wouldn't the kid just let it go? What was the point?

Ken made a noise of disgust deep in his throat, pushed away from the bar, and walked back toward the tables. When he reached Mandy, he stopped and said, "And fuck the damn footprints," before moving on.

Mandy laughed softly, quickly.

Ken turned around just as Neil did.

"Lady, I don't see you using your brains."

She stared at him, a mild smile.

He looked pointedly at her chest. "God knows you got enough of them."

She slapped him.

It wasn't hard, she didn't bring her arm back for a round-house swing, but it was loud. It stung. It widened his eyes. He looked at the others, finally looked at Neil, who watched him almost lazily, canting his head just a little, just the slightest touch of a dare, and Havvick snorted again in disgust, turned his back and walked away.

Is that what you are? Neil thought to his back; is that what you are?

And what are you, he asked himself.

A survivor.

It tasted bad.

Trish wandered off then, and Hugh followed, muffler in his hand and swinging at his side.

Mandy shifted to the last stool, swiveled a revolution, hooked her feet over the brass band near the bottom. There was no emotion in her expression. She merely looked at the snow, but he saw that she had buttoned his cardigan above the neckline, had one hand buried in a pocket.

"He's going to do something, you know," she said at last.

He nodded.

He knew it.

Havvick wouldn't let his own challenge go unanswered. He would mutter to himself for several minutes, check the outside, check his courage, finally announce to one and all that he wasn't about to sit on his butt anymore and let some freak scare him like he was a kid, or a coward. There was no telling how far he would get, maybe not even as far as the front door, before Trish begged him to stay.

Maybe he would.

Maybe he wouldn't.

Neil bet Nester's ghost the kid would go.

What he didn't bet was if the kid would live long enough to gloat.

"Jones," Mandy said.

He looked at her. "Sorry?"

She twirled a strand of hair around her forefinger. "Ceil's name is Llewelyn. Mine is Jones."

When she paused, he wondered what he was expected to say. His shrug said *okay, so?*

The speakers crackled, and they jumped, grinned sheepishly.

Tommy Dorsey.

He thought about the front window then, downstairs. And the rifle. He looked at the trapdoor and said, "Would you mind opening that up for me? I'll be back in a second."

To the front.

Ignoring the others watching him.

At the counter he picked up another candy bar, and the rifle, looked outside and saw nothing but moving lines of white.

Trombones over the speakers.

They were quiet when he returned, though he heard someone stirring in the booth, heard a low voice but no words as he propped the rifle in the corner and peeled the oilcoth away, let it crumple to the floor. A hand through his hair. A glance over his shoulder—Mandy was gone, he couldn't see Julia, he couldn't see anyone.

He was alone.

They had walked out and left him.

A chill rippled from crotch to throat, and he swallowed heavily until he saw a vagrant flash over in the corner booth. Skin. Gem. Eye. It didn't matter. His throat was parched, and he fumbled hastily over the bar to grab a clean glass, moved down and leaned over again, turned on a spigot and filled the glass with water. He drank it all without taking a breath. He felt the woods at his back, the glass, the man in black.

He refused to turn around.

His imagination, that's all. It worked on him the way it worked on the others, tricking them, teasing them, using the storm and the night and the wind and the trees to show them a black ghost who left no traces behind but the body of a man.

A man who came and went at will.

A man impervious to the weather.

A man who had murdered a drunken gambler who cheated on his wife and cheated at cards and cheated on every friendship he had ever had in his life. Not a terrible man, however; an ordinary man. Not a murderer. Never a murderer.

Came and went.

Killed and left.

Neil gripped the padded rim of the bar suddenly, hard, feeling abruptly nauseated when a brief, terrifying wave passed over him, through him.

He blinked.

Jesus.

Jesus God.

It was envy.

I t passed, *not envy, how can it be envy? jesus,* and he set the glass down with exaggerated care and lowered himself onto one of the stools. He folded his hands before him, stared at his reflection in the mirror, hiding behind bottles and the popcorn machine. Several deep breaths and a caution that this kind of thing wasn't going to do anybody any good. He had to remain calm. All the time. He saw Julia peer around the corner, frowning.

"Someone," he said, "should sit up front and let me know if that guy shows up there."

She didn't move.

"Please."

"Okay. Sure."

His reflection looked more impassive than he felt. A false study of confidence. A paradigm of granite. A riddle of a man who knew what was right and did it despite the denunciations of others. The question was the definition of "right." Protect, in this case, the people under his roof. Do it by staying, do it by leaving, do it by doing nothing.

A woman's hand passed twice in front of his eyes. He shifted his gaze but not his head, and Ceil, a cigarette in her left hand, tapped a finger on the bar.

"I'm a committee of one," she said.

He waited.

"They've decided. They want to leave."

He puffed his cheeks. "I said before, I'm not going to stop anybody. You want to try it, go ahead."

"That's what I told them you'd say."

Pressure from his foot swiveled the stool around to face her. "So?"

"Cow boy wants the rifle."

He laughed humorlessly, barely a sound. "Cow boy can whistle for the moon." He had no idea why he'd said that. Logic should have had him agreeing. He would keep the revolver, let those leaving have the bigger weapon. Havvick could probably use it, most young kids around here could, and probably use it well enough not to shoot any of his party by mistake. But he shook his head. "No." He pulled the gun from his waistband, held it out to her. She stared at it, neither fear nor excitement, and took it. "Cow boy doesn't like it, he can break up a table and use the legs for clubs."

She turned her head side to side, blowing smoke, creating a screen. By the time he blinked it from his eyes, she was walking away. Slowly. Hips not quite snapping. The hand that held the gun down at her side.

She hadn't reached the end of the bar when Hugh called from the front: "Company."

He was off the stool before anyone said a word, had the

rifle in his hand and was on his way down the steps before someone called his name.

Stay there, he thought; stay there, you son of a bitch.

He didn't look at the tarp.

He darted around the posts, bent over as the roof and stone floor rose toward each other, was on his knees when he reached the window, no more than two feet wide, half that high. Old boxes were shifted out of the way, shards of cement dusted from a ledge extending out from the sill. The outside level with the gravel, part of the pane now covered to the depth of the snow. He breathed downward to prevent the glass from fogging and unlatched it. It was stuck. He leaned close, and squinted.

Saw him.

Shadow against shadow in his usual place just back of the streetlight.

Diamonds of snow winking on his shoulders.

fairy dust

raven's wings

Running footsteps upstairs and harsh whispered voices, a chair scraping, something heavier, voices again and he wasn't sure but that he heard his name mentioned once.

He tried pushing the frame, but it wouldn't budge. It hadn't been open in years; the wood soft and rotted in places, splintered in others. If he hit harder, if he broke the pane, if the frame protested, the man would be alerted and leave.

If he fired through the glass, there was no telling whether the shot would be true.

It didn't matter.

The man would know they were armed, maybe take the opportunity to leave, and leave them alone.

And if he was lucky, then what the hell, he was lucky.

He eased back and brought the rifle to his shoulder, chambered a round that sounded like a gunshot itself.

Sighted on the man's chest.

Uphill.

Shadow.

You never hit those damn turkeys, you know.

The barrel quivered.

Footsteps heading toward the back. Hard. Determined. Someone definitely yelling his name now.

He inhaled very slowly.

A flurry of snow pattered against the window and fell away, making him blink.

Very slowly he exhaled until the barrel stopped moving.

He held his breath.

The man in black didn't move.

Neil fired.

Twice.

Someone screamed.

Distant.

Muffled.

Footsteps running.

Distant.

Muffled.

The night spat at him, snow and wind through the shattered pane. His ears rang. His head ached. He blinked to clear his vision and finally saw the empty space by the streetlamp. Nothing on the ground. Nothing in the street.

His ears rang.

His head ached.

He chambered another round and stared, waited, ignoring the sounds above his head, waiting for something to move, out there in the dark. But there was nothing to see but short streaks of white. Nothing to hear but the snow hissing at him, flicking across his face, pricking his cheeks and brow until it melted and he reached down and grabbed a small burlap bag and stuffed it clumsily into the hole one-handed.

You missed.

He nodded.

It's not that you hit him and he didn't die; you missed, that's all.

He nodded again and backed away stiffly, lungs working like shallow pumps as if there were a stench he was trying to avoid. His gaze didn't stray from the window, and when his head brushed against a beam, he ducked in fear, couldn't spin around, scrambled back and backed away when he could stand.

The window shrank.

You missed.

Not much bigger than a large cat's eye.

By his left shoulder, a bulb whose light was a flash in the corner of his eye. He turned from the window slowly, thinking it had been a damn good idea anyway, it didn't matter that he missed because, as he said before, the man now knew they weren't going to sit around all night and let him pick them off. One by one.

They weren't.

He shuddered.

His right hand burned, throbbed a little, and he realized he was gripping the rifle much too tightly. After looking at it stupidly, a conscious effort to relax. The rifle shifted to the other hand. He flexed his fingers. Blew on them. Looked to the tarp huddled against the wall and apologized to Nes for disturbing his sleep.

And stopped.

A hand lay on the rippled concrete floor, poked out from under the cover, fingers curled upward, thumb folded into the palm.

Oh Jesus, he thought, and hurried over, reached down, changed his mind, and used his foot instead to push the hand out of sight.

Another apology, and a sudden and difficult swallow that made his eyes water. He shook his head and walked toward the stairs, listening now for the others, and hearing nothing but soft voices, sexless and flat.

The music ended.

The wind took its place.

He climbed out of the basement, feeling as though he were surfacing from a dive, out of a deep-water cavern where all the light went to die. Monsters down there, and a cold that penetrated every cell, every bone. His head, and he saw the floor; his shoulders, and he saw Davies standing by the window, looking toward him, Ceil and Trish on either side; his waist, and he laid the rifle down, gave them a weak smile and a shrug before using his hands to push the rest of the way clear, pick the weapon up again and place it on the bar.

"There's a box of shells in my coat," he said to no one in particular.

Somebody moved; he could hear heels on the flooring. It was Julia.

"I think you missed," the radio man said.

He nodded. "I think so, too."

"I thought," said Ken from someplace he couldn't see around the corner, "you said you could shoot."

"I said I could use a gun." No anger. His ears weren't ringing, but his head still ached. "I never said I was Annie Oakley." A pause. "He got the message."

He leaned against the bar for a minute, pushed off and headed for the tables. He was thirsty, he was tired, he didn't want to talk and couldn't figure out why. Ceil moved aside to let him pass. He looked at Davies, who looked back without expression; then he dropped into a chair and stared out the window.

The creek, the trees, the snow, the night.

"All right!" Ken said urgently, clapping his hands once. "Now let's get going, okay?"

Neil lowered his head, chin resting against his sternum. "What the hell are you talking about?"

The young man shifted to stand in front of him. His coat was on, gloves sticking out of his pockets. "You've scared him off, so now we can haul ass before he decides to come back, right?" He waited. "That was the idea, right?"

Neil didn't answer, not even when Havvick nodded, taking the silence for assent. He hurried away, and Neil watched the snow.

I missed him, he thought; honest to God, I missed him, but if he has any brains, he'll already be in the next county.

A shout.

He turned quickly and saw Willie standing in the kitchen doorway. Havvick tried to push past him, and Ennin shoved him away.

"Goddamnit, you jerk, we need those knives!"

"You can't have them," Willie protested. "Mr. Maclaren, tell him he can't have them."

Ken tried to pass again, and again Willie blocked the way.

Neil pushed himself out of the chair.

Ken grabbed the little man's shoulder and yanked him forward, put a hand in the middle of his back, and shoved. Hard. Willie went down, and Julia stomped toward them behind the bar, dropping the box of shells by the register, her face dark and her eyes narrow.

Ken vanished into the kitchen, swearing loudly.

Willie sat up.

Neil felt abruptly cold.

"Hey," he said.

Julia rounded the end of the bar and held out a hand. Willie took it and let himself be pulled to his feet. But when he tried to follow Havvick, she refused to release him. "Let him go," she whispered, her arm stretched out, Willie hooked at the end.

"*My* knives," he argued.

"Let him go."

Neil saw the look that passed between them, and felt the cold again.

"Jesus Christ," Ceil muttered, back in her place, back in the booth.

Havvick kicked the swinging door open, a cleaver in one hand, a long carving knife in the other. He grinned at the cook, and winked. "Damn, you keep these things sharp, don't you." He nodded thanks at the bartender and made his way around them.

Neil watched.

Willie watched.

At the bar's corner, Ken dropped the cleaver and blade beside the shells and looked around. "We haven't much time. Maybe it's too late already. You ready to go?"

No one moved.

Havvick shrugged; he didn't give a damn. "Trish, get your coat? I'll get the rifle." He reached for the weapon, but Julia, still holding Willie's hand, pulled it out of reach. "You stupid bitch, what the hell are you doing?" He stepped back and grabbed the barrel, yanked it to his chest, and shook his head. "Jesus." He checked it, saw the shell box, and reloaded. Stuffed the box into his coat and patted it. "You coming, cop?"

Neil almost laughed. "He shot Nes when Nes was down. What makes you think he's scared? Or scared off?"

Trish had one arm in a coat sleeve; she froze.

"What makes you think I just didn't make him more cautious?"

Havvick snorted. "Y'know, Maclaren, sometimes I wonder about you, I really do. God." He picked up the cleaver and blade, awkwardly holding them in one hand. "Trish?"

Davies came to the top of the steps. "Sorry," he said. "It's too late. He's back."

Nobody moved.

There was no need.

Mandy heard Neil's sharp bark of a laugh and pulled her legs up onto the seat, hugged her knees, wriggled her toes. She sat in the first booth, leaves and spider legs trailing down toward her right shoulder, the paneled wall not quite chilly on her back. She had hurried there, practically run, when Neil had disappeared downstairs, stayed when the shots were fired, stayed when he returned, stayed when the cow boy decided to make his move and save them all.

She thought the little cook was going to kill him.

She thought Neil was going to kill him.

Then Davies made his announcement, and they all stood there like idiots, mouths open, Havvick ready to burst into tears, Trish flinging her coat in despair to the floor, Neil laughing just that once and dropping back into his chair and shaking his head. Once. Just once.

Swell, she thought; goddamn story of my life.

You get a stupid first name like Mandy, you get a miserably ordinary last name like Jones, and nobody believes you're for real. Jones? Mandy Jones? Try putting that on a motel register without a sly look from the clerk. Try hiding the fact that you weren't practically born in a Welsh coal mine, that you're actually someone with an ordinary middle-class past just like everyone else, and all they do is talk about your accent, how lovely it is, how like music it sounds, how come in all this time in the States you never lost it, aren't you proud to be an American now?

Try to keep age from taking everything away.

Try to prove you're more than a chest, that you've got a quick and decent mind, and what do you get?

She grinned.

Another day older and a-deeper in debt.

In less than an hour Neil would be her age, and he'd still be lost; in less than an hour she would be his age, and she'd still be lost.

Life's a bitch.

She wondered if anyone had noticed that nothing, not a single car, not a single truck, had gone by the restaurant since the sander.

The furnace grumbled.

Muted static from the ceiling speakers as someone turned the player off and on, off and on.

Mr. Maclaren, have you considered lowering the price for your establishment?"

"Every second for the last hour or so, Mr. Davies."

"Because I think I want it."

"Think all you want, Hugh. You're not going to get it."

"The publicity of this night alone is going to make one of us a fortune. I think, no offense, I'd rather it be me."

"You're nuts, Hugh."

"Like a fox, Neil."

"Well, you're still not going to get it."

"Don't count on it, Maclaren. Don't bet your life."

Ceil couldn't believe what she heard. Buy this place? Was he out of his goddamn mind? He thought this was good publicity?

Out here?

Live out here in the woods, ninety feet of snow in the winter, a million degrees hot in the summer, and she had heard Maclaren telling Mandy before, about the bear.

Out here?

No.

She looked at the rifle the cow boy still held, at the cleaver and carving knife. Smiled to herself.

One more word, she vowed, a chill of excitement making her grin; one more word, you smug Texas bastard, and you're going to die.

Trish decided she was going to bed Hugh Davies before he left for the city. No big deal. He was famous. He was in the newspapers. He was on the radio, and that made him more tempting than if she had to look at his face every night on a television screen.

She'd fuck him and then tell Kenny.

See what happens.

She would probably pay for it later, when she and Kenny were alone, but it would be better than sitting around here, doing nothing, waiting to die.

Mandy's left hand cupped her right shoulder, right hand cupped left shoulder, forearm pressed against her breasts, staring at the snow swirling over the creek.

A part of her mind, some distant part that giggled hysterically whenever she uttered her last name, suggested that this was going to be her last night alive. Heaven was the next stop; surely it wouldn't be Hell. She wasn't a saint, for crying out loud, not with her line of work, but she wasn't like that man out there, the man in the duster. She was human. And so were the others, which meant that they wouldn't be very effective when he finally decided to come inside. She wondered what he looked like without all those clothes on. A strong face? Beard? Dark eyes or blue eyes? Did he ever smile? Did he smile when he killed that obnoxious gambler man? Did he care?

She didn't think so.

That's what grew the ice in her chest.

He didn't care.

A slow breath.

Hugging her knees.

Watching Trish plop onto the last barstool and demand a drink from the bartender, who moved to comply, pulling the cook gently behind her.

Watching the dim glow of Ceil's cigarette. A pulse. Not quite a heartbeat. But fast enough to reach the filter in less than a few minutes if she didn't pay attention.

Watching without turning her head as Hugh stepped down from the restaurant and absently wrapped his muffler around his hand as he surveyed the lounge. His coat was still on. Trish whispered something to him. He looked to her, over to Ceil. He didn't seem to know what to do next.

Neither did she.

Nothing but sit.

And feel the building shrink.

It was; it was shrinking. The dark that had been born when the lights had been turned out was slipping out of the corners, crawling toward the tables in streamers and bands, stopping whenever somebody looked down, puzzled, moving again when they looked away.

Smaller; like the mines.

Deep in the mines, where the sun never shines, and a voice floated forever on the back of black light.

Smaller.

She hugged her knees.

Smaller.

She felt a tear.

Smaller, Havvick thought angrily, then fearfully, then angrily again; smaller.

It was like some damn movie or other he had seen on television, some guy in some cell in some damn foreign country screaming that the walls were closing in on him, were going to crush him, while the guards sat at a table outside and played cards and laughed at him and once in a while threw him a crust of stale bread.

Of course, it wasn't really growing smaller, this two-bit place of Maclaren's; but it might as well be.

It might as well be.

He set the cleaver and the blade down gingerly, as if they were made of glass, and arranged the rifle beside them. Then he yanked off his tie, stuffed it in his suit jacket and draped the jacket carelessly over the back of a chair. He didn't look at the others, certainly wouldn't look at the ex-cop, not after he'd laughed, like he was enjoying the whole thing and couldn't wait to see what came next. Ken wouldn't look at him, because if he did, he would do something stupid. He knew it. Not the way he knew Trish gave good head or had a mole under her right breast or didn't want him for anything but his money; it was a knowing that came with the shrinking of the room. A feeling. His father would call it a hunch, a businessman's hunch that would, if acted upon now, rake in the money before the rest of the world caught on and caught up. A feeling that goaded him, whispered to him, suggested snidely that he was a little coward, and the only way to prove he wasn't was to do something stupid.

Like kill the ex-cop.

Stupid.

Like the cop—correction: the *ex*-cop—would just sit there and let him.

The others he didn't care about. They wouldn't try to stop him. They'd yell a lot, maybe, and maybe they'd try to tie him up when it was over, but they wouldn't stop him while he was doing it. Not them. He knew them. He'd seen them before. They'd just stand there and watch, like they just stood and didn't move when he'd told them, he goddamn *told* them it was time to get their asses in gear and get the hell out.

Until it was too late, and the room began to shrink.

He snapped his fingers, unfastened his shirt's top button, walked to the window and counted the steps; walked back to the bar and up into the restaurant to the front door, and counted the steps; walked back down to the bar and the back window, and counted the steps, and didn't believe it when they were the same, give or take, because he had to move around the tables. Didn't believe it. The room was definitely smaller.

Snapped his fingers.

Watched Trish empty a glass, head back, chest out. Talking softly to the radio man, who smiled at her. Blankly.

Watched Ceil smoking, and staring, and smoking, and wondering what the radio man had that he didn't have that she would be so damn snotty to him. It wasn't like he hadn't been called something like cow boy before; it wasn't that. It was the way she said it, like she was talking to a pet dog. Worse than a pet dog, one of those tiny pet dogs not much bigger than a rat.

He could kill her too.

And nobody would stop him.

The radio man would probably give him a reward.

He grinned.

Snapped his fingers.

Glanced around the room and felt his throat dry when he saw Willie Ennin staring at him.

Just . . . staring.

Behind the bar.

Staring.

While the room grew just a little bit smaller.

A lot smaller, thought Hugh when he moved away from Trish Avery, wandered a bit, halted at the window and looked out at the yard. When it wasn't snowing, and the floodlights were still on, it had looked a lot bigger. Now it wasn't. Now it looked small, almost phony. Like a stage in a run-down summer theater. Stare hard enough at the trees and you would swear they had been painted on some kind of rough wrinkled canvas. Not real. The water not real, just smooth and silver and black and nothing wet. Even the snow wasn't real now because everything was white and you couldn't check to see how deep it was. It just fell. Fell and disappeared into itself.

Hands in his pockets, he shifted sideways, listening to that delectable Avery girl complaining to the bartender, listening to that insufferable boy whine about lost chances, listening to Ceil suck dully on a dead cigarette. He wondered if Trish—what a ridiculous name for a full-grown woman—was serious about wanting to meet him somewhere quiet. Have a talk. Ask about his show. Like an interview, she had said, spilling a drop of liquor on her chest and wiping it off, very slowly.

Like a private interview or something.

Good lord, he thought; the possibilities this nightmare had opened to him tonight.

His left leg bumped against the booth.

"I've had enough of this, Hugh," Ceil said quietly. "I want to go home."

Well, heavens, of course you do, he thought; the party isn't fun anymore, there isn't anything in it for you, I can't tear off your clothes and ball you on the table like we did that time in Los Angeles a hundred years ago, unless it was last summer, so of course you want to go home. You're a queen at home. You command, I obey, you sneeze, I bless you, you shit, I wipe you.

"Are you listening to me?"

Every blessed day, my darling. Every blessed day, every cursed night, at home and at the studio and at the restaurants and in the car and on the street and with friends and when we're god help us alone.

"Get the damn gun and let's go."

He looked at her.

She didn't smile. "At least try the car again."

He didn't smile either.

It was a long-standing joke between them that he wasn't the slightest bit mechanically inclined. Even an alarm clock's buttons baffled him. He didn't mind. It wasn't what he did. There were plenty of others to do that sort of thing for him, so he didn't mind at all. What he did, what he did better than anyone else in the world, was make friends with voices, make love to voices, make voices weep with him and laugh with him and travel with him to places they had never been before and would never see again, not even if they actually went there on their own without him. That's what he did. He didn't fix clocks, and he most definitely didn't fix cars.

He fixed voices.

And people knew his name—

"Hugh."

—but they didn't know him from a hole in the ground or a bum on the street or a clown in the circus.

Like that man out there, he thought, smiling suddenly, suddenly slipping into the booth and reaching out to light another cigarette for Ceil.

That man, whoever he was, whatever he was, was anonymous.

Just like him.

Dark clothes and deep voice.

Wandering the night, and the night air, alone.

Twins.

No identity.

He glanced down and saw the muffler lying on the table.

"Hugh!" Ceil screamed.

He looked and saw that his lighter had burned her hand.

Neil snapped around at the shout, saw Davies scramble out of the booth and run for the bar, calling to Julia to get him some ice, his lady had burned herself and he wanted to stop the pain.

Ceil wept.

No one else moved until Willie beckoned to him, and he walked over, glancing back once as Davies rushed back with an ice pack, then dropping onto the stool by the register. Trish was still at the end, still drinking but slowly, and staring at the door that led to his office.

"Mr. Maclaren, I'm going to check the cars again."

"You already checked them once."

Willie shrugged, glanced at Julia washing her glasses around the corner. "I could've been wrong."

Were you? he wanted to ask, and didn't. He shrugged, and the cook smiled fleetingly, rubbed his hands and hurried away, climbing the steps and vanishing as if the plants had taken him.

"What the hell's he doing?" Havvick wanted to know.

"Double-checking the cars," Neil answered. "He thinks maybe . . . I don't know, maybe the cold might have gotten to them."

"Bullshit."

Neil didn't care what the young man thought; he just wished the kid wouldn't think it aloud.

"Maybe," Havvick said, his lower lip drawn between his teeth and let loose, "I should go down, see if I can get him next time he shows up."

Neil's first reaction was to tell him he was crazy. The one thing they didn't need was the man in black's anger. But, he countered almost immediately, if the first shots hadn't brought him in, shotgun blazing, why should any more? He didn't know. It was a stupid question, and a stupid answer, and he nodded to Julia, telling her to let Havvick take the rifle, what the hell.

"Good," Kenny said. No gloating. Not smug. Just: "Good," again as he picked the weapon up, blew a kiss at the barrel, and headed for the cellar.

"Ken."

Havvick paused on the top step.

"Just don't open the door too wide, okay? If you use it. Keep it locked otherwise."

Havvick's look—*thanks, man, but I'm not completely stupid*—kept him from offering more, obviously unwanted, advice. Instead, he watched the boy disappear, wished him well. Julia put a glass in front of him, scotch. He lit a cigarette, blew smoke over the liquor, wondered what had come over him. Like a spell. A wearying spell. What he ought to do was go to the door, try to attract the man, set him up for a killing shot; what he ought to do was try to get back to the house, see if the telephone there really was out; what he was doing was sitting. Like an old man. Not scared, although he wasn't exactly brimming with flaunted courage. Just . . . he shook his head to rid it of *indifferent* because he was anything but that. Just like the others, he had no intention of dying before his time, whatever the hell that meant. It puzzled him, then, his lack of action, but what bothered him more was the fact that Ken and Ceil, maybe Davies too, were more bothered about it than he was.

He figured as he sipped that there must be a psychological term for it, an explaining away. He almost laughed aloud when he realized he didn't care about that either.

Ceil shouted, angrily.

He spun the stool slowly around to face the room and put the glass on the bar behind him.

She was pushing out of the booth, tears on her cheeks as Davies backed away from her, palms up and out as if trying to hold her back in.

She had the revolver.

Damnit, she had the goddamn revolver.

"For god's sake, Ceil," the radio man said calmly.

She held the gun in one hand; it didn't waver.

Davies looked around, saw Neil, jerked his head toward the woman. "Would you mind telling her that I didn't burn her hand on purpose?"

Neil frowned. "What?"

"Ceil, stop it," Mandy said from her booth by the plants.

Slowly Davies lowered his hands, but he didn't stop moving. One gliding step at a time. "I burned her hand. She thinks it was deliberate."

Ceil didn't say a word. She didn't move. The gun remained aimed at the center of his chest.

"Ceil!" Mandy snapped.

Neil didn't know what to do, had no rules for something like this, and so remained on the stool. "Ceil . . . Miss Llewelyn . . . I think we have enough trouble already, don't you?"

Her eyes shifted; the gun didn't.

"If you want to kill him, hurt him, why don't you just send him on to Deerfield for the cops? Our friend outside will take care of the rest."

Mandy slipped out from behind her table.

He heard Trish put down her glass too hard.

With her free hand Ceil reached behind her and pulled

her purse to her hip, fumbled inside and pulled out a pack of cigarettes. She shook one out. She put it in her mouth. The gun didn't move.

"Ceil," said Mandy disgustedly, "for god's sake."

Davies stopped moving.

Neil wasn't sure if the woman would fire or not. He couldn't tell by her expression; there was nothing in her face. He tried to think again, picturing himself walking cautiously along the side of an automobile, knowing the driver was drunk, not knowing how drunk or belligerent he would be. Not knowing anything except to be careful. There could be tears, there could be a gun, there could be a shattered bottle, there could be nothing at all but a beer-based belch and a staring straight ahead.

"Miss Llewelyn—"

"Ceil," she said.

"Ceil." He nodded, put his own cigarette out and picked up the glass. "Ceil." Sipping, pushing the liquor around his mouth as if testing both taste and name. "If you shoot that thing, you know the kid's going to come up from the cellar like John Wayne. He's scared enough to do it." He drank again, emptying the glass. Tested. Tasted. "I would rather not have him miss and hit me, if you don't mind."

Dumb, he thought; boy, that was dumb.

Mandy started toward the woman, and stopped short even though Ceil didn't offer a threat. "Ceil, please, put it down. You can't . . . this is nuts. What in god's name is it going to prove?"

Ceil found her lighter, lit the cigarette. Davies started to move away again, this time toward the tables, and her arm stiffened sharply. He stopped. She blew at the ceiling without taking the cigarette from her mouth.

Mandy, one word at a time: "I can't take much more of this, Ceil."

"Too bad," Ceil answered. "My hand hurts, and he did it."

"Oh, really, Ceil." Davies shook his head. "You know it was an accident. This is just too goddamn melodramatic for words." He wiped a hand over his face. "You know what I'm going to do, love? I'm going to sit down at this chair here. I'm going to sit down and watch the snow, and maybe Willie will come back and tell us the cars are working so we can go." He wiped his face again. "I'm going to sit down right over here, and you can sit over there, is that all right with you, love?"

He moved.

She jabbed the air with the gun. "No," she said. "I don't think so."

He stopped.

Neil couldn't see the man's face, but he imagined there was surprise.

The front door opened noisily.

Neil reached behind him, his hand drifting over the bar until it found the cleaver's thick handle. He picked it up and held it in front of him, the flat of the broad blade like a shield before his chest. He cleared his throat, and she looked at him.

"In a minute I'm going to get up," he said, though he didn't move at all. "You'll think I'm going to do something brave and stupid, so you'll take a shot at me. I don't know if you're good or not, but nothing will happen, because the bullet will ricochet off this blade here, lots of sparks and stuff just like in the movies, and while you're so shocked you won't be able to move, I'll throw it at you, probably hit you in the chest. Your gun will go off and hit Davies in the balls, but it won't make any difference because you'll already be dying." He grinned. "Pretty gruesome stuff, Ceil."

She smiled.

There was little humor there, but it was a smile.

"Willie," he went on, "will be royally pissed."

"Why?" Willie asked from the stairs. "Did that kid steal more of my knives? Nobody steals my knives, not even you."

Ceil looked at him, looked at Neil. "In the balls?"

Neil shrugged.

"Might be worth it."

"Ceil!" Davies exclaimed.

Mandy whispered, "Jesus."

"Mr. Maclaren?"

"It's okay, Willie. Miss Llewelyn here is just letting off some steam."

The cook took a step down.

At that moment Neil heard, incredibly, Julia still washing glasses.

A voice from the cellar, faint: "Hey, I can't see him. Can you guys see him?"

Neil looked out the window, saw nothing but snow, and dark trees, and dark water.

"It's the gas," Willie said then. "Mr. Maclaren, it's the gasoline. It's gone, that's why they won't run."

Neil grinned. "You're kidding."

Ennin shook his head. "Swear to you, Mr. Maclaren. The gas is all gone."

Davies sidestepped toward the nearest table. "No ghosts," he said, voice trembling with relief. "For a minute . . . good lord, no ghosts."

"Of course not," said Ceil scornfully. She dropped her arm, didn't seem to care when Davies fell heavily into a chair, legs stretched out, head hanging. "Christ, did you think he was an avenging angel or something?" She sat on the edge of the booth's seat, right elbow propped on the table, right hand plucking the cigarette from her mouth. "Hugh, sometimes I wonder what country you live in."

Mandy walked quickly across the room and took the

stool beside Neil, pleaded to Julia with a desperate look and was given a glass and two wide fingers of brandy. "Once," she said, swirling the liquid around, "she told him his medicine, some kind of sinus thing, was really crack. He flipped out, made the doorman drive him to the hospital to get his stomach pumped. When he came back, she was on the dining-room table, naked, her stomach covered with lines of flour. She told him it was cocaine."

"You were there?"

"He told me. She said he was lying."

He looked across the room; she still had the gun.

"She nuts or what?" he asked softly. When there was no answer, he looked at her. Her chin quivered, her hands couldn't hold the glass, an ordinary tumbler, still. He put his hand over her wrists and pressed until the glass was back on the bar. "War is hell."

"Thanks, Sarge," she said sourly. "That helps a lot."

"Where the hell is he?" Ken called from the cellar, sounding as if he were standing at the bottom of the steps.

"I don't know," Neil called back. "If you're getting cold, come on up."

Trish laughed into a hand.

There was no response from Havvick.

Willie finally stepped down into the bar, bewilderment contorting his face until he looked as though he would cry. He stepped behind the bar, pushed the hall door open, and looked at Julia. "Do you want a steak?"

Julia shook her head.

"It's warm," the cook told her earnestly. "You look like you're cold. A good steak is warm."

She looked at Neil, helpless. "Willie, I don't think I could eat anything now."

"That's okay."

Then Ceil said, "In the balls, huh?" and fired, and Hugh Davies screamed.

Trish screamed.

Mandy yelled.

Neil came off the stool without thinking, not realizing he was holding the cleaver over his shoulder, ready to throw it, until he saw the expression on Ceil's face—from smug satisfaction to wide-eyed terror staring at the blade. Cordite stench. Acrid urine. He looked at Davies lying on the floor, moaning, writhing, looked up at Ceil, who had dropped the gun on the table beside her, had pushed herself back into the corner, shaking her head, warding off his approach with her cigarette.

"I didn't," she said, pointing shakily at the ceiling. "I didn't."

He knelt beside Hugh, touched his shoulder, gripped it tightly when the radio man tried to shake him away, and rolled him gently onto his back. He looked. There was no blood.

"I didn't."

A check over his shoulder at a noise, and he saw Willie standing next to Julia, the carving knife in one hand, the other waving at the air protectively in front of the bartender's chest; Trish was crouched, terrified, under the bar flap; Mandy was on her feet straining but not moving.

"I didn't."

"Where is he?" Ken screamed from the trapdoor. The rifle was up; he looked around wildly. "Where is he?"

Neil felt the cleaver transform into lead, and he let it fall beside his feet. "You okay?" he said to the radio man.

"False alarm," Mandy said to Ken. "I think."

"I didn't."

Hugh's eyes watered but didn't flow; there was blood on his chin from biting into his lip. He shook. Everywhere.

And whimpered while Neil patted his shoulder, trying not to pant and not being able to help it. There was a rage he had to suppress, one that had his hand reaching again for the cleaver until he saw it and pulled it back.

"I didn't."

"For Christ's sake," Mandy shouted, "will you stop saying that?"

"What the fuck's going on?" Havvick demanded. "Trish?" He climbed the rest of the way out of the cellar. "Trish, where are you, honey? Are you okay?"

She stuttered his name, not quite softly.

Neil wanted to say something—to Hugh, to Ceil—but he could only grip the man's arm, tell him with the touch that he hadn't been hit. Hugh knew what he meant, and finally, rolling into a sitting position, he gave him a death's-head smile.

Neil glanced into the booth. "You can slug her if you want. I don't give a damn."

As if sprung from a wire, Mandy stomped across the floor and snatched up the gun, reached into the booth and slapped her hard, twice.

"It's all right," Hugh said. "I need . . . I need the bathroom." A look to his groin, and he wrinkled his nose. "I pissed myself, I think."

Neil helped him up, surprised at how light the man seemed for his size. "Willie, take him in the back."

"No need," Hugh said stiffly, stretching his neck, searching for his dignity. "I can manage."

"Willie," Neil insisted.

Ennin pointed toward the door. "This way, Mr. Davies." He laid the knife on the shelf below the bar. "C'mon, the light's tricky, I have to show you."

Davies didn't move until Neil prodded his waist; then he walked toward the cook, not missing a step when Havvick brushed past him and knelt beside Trish. Whispered to her, still holding the rifle in one hand. She shook her head quickly, looked up fearfully when Davies lifted the flap and stepped around her. Havvick started to say something to him, and changed his mind, rose instead and glared at Ceil.

"What the fuck," he said evenly, "are you trying to do?"

Neil felt it then—the cold.

Ceil sobbed dryly, Mandy slammed the revolver onto the table beside him and walked up into the restaurant, and there was so much cold he couldn't understand why he couldn't see his breath. His neck was freezing, his feet were freezing, he checked the back window half expecting to see the pane rimmed with frost. It was so bad he knew that if he stood still one more second his teeth would begin to chatter. But if he moved, he also knew he was going to jump into that booth and wring that goddamn woman's throat.

"Mr. Maclaren?"

He looked without turning his head.

"Mr. Maclaren, Mr. Davies, when he . . ." Willie's hand skittered nervously over his white jacket. "He needs . . . something to wear."

Neil took a breath. "In my office. There're some jeans and a shirt in the closet. They won't fit, but what the hell."

Willie disappeared with an awkward salute.

Ceil sobbed, hands clamped to her face.

He didn't care.

"God damnit," Ken said, still kneeling by his fiancée.

Neil picked up the revolver and walked over to the bar, looked down and said, "Don't worry about it." It was an order, and he didn't care that Havvick looked as though he were going to do some shooting himself. "Just leave it be." He leaned against the bar and pressed a hand to his forehead to stop his fingers from trembling. "Trish, you okay?"

"What do you think?" Ken asked belligerently.

"I think," Neil said wearily, "I didn't ask you."

Havvick rose, almost lunged to his feet, but Trish took his arm and hauled herself up clumsily, swung onto the stool and hugged herself, rocked herself, while Ken rubbed one shoulder.

"I want to go home," she said, and turned her head toward him. "I don't care what's out there. I want to go home."

"The gas," Mandy said from the steps.

Ken stared at her. "What about it?"

She pointed to the swinging door, explained what Willie had said, and Ken started toward her, turned back slowly in disbelief. "No gas? You're . . . no gas?" He appealed to the ceiling. "You mean we've been stuck in here all this time because there isn't any fucking gasoline?"

Neil almost said something, decided not to and tried instead to think. He felt like a jerk. An idiot. Once again failing to protect his charges even though, he reminded himself, protection was hardly in the job description of a man who ran a small restaurant in the middle of nowhere. Then he looked at the floor and felt his lips twitch.

"The generator."

"Gas or kerosene?" Havvick wanted to know.

He smiled. "Gas."

Idiot.

Fool.

So he didn't object when Ken rushed past him, took the bar's corner at a skid, and practically leapt down the cellar stairs. He just looked at his hands, shook his head and suggested to the others that they get their coats, it was time to go. No one asked about the man outside; no one wondered aloud how far a couple of gallons of generator fuel would get them. Far enough; that was all that mattered. To the development or the police; one was as good as the other.

Pushing chairs out of his way, he picked up the revolver, hurried up into the front room and stood beside the door. Looked out. Held his breath.

Dim light across the way, sparkling with small flakes

falling straight to the ground. No wind. The road was covered. None of the vehicles were facing out. They'd have to back up, slip and slide up the gravel and make a left turn, all at the best speed they could manage without skidding into the fence or the tree. And if the man was out there, he would have plenty of time to pick his shots.

The driver.

The tires.

The engines.

He felt giddy when he realized they would have to go out with guns blazing. A goddamn mobster movie.

It wasn't real.

How the hell could it be real?

He heard Hugh's voice raised in confused question at all the fussing, giving a hearty hooray when he heard the good news and immediately making sure, loudly, that everyone had everything they needed. There was no question but that they would take Havvick's van—it had more traction, and more room for them all.

Neil nodded agreement, looked out, and saw nothing.

A hand touched his arm; it was Mandy, his sweater still on beneath her unbuttoned cloth coat, fur collar, fur cuffs. "What's the matter?"

He almost laughed, caught himself by clearing his throat. "It's too easy, don't you think? I mean, after all this, don't you think it's too easy?"

"You just figure that out?"

He said it aloud then, but only to her: "Do you have any idea how I feel right about now?"

Ken begged for assistance, the damn cans were damn heavy.

Hugh answered.

"I think so," Mandy said. She sniffed, wiped a finger across her upper lip. "So what? I saw it down there, Ken did too. We didn't figure it out, why should you?"

There was something wrong in that logic, but for the

moment he felt too good to want to figure it out. Instead, on impulse, he leaned over and kissed her cheek, felt her fingers touch the side of his neck and drift away as she pulled away and promised to return his sweater as soon as she could. In person, if he didn't mind; she didn't trust the mail.

Trish stumbled toward them, fumbling with her mittens, beret already yanked on. "I didn't see him," she said to the floor. "He was out there, the bastard, siphoning the damn gas and I didn't even see him." She looked at Neil. "How could I have missed him siphoning the tanks, Mr. Maclaren?"

"How," he countered, "could have I forgotten about the gas?"

She giggled. "Pretty silly."

He smiled back. "Stupid is a better word, I think."

She giggled again and called for Ken over her shoulder, told him to hurry up, her folks were going to be royally pissed he'd kept her out so late.

Mandy looked at her watch. "Hey," she said.

Neil looked.

"Happy birthday."

Snow ticked against the door's pane.

A soughing in the eaves.

I'm not going!" Ceil screamed. "I'm not going and you can't make me!"

Willie looked up from the counter when he heard the commotion in the bar. He blinked slowly. He shook his head, slowly. He dropped the damp cloth back into the sink and clucked softly when he saw the speckles the splashing water had made on his clean suit. That was all right. It would dry. If there were stains, he would take it to the laundry and let them fix it. He dried his hands, folded the towel, checked his alcove and saw the shoe box. Oh lord, he'd forgotten the mouse, all the noise and excitement and he had forgotten to bury the poor mouse. More cries from the bar. He bit down on his lip and closed his eyes tightly, shutting out the voices and the freezer's hum and the sound of the wind that had risen again. He thought. He prayed. He decided it would be all right if the mouse waited until tomorrow. First thing in the morning he would take the box and bury it, just like always, by the creek. On the other side, in the trees where no one would find the grave. It would be all right.

Satisfied, feeling much better, and knowing he'd better hurry if he didn't want to be left behind, he double-checked to be sure the cleaver was back in its place, washed and dried once again. Then, from the counter, he lifted the carving knife and held it up to the ceiling light. It glinted. A trickle of light slipped along the cutting edge.

That woman crying again.

They would be outside soon, with two guns and the raven.

He looked at the blade, brought it close to his eyes and watched his reflection twist and spiral out of shape.

He didn't like guns. They were noisy and messy and they weren't clean at all.

But he knew how to use a knife.

He buttoned his suit coat, smoothed his tie. Opened a drawer beneath the counter and pulled out a worn leather sheath he slipped over the blade. A perfect fit. He had made it himself. He could put it in his lower inside pocket and nobody would know in case he had to help them. Put his arm against his side and the knife wouldn't fall out.

He smiled.

He walked to the door and switched off the lights.

In the dark he heard the freezer, and the snow, and the slow rising wind.

In the dark he whispered, "Julia," and hurried out to the bar.

Get your goddamn hands off me, Hugh, I am not going to go!"

Julia took her coat from the rack without looking away from the radio man trying vainly to pry Ceil Llewelyn out of the booth. She was tempted, as she jammed a wool cap down over her hair and ears, to walk over there and grab the hysterical bitch by the throat, yank her to the floor, and drag her by her heels into the parking lot. That's all she deserved. Maybe not even that. She certainly didn't deserve the way the radio man treated her—wheedling and chiding and fearfully close to begging. It was horrible. In a frightening way it reminded her of Nester and the way he looked at her and teased her and tried to undress her with his eyes.

She didn't know why.

Demeaning, maybe; then again, maybe not.

She pulled on her gloves, wool fingers, leather palms. Hard. Angry that Maclaren hadn't thought of the gasoline before. Angry that she hadn't thought of it before him. Angry that nobody, not even her, had had the guts to go out there and try to talk to the man in black, to find out what the hell he was after. Somebody should have. She should have when nobody else would. Why not? She knew how to use a gun. She knew how to run. She knew how to talk. Why the hell hadn't she done something when nobody else would?

She buttoned her coat and felt instantly too warm.

The hall door opened and Willie came out.

She handed him his topcoat. A hunting jacket, really, that was too long and too wide, and made him look kind of silly against that ice cream suit of his.

"Are you all right?" he asked.

She shrugged. What kind of an answer did he want? She was mad, she was scared, she was tired of waiting around, she wanted to go to bed, she wanted to start the day over, she wanted him to stop looking at her as if she were a child just waking from a nightmare.

"Yes," she said.

He nodded.

Ceil lashed out with a foot and caught Davies in the chest. He bellowed, and slapped her.

Ennin shook his head sadly. "She's just scared, you know. He shouldn't have to hit her."

Julia smiled, briefly, softly. "Sometimes you have to, Willie. Sometimes you have to knock the scared right out of someone before they'll do what they have to."

A one-shoulder shrug. He supposed she was right, but he wasn't convinced.

"Willie," she said, "don't worry about it, let's go."

Then Davies hit her again.

And Willie took out the knife.

Let! Me! Go!"

Trish ordered herself not to cry. It would be stupid to cry. Besides, she had had too much to drink and nobody would listen to her anyway because she was, probably, just a little drunk. And who listened to a drunk? Especially a drunk woman? Especially a drunk woman who, if that woman didn't stop her shouting, was going to do some shouting herself.

This was dumb. This was crazy! All she had said was that she wanted to go home, and suddenly everybody knew how to go home. Just like that. It didn't make any sense. And she wouldn't even get to fuck the radio man, not here anyway.

Now, suddenly, it was all turned around and nobody was going home because that . . . that *bitch* was acting like they were asking her to walk naked down the middle of the street in the middle of the day with the goddamn minister watching from the steps of his church, for god's sake. What was wrong with her? Didn't she know that they would die if they stayed here and they would live if they left? Was she nuts?

"Ken," she said. "Kenny?"

He stood at the top of the stairs, looking down into the bar, the gasoline cans parked at his feet, his hands clamped on his hips. She knew that stance. He did it all the time when he couldn't figure out why nobody was doing what he wanted, when he wanted, how he wanted. It was like, disgust and impatience and thinking they were out of their minds and wondering why they didn't simply move now and ask their dumb questions later. She knew that stance. It was the one he had used when he had asked her to marry him the first time, two months ago, and she had said she wasn't sure, that she'd have to go home and think about it. She also said she wanted to have her clothes on, too. It was a joke. He didn't get it. He just stood in his bedroom door with his hands on his hips and his head kind of forward a little and his eyes moving from frowning to wide.

"Kenny!"

She knew that stance.

He was ignoring her.

The room tilted a little.

Behind her she heard Mr. Maclaren whisper something to that other woman, the Mandy one, and heard the Mandy one say, "To be honest, I don't care if you leave her here all damn winter."

That shocked her, but she didn't turn around.

Instead, she gave Ken one more chance to stop playing the tough guy and get that gasoline out to the cars.

"Kenny, damnit!"

And when he didn't move, she whirled around and grabbed for Neil's gun.

You goddamn son of a bitch, get the hell out of my life!"

The wind rattled a drainpipe.

Blowing snow clawed at the windows.

And what would you like for your birthday, Mr. Maclaren, he thought as Ceil yelled and his temper surged to
break free of its restraints; how about a little peace and
quiet, just for starters?

He collided with Trish as he started for the lounge,
grabbed her arms to keep her from falling, and they per-
formed a clumsy sidestep dance until he gently pushed her
away and told her to take it easy, don't be in such a hurry.
Her answering stare was wide-eyed, close to glaring, but he
paid it no attention, marching instead across the floor to
Ken. Tapped him on the shoulder.

"The gas," he said, jerking a thumb over his shoulder.
"You want to get out of here, let's do it."

Ken's loathing was just evident enough to give the temper another boost.

Neil touched one of the cans with a toe. "Now, okay?
I'll get the others."

He took the two steps down slowly, shouldering aside
Willie when he reached the floor, not taking his gaze off
the couple struggling in the corner. Maybe Mandy had the
right idea; just leave the woman here and get on with it. A
thought that made him smile when he reached them, took
hold of Davies's arm and pulled him away.

"C'mon, Ceil," he said.

She shook her head. "I'm not going out there." Not yelling now, no less adamant. "He's going to kill us all."

Bad movie, he thought; she lives in a bad movie.

She squirmed deeper into the corner when he reached for her, and his temper finally broke loose. He leaned in and snared her arms, ignored the shoe heel that connected with his thigh, and dragged her out of the booth.

"Ceil, for heaven's sake," Hugh said.

She struggled, but Neil had her firmly to his chest. "Get her coat," he said to the radio man. Then, to her: "You wanted me to do something. I'm doing it. Knock it off."

He hadn't yelled, hadn't sworn, but he could hear the threat in his voice, level and all the more cold for it; she had heard it as well, and didn't object with more than a choked whimper when Davies held out the full-length fur, waited until Neil felt her submit. He released her. She stepped back, accepted the garment without a look behind her.

"Out," he said.

He didn't move.

They hesitated.

"Damnit, out."

They moved slowly then, and he remained behind them, herding without touching, without speaking, until they were all up in the restaurant. Silent. Gathered at the door. Listening to the wind. Watching as he turned around at the head of the steps and looked out the rear window. Dots and dashes of white, and the trees nearly smothered. Chairs and tables highlighted, reminding him of some baroque theater, no patrons, and the film filled with grain and shadow.

It was unnerving.

The glow of the CD player's digital display attracted him. He signaled a *wait a minute* and hurried to the bar, switched it off and glanced at the trapdoor.

Back in a while, Nes; somebody'll be back in a while for you, you poor sap.

At the door he took the rifle from Ken and handed it to Julia. When Havvick protested, Neil didn't ask him if he could carry the gasoline and the weapon, too; he just looked it. Ken rolled his eyes, and Trish stroked his arm to tell him it was all right, honey, this was no time to start.

"We do the gas first," he instructed them. "If the van starts, come running. We don't want to waste any time."

"Then what?" Hugh asked.

Mobsters; gunmen.

Al Capone streaking down a twilight Chicago street, guns blazing, tires screeching and smoking, sirens wailing, panicked pedestrians scattering and bodies falling all over the damn place.

He opened the door and nudged Ken out ahead of him as he hefted the revolver in his right hand.

The streetlamp was alone.

The snow on his face, small bites, and bitterly cold. His left ear began to sting as they squeezed around Davies's car; his lungs felt filled with ice when he finally opened the gas cap after several fumbling tries.

Ken set one can on the ground, unscrewed the top of the other and said, "If this isn't unleaded, it's going to ruin my engine."

Neil almost shot him. He was that close.

That close.

Havvick bent over. "You forgot the tube. It's going to spill all over."

Nothing at the streetlamp.

The road was deserted.

"Pour," he ordered. "Just pour the damned gas. Jesus Christ. Some of it's going to get in."

Havvick did, and the fumes' abrupt assault made Neil's nose wrinkle and stomach lurch, made him step away when what seemed like half the fuel slopped down the vehicle's flank to the ground and was taken by the snow. He moved to the back and scanned the parking lot. No trace of Nester's murder. No tracks. And nothing on the road that he could see but unmarked snow. Sleeves of it stretched over the fence railings. Caps of it on the posts.

The wind blew more softly, more quietly, and the quiet was what made him check the restaurant several times. Not a sound. No whispers. No moans. No creaking of wood. Just the snow falling gently, the gurgle of pouring gas, and the cold that turned his flesh brittle. He walked around to the passenger side and made sure the door was unlocked, swiped the snow from the side mirror and the window.

Watching the streetlamp.

Hurry up, he thought.

Always watching the streetlamp.

The cold seeping through his shoes, settling on his hair, freezing his hand around the butt of the gun.

Hurry up.

"Okay," Ken said cheerfully, and tossed the last can away, bouncing it off the rear fender of Hugh Davies's large black car. A quick step to yank open the driver's door and he scrambled in. Neil watched the key slip into the ignition, watched Ken's eyes close briefly when he turned it.

The engine sputtered.

Gas, Neil thought; how could it possibly come down to just a little gas.

A large flake burned the rise of one cheek; he slapped it away with the back of a hand.

The engine coughed.

Shadow movement in the doorway, anxious faces without features, the only light reflecting off the snow from the streetlamp.

He slip-stepped to the front and cleared the windshield, saw Havvick's face distorted in the dashboard glow, scowling each time the engine refused to fire; he took a swipe at the headlamps, looked up, and swallowed when he saw discouragement in the young man's face. He shook his head, raised a hand to tell him not to give up, and for god's sake don't flood the engine, you jackass.

Havvick nodded, and tried again.

The restaurant door opened.

The motor bellowed, guttered, settled to a racing while Havvick yelled triumph and pounded the steering wheel with both hands, switched on the wipers, pounded the wheel again.

Neil waved an urgent arm to the others and moved to Ken's side of the van. Watching the road. Impatiently blinking the snow from his lashes. Watching the street-lamp. Paying little heed to the slipping, the curses, as the others scrambled off the stoop and across the gravel. For no particular reason wondering why the sander hadn't re-turned. But there was too damn much "why" and not enough "because," and when someone barked his name and told him to get in, he almost didn't move.

He could feel the van rock slightly, creak a protest, as they crawled around to their seats; he could feel Maclaren's Food and Lodging at his back, suddenly huge and suddenly empty.

No.

Not empty.

Deserted.

Squatting in the dark, with the cabins back there, cold and unlighted. A ghost town waiting to happen.

He almost didn't move.

And realized with a start that he was waiting for the man in black.

"Brother," he whispered, and hurried around the side, yanked open the door and fell into the high-back passenger seat.

"Took you goddamn long enough," Havvick com-plained.

"Can we go, please?" Trish said.

Neil nodded.

The headlamps flared on, a momentary blindness.

The van backed away, slowly.

Neil shifted to look through the gap between his seat and Ken's. A bench seat directly behind, three women there, huddled together; Trish directly behind Ken, staring anxiously through the window, Ceil in the center with lips pursed and throat working, Mandy on the outside, hands trapped between her legs. He smiled, not to worry, Ken knows how to drive in snow. The seat in back, with Davies and Ennin, and Julia with the rifle. He could barely see them, they were shadows. Mannequins draped in mourning.

"Shit," Ken muttered as Neil turned to face front. The van lurched; he'd run over one of the cans.

"Be cool," Neil told him. The gun was in his lap.

The blower forced heat into the cabin, melting the snow on his head, trickling it down his chest, his back. Melting it on his jacket, quivering gems.

fairy dust

Jesus, knock it off.

"A little speed if you don't mind." A deep voice from the back. Disembodied. A radio voice.

Neil saw the tension in Havvick's rigid arms, in the taut planes of his face, knew the screaming debate the kid was having with himself, speed and caution in equal strength, and caution stayed his accelerator foot. Just barely. He was surprised. He had expected Ken to try to break the sound barrier, maybe even try to just smash through the fence just to get to the road.

Carefully backing.

Tires crunching over the gravel, slipping, holding, grinding the snow.

"I imagine I could crawl faster."

Radio voice. Confident. They all were, he thought, when no one could see them. Little gods, and fearful they would be switched off with a knob or button.

"The gravel should help," he said calmly as the van inched forward, a little faster this time. "It's just that bit there before the road that gets a little steep. I keep meaning to even it off and never got around to it."

"Ice?" Ken's voice was strained.

"I don't think so. You got the weight and traction. The road'll be the worst part."

Ken shook his head. "Nope. The road's a runway, man. We gonna fly."

"Don't be stupid, honey," Trish said, leaning forward to look over Ken's shoulder. "Just—"

"Yeah, yeah, yeah," he muttered. "Yeah, yeah, yeah."

Forward then, the van slightly canted in the direction of the slope, passing the radio man's car, the front door, swinging uphill and aiming for the empty road.

Neil checked the back again, thinking the man might be hiding at the side of the building, saw nothing but a shredding spiral of exhaust, looked front, one hand braced lightly against the dash for no reason at all. The gun in his lap. Feeling the urgency now, the unspoken demands from the others for speed, for flight, for disappearing here and reappearing somewhere else, anywhere else, as long as it was done *now* and the hell with the laws of physics. Watching the glitter and sparkle of snow pass over the streetlamp as the wind gusted and settled. Focusing on the merge of driveway to road and frowning a little at the height of the snow there at the junction. There was a small bump, but it shouldn't have been . . .

"Son of a bitch."

The van picked up speed, fast walking, and thumped against the rise.

Stopped.

"Wonderful," Davies muttered.

"What?" Trish asked, panic too close to the surface. "Honey, what's wrong?"

Neil squinted down over the van's blunted nose. "I think it's a log."

"The bastard." Ken rocked up to look over the wheel, grunted and looked behind him to the slope falling away. "No big deal."

He backed up, and the exhaust filled the rear window with fog; backed up until the corner of the restaurant was even with the rear bumper.

"Don't stall it," Trish whispered fearfully, and his left hand jumped off the steering wheel into a fist that immediately opened to grab the rim again.

The engine raced, his foot came off the brake, and the van didn't move, not for a second much too long, rear wheels spinning, spitting gravel, rattling, the back end settling until the tread caught and the van lurched forward and the tire tracks he'd left became shorter, the road wobbling, steadying, vanishing when the tires struck the buried log and the van nosed upward. Straining. Thumping and scraping over the low obstruction and banging down hard enough to make Trish squeal and Davies swear. Havvick adding gas and grunting as he wrenched the wheel around to aim the vehicle west, and the back end continuing to glide smoothly over the road, fishtailing, the windshield facing the trees across the way, the road, the restaurant, the road heading east, the trees again in a blur while Trish screamed and Neil's grip on the dashboard tightened.

Havvick lost control.

Neil yelled at him to take his damn feet off the pedals, but the cow boy didn't listen, wouldn't listen, spun the wheel, raced the engine, pumped the brakes, while the night and the snow made a dizzying carousel until the van slammed into a fencepost and he was thrown forward, arm rigid and his shoulder wrenching back.

"Son of a *bitch*!" Havvick yelled, and slammed the gears into reverse, trying to back away from the fence.

The van whined, rocked, and didn't move an inch.

No one in the back spoke.

Havvick ground the heels of his hands into his eyes, took the beveled wheel again and ran his palms around the rim. Finally, eyes half-closed: "You guys all right?"

A murmuring.

Snow from the roof slid over the windshield. The wipers took it away, ice crusting on the blades, leaving a smear behind.

"Well?" asked the radio voice.

Havvick reached for the handle but Neil stayed him with a touch. "I'll check." He pushed open the door, shuddered when the cold grabbed him and pulled him out, cursed when the wind buried him in a wave and rode him toward the fence. One step at a time, he told himself; don't think. Just move.

With one hand fingertip-braced against the van's side, he examined the front and saw that the post had been knocked askew but not over, not split; the van's blunt nose was dented. Nothing serious, nothing caught on anything, and he blew his relief, banked his anger, as he made his way to the back, hunkering down to look beneath the rear tire. It was clear. He thumped a fist once against the side, a signal to try again. When Havvick, less anxious or more sensible, barely touched the accelerator, the tires spun and didn't grip, only spat dirty snow onto the road.

He thumped again, twice.

The engine wound down.

He tucked his left hand under his arm and rubbed it against his coat to bring the feeling back, then brushed away the few flakes remaining and touched the road.

It looked fine.

It was ice.

All right, he thought as he levered himself to his feet; no big deal, Ken'll have sand or chains or something, five minutes and we'll be out of here.

Someone rapped frantically on the side window. He

couldn't see in, the tint was too dark and the night not light enough, but he knew.

And he turned without haste.

On the hill behind the restaurant an easy wind shifted through the trees, and the trees shed their snowcoats to make room for more. The creek was a narrow dark line as ice crept outward from either bank; and in spots humped ice bridges had already been formed. Icicles in tooth-ridges hung from the restaurant gutters. Steam from the van's blunted hood. The county road was torn up by the skidding; miniature snowbanks marked the ruts of the van's passing.

A branch snapped in the cold.

And in the cold the snow stopped falling.

Slowly Neil backed toward the still open door, not taking his eyes from the man in black.

"Stay here."

"The hell with that, give me the rifle," Havvick growled, twisting around in his seat.

"Stay here."

He closed the door carefully, not slamming it, pushing it until he heard it catch. He had no idea why he was being so cautious. The man could see him. Unless he was blind, he could see everything. Had maybe even watched the whole thing from the moment the van had left its parking space.

Had maybe even laughed.

Neil kept the gun at his side, flexing his arm's muscles to keep them loose in the cold. In case. Just in case. Keeping the van close to hand, he moved forward again. One short step at a time. Not hurrying, not threatening in spite of the gun, his left hand folded into his jacket pocket, his head ducked slightly even though the wind had stopped. Checking his footing all the way, shifting weight from one side to the other in a deliberate, barely noticeable swagger in case he had to leap one way or the other. He wanted control. As much control as the weather and his clothing would allow.

A yard from the van. Plumes of exhaust tucking around his legs. He could smell it, and smell hints of gasoline somewhere on his jeans, his shoes.

One more step.

Automatically checking the sound of his voice in his head before he spoke, filtering out the quavers, the anxiety, a quick grin no one saw because like it or not there were apparently some things you just never forgot.

"Who are you?"

He didn't have to speak loudly. There wasn't that much distance, and sound carried in winter, made the words crisp though he hadn't intended them that way. He just wanted to know. And that, as much as anything, made him uneasy.

envy

"Who are you?"

don't be stupid knock it off

A fleeting frown. He shouldn't just want to know. He should be demanding just cause, demanding identification of more than just a name. Explanations would do for a start; retribution would come later. His anger should be doing more than simply sparking around the edges; his concern should be vital, not merely personal curiosity.

"Who are you?"

Another step.

The van creaking; someone was moving.

The fall of the streetlamp hadn't changed—pale, barely illuminating, and the man standing back there, just out of reach, a quick glance and he wouldn't be there, he'd be just another shadow. Vague. Disturbingly as if he were just this side of transparent. A fog image. There, and not there.

"Why'd you shoot Nester?"

It wouldn't be so bad if the man would move; shift, hitch his shoulders, twitch a hand, bend a knee, tilt his head. It wouldn't be so bad if the man would only speak; throw a challenge, send a warning, laugh, give his name.

Who the hell are you?

Thinking it odd that here, now, he felt no intimation of danger. Nester was dead, but Neil didn't believe the man would kill him, too. Or try to. Not a sensation of safety, too much had passed for that; but a feeling that he himself wasn't really a player in this bizarre dilemma. No; he was. Absolutely, he was. But his role hadn't been written yet, hadn't yet been defined. Which made him all the more uncertain.

"Who are you?"

He raised the gun.

"I can use it."

The man in black didn't move.

Neil felt like a fool.

And he felt, for no reason, that the man in black knew him.

He almost laughed at the preposterous notion, used the gun to direct the man to come forward. An order. Move now, or I won't miss this time.

A single snowflake floated into the light, leaving a trace of itself behind as it crossed in front of the stranger, a pale comet's tail, a grey slash against the dark.

The creak of a van door opening slowly.

The man in black moved. A shrug, slow and quick at the same time, barely visible back there beyond the light.

But Neil saw it.

Slow. Quick.

Raven's wings, unfolding.

Then the shrug became the man's right arm reaching into his long coat.

Neil's eyes widened, and he backed away swiftly, finger tightening on the trigger, left hand out and waggling for balance and distraction. In spite of everything, he wasn't positive the stranger would actually complete the draw, not until he saw the glint of a darkwood stock, the gleam of a barrel.

He fired.

The shotgun fired.

Ken Havvick yelled and fired off-balance as he leapt to the ground, stumbled to one knee and fell shoulder-first against the van.

Neil threw himself back and to his left, firing a second time wildly, coming up against the van, pressing a shoulder to its flank, and firing again. Trying to shut out the explosions that came too fast. Fire. Havvick, firing. Someone yelling inside, just above his head.

The shotgun.

Sparks and smoke and the van's rear panel rang.

A woman screaming.

The shotgun.

Neil fired.

The left rear tire exploded, and the van shuddered, bounced and settled as if it had been dropped.

The stench of charred rubber.

He heard Kenny swearing at the top of his voice as if the words would serve as ammunition while he reloaded his weapon; he heard people scrambling frantically in the van, heard the door open behind him, and before he could turn and warn them back inside he saw Mandy and Davies slip to the ground together, the others piling after them and using the open door to slingshot them to the fence.

Havvick fired twice.

Neil spun around on one knee, squinting through the drifting smoke, shaking his head to clear his ears, settle his vision.

Havvick fired a third time.

There was no answer.

Faint echoes off the hills; nothing more.

Neil used the van to help him to his feet, moving slowly, almost sideways, into the road. One step at a time. Breathing heavily, heart racing. Once in the open, a shuffling movement on his right—Havvick in a half-crouch, the rifle clamped to his side. They looked at each other, looked across the road.

The man in black was gone.

Neil crossed his left hand over his chest and signaled Ken to reload and move to the right.

Someone weeping quietly; he couldn't tell if it was a man or a woman.

Moving, angling left, keeping the gun up, keeping it steady, staring until his eyes began to water at the place beyond the streetlamp where the shadow had been standing. Seeing nothing but a languid curl of smoke drift and shred beneath the bulb. Hearing nothing but the crunch of his shoes in the snow, and Havvick's panting.

Checking the trees, the closing distance giving them faint definition, bringing them toward him, from dark wall to shadow to scabrous bark pocked with snow.

Seeing nothing.

Feeling his chest rise and fall, rise and fall, hitch once when something crunched deep in the woods, then rise and fall as the cold he had forgotten reintroduced itself, steaming the air in front of his eyes, momentarily blinding him until he directed his breathing aside. Swallowing when he reached the midpoint and paused for a moment, checked to be sure Ken hadn't already darted into the trees, and moved forward again, sliding steps, thighs tight in anticipation of a slip, or a dive.

Gone.

The stranger's left.

He straightened, but in stages; his fingers loosened, tightened repeatedly around the revolver's grip. A shake of his head for Ken when he knew they were alone, but he didn't return the gun to his pocket when he reached the other shoulder; he didn't stop looking just to the side of every tree for a sign of movement contrary to the wind that had begun to tease once again, slither again, little more than a taunting breeze.

Ken hissed at him.

Neil signaled him to wait, to be watchful, and stepped down into the shallow ditch, sliding a little to the rocky bottom, slipping a little on the way up the far side. Snow worming over the tops of his shoes, clinging to the bottoms of his jeans. Staring now at the ground where the man in black had stood, almost crying out, almost laughing, when he saw the scuff marks, the depressions.

I'll have to show Trish, he thought.

Then he looked closer, and changed his mind.

Ken hiked the rifle under one arm, barrel pointing down. He sniffed. "Now what?" A hushed voice meshed with tension. "We go after him or what?"

Neil stared into the woods. "You really want to go in there?"

"The snow's deep. How fast can he move?" He climbed into the ditch, stood at the bottom. "Two against one."

"In the dark."

Havvick shook his head, not understanding. "I don't get it. What the hell's the matter with you, Neil? This guy's been busting our asses all night, we got to have hit him at least once, all that shooting. You really think he's in any condition to fight back?"

Neil pointed at the snow. "If we hit him, he's not bleeding."

Voices in the air, hanging there and distant.

He turned to watch the others, still huddled by the fence, standing at the front of the van as if debating whether to push it back onto the road. Which, as Davies noted with a disgusted gesture, would do them no good at all unless there was a spare tire and the rim hadn't been damaged.

"I don't get it," Havvick muttered. Inhaled with a hiss.

Neil looked at him sharply. "Hit?"

Ken sneered away the concern. "A couple of dingers in the leg, that's all. When he shot the tire, I guess."

When he shot the tire.

Neil searched the woods again, branches groaning, snow falling in knots and chunks to the ground, and returned to the road. Havvick followed him reluctantly, but he didn't look around. The kid wasn't seriously hurt, neither was he, and that was the point. The man in black hadn't fired directly at either one of them; he'd kept them at bay while he took out the tire. Immobilized the van. Which was curious since they still had other vehicles to use—Davies's car, Willie's and Julia's. Why would he bother with just one? Because, he concluded as he reached the rest, it was the one they had been using at the time, no more reason than that.

And he would be back if they tried it again, in a car.

He wouldn't kill them.

He would just keep them here.

By the expressions he saw, he knew the others had already reached the same conclusion. No one had bolted for the safety of the restaurant once the shotgun had stopped blasting. They leaned against the fence, stood beside it, dusted at it idly, breath in streams of fog, hands jammed into pockets or under arms, feet stamping, shifting them without moving them. Watching him expectantly. All except Ceil, who stared at the sky.

"I guess," he began, and stopped when Ken dropped the rifle onto the front seat and slammed the door.

"So who's gonna help me push this lame son of a bitch off the road?"

Nobody moved.

"Aw, Jesus, c'mon, I can't do it myself."

"Why don't you leave it that way?" Mandy suggested.

"Are you nuts? Some asshole will come by, probably smack the hell out of it."

She conceded the point. "And maybe, seeing it like this, he'll stop. Tie a cloth or something on the mirror. You know, one of those help-signal things."

Ken's mouth opened in a retort, closed again as he considered the possibility she was right. He brushed a palm over the door and walked around the back, out of sight. Mumbling. Shaking his head disconsolately. The sound of a foot kicking angrily against the shredded tire. Trish flapped her arms helplessly, then stumbled after him.

"Mr. Maclaren?"

"Yeah, Willie?"

"It's a lot warmer inside."

And safer.

Just because the man in black hadn't shot at them this time, it didn't mean he wouldn't the next time. Nester Brandt was dead.

He nodded.

With no further prodding they moved off hurriedly, Mandy lingering for a second before trudging after Davies and Ceil. Julia, however, hands in pockets and arms tight at her sides, came to stand beside him while he checked the length of the road in both directions, unbroken white that shaded to grey in the dark. Aside from Trish and Havvick's murmuring on the other side of the van, there was silence. In ordinary times, an ordinary silence. The muffled hush that snow creates, and out here, touched by waiting for the distant sound of tire chains, an approaching engine, the grumble and harsh scrape of a plow.

"Where are they?" she asked.

He didn't need a translation. "I don't know." A curious jolt of surprise when he realized she doubted. "Accident, maybe? Blocking the road?"

"All night?" Just as curiously, she didn't sound worried. "Both directions?"

A breeze fluttered the hair that stuck out from under her cap.

He waited.

She looked into the woods, looked up. "You know that night, when I hit Nes?"

"Sure."

"I wanted to kill him, you know."

He bumped her shoulder with his. "We all did now and then, no big deal."

She shook her head. "No, Neil. You didn't hear me. I wanted to kill him."

"Uh-huh. So why didn't you?"

She raised her shoulders, pulled down her head. "Beats the shit out of me." Looked up at him, still pulled in like a turtle. "I'm sorry, but I'm not sorry he's dead."

A frown in irritated disbelief, comments almost voiced: *hey, you may not have liked him, Julia, but for god's sake, he was still a man; how the hell can you say something like that?; Jesus Christ, what kind of talk is that?*

Almost voiced.

Not spoken.

Her expression suggested she didn't care what he thought, how he felt. Him, or anybody else.

But he couldn't stop a grunt of disapproval, or step away without moving a step.

"Hey," Trish called, "you guys coming or what?"

"He looked at me, you know," Julia said with a slow and long exhalation, shaking her head through the cloud that formed in front of her face.

"Who?" he asked, disinterest a penalty for her unexpected heartlessness.

"The bird. That raven."

"Oh." He figured it was a nervous reaction to what had just happened. A failed escape; bullets flying as if they were back in the Old West; the crash; the tension; all of it. He was, now that he thought about it, a little surprised that at least one of them hadn't tried to run away. Literally. Taken off up the road toward Deerfield, the way Ken had originally wanted them to.

He was more than a little surprised that he hadn't done it himself.

Lie, he thought then; that's a goddamn lie.

"So who is he?" she asked.

"Hey!" Trish called. "You guys still alive or what over there?"

"Who's who?"

She nodded toward the streetlamp. "The raven."

Great. Now she's given him a name. Perhaps not a bad idea, because it made him more human. Unless, he thought, watching her closely as she turned away, she thinks he's some kind of supernatural creature.

Quoth the raven.

"Julia, why don't you just go back and—"

"Mr. Maclaren, will you—oh!"

He whirled as Ken swore, flung open the driver's door, and lunged into the van, grabbing for the rifle. At the same time, Trish bolted for the restaurant, spinning around the end post and falling, yelping, sliding all the way down the slope. Julia didn't move except to tap the wrist that held the gun.

"Getting to like that thing, aren't you."

She left, unhurried, and climbed over the fence.

"C'mon!" Ken shouted, standing in the road. He put the stock to his shoulder. "C'mon, you bastard!"

Neil hadn't realized he'd drawn the gun until Julia had touched him. But there was nothing he could do now anyway. He couldn't see anything but Ken, shifting side to side, forward and back, yelling, daring, taunting. Firing twice into the air and breaking into a run before Neil could stop him; tripping, falling prone, arms extended, the rifle spinning away to the right. Neil rushed to fetch it, slipping to one knee himself and sliding, revolving slowly until he faced Havvick, who was on his knees now and pounding the road with his fists in frustration.

The road was empty.

Neil took his time getting to his feet, took his time crossing over to Ken, who stopped once he realized he wasn't alone. A hand out, and Neil pulled him up, backed away as Ken slapped the snow from his chest.

"What does he want?" Ken asked. Bravado had vanished. A small boy stood there now. "Christ, Mr. Maclaren, what the hell does he want?"

He didn't know. "Let's get inside before we freeze to death."

The eaves lights in the corners came on as they made their way to the parking lot; the inside lights stayed off.

"Bastard," Ken muttered. A litany. "Son of a bitch. Bastard."

Then the shotgun fired again, and Ken's van exploded.

A night blossom.

During the day it would have been pale, most of it invisible, and except for the destruction, almost insignificant.

Night gave it color, made it bright, sound and fire, as it fanned out from beneath the van, lifting the vehicle off its rear wheels. The woods vanished for an instant, the sky became a rippling ceiling and the stars no longer there. Not spectacular, however; there wasn't enough fuel left for that. But it punched through the floor, and when the initial glare faded, the trees drawing the dark back around them, the blossom burned bright and fiercely across the seats. Snow steamed and melted in patches where flaming gas leapt free of the tank. Smoke. The tortured squeal of twisting metal.

An instant.

Sound and fire.

That passed all too quickly into the constrained, muted voice of the fire.

Which itself didn't last very long at all.

Not nearly long enough to match the explosion's sound and fire.

He watched the others gasp and cry out as the restaurant filled with light, and darkened again. He watched them press close to the door, to the windows, to watch for a while and curse, Kenny with his impotent fists in the air but not enough courage to race back out, whimpering at last more at himself than at the loss of his van. He watched them, silently, drift away as if the flooding light had taken something of them with it when it receded and confined itself to gathering around the scorched and burning van. He watched Maclaren stand at the doorway, his face unreadable, his left hand drumming tightly against his thigh, his age more pronounced in the flickering fire glow. Age. And something else. He couldn't figure it out and so dismissed it as unimportant, instead watched Mandy Jones come up behind him and touch his arm hesitantly, as though afraid he'd strike out at her. Maclaren didn't. He only grunted and turned away, not deflated like the others, but trembling. A man in conflict. Enraged enough to do something stupid, and not stupid enough to do it. She whispered. Maclaren nodded, put the revolver on the counter and walked with her to the steps that led down into the lounge. The pass of a hand through the web of spider plants, the same hand passing next through his hair.

Shadow-show, Davies thought.

Ken and his girl already at the bar, Havvick complaining about his leg, and the girl, whose lips had tasted so sweet, responding in a voice that tolerated no whining. A soft voice with razor edges. Something the boy probably wouldn't hear for years, if at all; and if not at all, then marriage and hell would be synonyms for bliss.

Shadow-show.

The bartender snapping ill-tempered at the cook, who

seemed, suddenly, not to be so dense as first he'd appeared.
At least by the sound of his voice. A man in there somewhere, he thought in mild surprise. A normal man. Hugh
wondered if the bartender had noticed how the cook
looked at her. Not quite worship, not quite lust, a thrill-
ingly dangerous mixture of both. If they ever made it to
bed, he'd make no bets as to who would survive.

Shadow-show.

He didn't know where Ceil was, hadn't seen her since
she had fallen over the threshold, caught herself on the
counter and made her way blindly, mothlike, toward the
light at the back window. Perhaps she was in her old seat,
cowering in a way only she could manage—defiantly. A bit
of magic in that woman. One of these days he might figure
out how to love her.

Shadow-show.

He sat in the last booth on the left, one finger holding
the end of the drapery aside so he could look out, check the
fire, check the whereabouts of the man in black.

Alone.

In the dark.

The way it was meant to be. The way it had always been
meant to be.

My friends, tonight we bring you something entirely
different. Something special. The poets will rest, the son-
nets will be silent, and what words of love there are will not
be spoken. Tonight, my friends, and I can hear you out
there, sitting alone, like me, in your chairs, your beds,
driving down an empty street with no one but me to listen
to your weeping; tonight, I'm going to bring you Arma-
geddon. A resonant name, what they called in school a
proper noun. But not terribly proper, is it, when it signals
the end of all that you knew, and the beginning of things
you will never know. But don't be afraid. It needn't be
inevitable.

It needn't be.

He glanced out the window—who the hell are you?

Amarillo was, at one time, thought to be inevitable. Songs about it, stories about it, dust devils in summer skipping across the streets and through the yards and into the fields on the outskirts of the city; pretensions to city while hanging on to the honky-tonk, the scuffed boots, the worn shirts, the man in the frame house who took hold of his son and told him, every night, that places like this weren't places to go, they were places to be from. No offense to the founding fathers, whoever they were. Too far from Dallas, too far from Houston, too far from any place at all, and not far enough. The son, he didn't listen. Sons don't, you know. The son worked his . . . buns off and escaped the frame house and discovered, by turns, Oklahoma City, Lincoln, St. Louis, and finally Chicago, where he learned for the first time that his voice was somehow different, especially after the accent had been exorcised. Died in front of a hundred grime-streaked mirrors in a hundred hotel rooms on a hundred side streets with bars on all the corners. Others were deep, others were fluid, others were soft even in anger. But others didn't have the heart. Others couldn't wring a tear or a sigh or a smile or a memory or a touch or a kiss from the air.

He looked outside.

The flames were gone.

They accused him, my friends, of being a heartless mimic, those old enough to remember.

He slid out of the booth and stretched, grimaced at the way Maclaren's jeans didn't fit, and it took him a while to recall why he had them on.

They accused him of copying a personality from long ago. A man before his time. The Continental. A television star when television was without color. A suave man, with an accent, who wore a dressing gown and sometimes a cravat and smoked a cigarette and offered champagne to his audience while he read to them. From books. From memory. But he had been seen. And there had been some who thought him grotesque. Or plain. Nothing special, nothing continental, at all.

But the voice, my friends, the voice . . .

He listened to Havvick chiding Maclaren for his cowardice, demanding, though not loudly, that they not waste time, this time, trying to figure things out. The man in black had started a war; they would either have to finish it, or perish in it.

Hugh lifted an eyebrow.

Perish?

The boy knew the word?

Amazing.

He picked up the gun, broke it open, checked the chambers, saw that somewhere between the road and the building, Maclaren had reloaded. One chamber empty. For the hammer, he supposed; they always did it in the movies.

The voice.

Invisible, and powerful. All things to all people. All women. Erotic for some, comfortable for others who needed the comfort. Every so often, and not every night, just the vaguest, deliberate hint of Texas Panhandle.

On enough stations to make his name known along most of the East Coast and a few hundred miles inland. Soon. Tomorrow. A full national audience. But never television. Never. It was the voice, not the man. God knows, it wasn't the man. Not that it made a difference tonight. Voice, or man; nobody, but nobody was going to stop him from slipping into the night lives of the people who listened. It was, he had learned on that first night out of Texas, a simple equation—control the nights and you control the lives. During the day, people gained power from the light and in the light and in the way they were seen.

At night they were themselves. In their homes. Alone. No light. Just the dark.

Control the dark.

Or, like the man in black, be the dark.

Be the voice.

He pressed close to the door, squinted in an attempt to see beyond the dying flames. Who are you? And decided it just didn't matter.

He sighed, and turned around.

Ceil walked in front of the long window.

Shadow-show.

The bitch.

He opened his mouth.

He laughed.

Willie perched on the edge of the last stool by the trapdoor, and watched Julia fuss with her glasses, her bottles, the CD player turned back on, avoiding his look.

He smiled and spun around, not too fast, not too slow.

He could feel it anyway, without her corroboration. The energy. Despite the fact that they sat at the bar or a table or walked in front of the back window, looking like corpses robbed of their funerals, they had energy. Had built it up. Banked it. Blew on it. Had begun to vent it when they'd made their escape, and couldn't control it now that they were back, their escape unexpectedly shunted to a side rail that wasn't acceptable at all. He suspected that if he jumped up onto the bar and shouted, "Boo!," they'd either all drop of heart attacks, or tear him limb from limb. He wished Nester were here. Alive, that is. They'd have a good time making book on which one would break first. Too bad. Brandt was dead. A ridiculous man. A pathetic man. A man disliked not because he was ridiculous or pathetic, but because he made bets and won, most of the

time. Won big. Big money. Seldom working an honest day
in his life. Willie didn't know his past, but he figured Nes
didn't know the meaning of an honest day's work for an
honest day's pay.

Willie worked hard. Very hard. A course in Rhode
Island in that famous school he couldn't remember, and
one in San Francisco, and one in Kansas City. Learn the
recipes and make your own adjustments. Experiment. Fool
around. Talk to the food and make it laugh. Dress it up.
Dress it down. Strut your stuff in New York hotels, in Los
Angeles hotels, in Miami hotels, in Phoenix hotels. Watch
'em eat. Talk. Eat. Talk. Drink. Talk. Eat. Drink. Paying
no attention to what they put in their mouths. All that
work and all those schools and all that traveling and all
those goddamn snobs with their goddamn tuxedos and
their goddamn phony accents and their goddamn fucking
shiny black shoes who wouldn't have their goddamn fucking jobs if it hadn't been for him and his kitchen, all of
them bowing and sneering and smiling and sneering and
opening their eyes panicked wide when he told them, fuck
it, I quit, shove your shoes up your ass, next to your head.

Mr. Maclaren was different. These people here, and
those who traveled through, they were different. They ate,
and they drank, and they talked, and they were, most of the
time, aware of what they put in their mouths. Most of the
time they liked it. Some of the time they didn't, and he
always, but always, tried to find out why.

Sometimes he did.

Sometimes he didn't.

Sometimes, even when there wasn't a lot of business and
not much to do in the kitchen, sometimes he just went
away for a while. A temporary vacation, like he once told
Mr. Maclaren, without leaving the room. A trick he had
learned during the hard times, when people shouted at him
and he couldn't shout back, when people scoffed at his
creations and he couldn't scoff back, when people derided

his tastes, and he couldn't cut their throats. Vacations. Quick. Long. They were, all in all, often better than here. He liked them. He trained them.

Sometimes they came when he wasn't even ready.

Vacation time.

Maybe later.

When he stopped spinning, faced into the lounge, he saw the pale woman pull herself out of her booth and stand at the window, looking out at the snow, arms at her sides. He wondered if she wished she had the gun back so she could shoot the man she came with. The radio man. He had heard Davies several times, not because he liked the show, but because he had once overheard Julia talking about it, making fun of it.

She was lying.

He knew.

She was lying.

His right arm pressed against his side, pushing the sheathed carving knife into his ribs. He fought not to giggle when he felt it, thinking that he would have really looked like a fool, pulling it out to fight the man in black when Mr. Maclaren and the cow boy had all those guns.

A glance to the trapdoor.

Nes was down there.

Rotting.

"Julia?"

She turned after slipping a disc into the player.

"You think maybe I should open the kitchen again?"

She came toward him, shedding her coat, making him stare because it was like she was shedding her blouse and pants. Stripping. In the faint light. Just for him.

She shrugged. "I don't know. What do you think?"

"I think," he said when the radio man laughed, "I'm getting a little pissed off."

Ray Anthony and his trumpet.

Muted and slow.

Mandy sat at the table nearest the restaurant steps, glanced up at the beams and failed to locate the speakers, glanced over her shoulder and failed to find Hugh. That he wasn't with them made her nervous. That the light from the single bulb still working outside barely reached her, barely defined her, made her feel too exposed. That they all seemed so passive made her believe, just for a moment, that they were already dead, just playing a role in some celestial cinematic allegory from which they were to draw meaningful lessons before being sent to Heaven, consigned to Hell.

Trumpets, muted.

It was warm in here.

She unbuttoned Maclaren's sweater, fanned the tops of her breasts, scanned the room again and realized she was wrong. They weren't passive at all, and that scared her even more.

Once, so long ago the exact date had become unimportant, she had gone to the zoo. She didn't remember what city. She did remember the animals. The big cats, the monkeys, the apes, the small creatures in a place designed to turn day into night. They had all been the same that day, and no one had been able to offer an explanation—they prowled. In the middle of the afternoon in the middle of August, every blessed one of them prowled. Cages smelling of urine and old straw and old meat and old age; eyes searching the walls, the bars, the people who watched and didn't quite know what to make of what they saw; claws barely retracted, paws slapping or grasping, noses twitching endlessly in search of a scent only they would recognize.

Yet not a single one of them had moved with any speed. Deception was the rule. A few steps here, rest, a few steps there, rest, a lifting of the head and a few more steps closer to her.

Ceil shifting in front of the window; Willie spinning on the stool, seldom stopping; Julia behind the bar, at the player, the sink, the bottles, back to the sink; Ken trading stools with Trish Avery, trading a second time, moving toward a table and changing his mind.

Neil standing motionless on the other side of the bar's flap, watching, moving without moving, once almost turning to go through the door, looking at her, smiling, finally lifting the flap and joining her. She took a deep breath, not caring if he watched her chest. She needed air. They were prowling. But worse than the zoo, because here they were all caught in the same tiny cage.

In the dark.

With the trumpets.

He propped his elbows on the table, clasped his hands, rested his chin on his fingers, tilted his head and rested his cheek instead so he could look at her squarely, face in shadow except for a tiny glint in one eye.

She couldn't help it; she smiled.

She couldn't help it; she said, "What are you looking at?"

"For god's sake," said Trish wearily, "get up on the damn bar and take off your damn pants."

Neil laughed, a short bark. "You, I suppose."

"You're not a doctor, you know," Havvick complained.

Trish groaned loudly, a martyr in the making. "Nobody gives a damn what you look like, okay? We gotta see what's what, right? So take off your goddamn pants and let's have a look."

Mandy caught Ken shifting from the corner of her eye,

saw Trish with hands on her hips. Havvick mumbled, and Trish asked Julia if she had any disinfectant, something to put on the wounds if they were as bad as he made them out to be. Julia reached under something, pulled out a small bottle and slid it down the bar's length, where it bumped to a halt at Havvick's hip.

"I don't think I want to know," Neil said.

Ken's pants dropped to the floor, loose change spilling, the belt buckle thudding. He mumbled again, and Julia slapped his knee. "Nobody cares what you're wearing," she scolded. "Now hold still while I have a look."

Mandy grinned, looked at Neil. "Bikini. Monogrammed. I could've guessed."

"Psychic, huh?"

She shook her head. "I like to know these things sometimes. Helps me make sound business decisions."

He frowned.

She cursed herself, cursed her tongue for refusing to obey orders.

Ray Anthony's trumpets became Billy Vaughn's saxophones. Not as angelic or driving; more like sugar-coated sex.

"So?" he said.

Does she, or doesn't she? Mandy thought as she leaned back, palms pressed against the table's edge. Damn. Then: Ah, the hell with it.

"It's been known in some circles as personal services," she answered, resisting the impulse to be coy.

A frown ridged across his forehead, began to lose its puzzled cast.

If she hadn't liked him so much, she might have been amused, watching him work through his puzzlement, then considering, then dismissing, then considering more seriously; as it was, she felt a shiver of apprehension, and forced herself to relax. What the hell. When she figured he had it, and wasn't sure whether he wanted it, she winked and smiled. And let a hand drop into her lap when his own smile, slow in coming but coming nevertheless, said *no shit, how about that* with no judgment that she could see.

Ken yowled at the sting of the disinfectant.

Trish told him to grow up and shut up, they're just goddamn scratches.

"Kind of dangerous these days," Neil said. "Isn't it?"

Mandy knew he wasn't talking about disease. "I'm a big girl." A waggle of her eyebrows. "Besides, I have what you might call protection."

Ken called his girl a bitch and hopped down off the bar.

Trish called him a prick and asked Julia for a drink.

Hugh Davies laughed.

Billy Vaughn sputtered off the speakers, was replaced by Glenn Miller, back for a second round.

Havvick pulled up his pants, set zipper and belt, reached around to the bar and picked up the rifle. "I'm going after that sonofabitch," he announced flatly. "The bastard killed my van. You chickens coming, or you just gonna sit here all night and wait for the goddamn cops."

Ceil, at the window, said, "Cow boy . . ." And stopped, wagged a disgusted hand. Her palms pressed against the pane. "What difference does it make?"

Hugh Davies laughed again.
And shot her.

Thinking the man in black had finally made his move, Neil kicked out of his chair, grabbed the rifle from Havvick's grasp, and yanked Mandy to the floor as he dove into the low corner where the steps met the higher level of the restaurant floor. He peered between two fat clay pots and saw the door wide open, a figure ducking to the left outside. Not long, but time enough for startled recognition, and he didn't stop to ask why, but leapt into the restaurant, knocking one of the pots aside, and crouched-ran to the counter. Paused. Listened to Havvick yelling at a hysterical yelling Trish while he inched forward, holding his breath, a cold breeze slithering across his face, pushing hair in and out of his eyes. Stronger when he reached the threshold and dared a look out. Straining. Cocking his head. Hearing the crunch of footsteps as Davies ran toward the cabins, or into the woods between the cabins and the road.

Like an old man he stood, one year at a time.

"Killed her!" Havvick bellowed. "The bastard killed her!"

The van was scorched and silent.

Neil couldn't remember if the radio man still wore his coat, and though he took a step out and down, he couldn't bring himself to give chase. If he went, the others would have nothing but what Willie had in the kitchen in case the man in black returned; if he stayed, Davies might get away. But he sure as hell wouldn't be running to any cops. Assuming he even got that far. Assuming the shotgun didn't find him first.

Jesus.

"What the hell *is* this?" Ken yelled, anger and frustration and not a little fear.

Jesus, thought Neil again and hurried back inside, slamming the door, stopping at the head of the steps when he saw Willie kneeling beside Ceil's body, a carving knife in his hand. Ken stood nearby, Mandy beside him, face drenched in tears.

Havvick pointed at the cook. "He won't let us touch her."

Neil took a step down. "Willie."

Julia opened the flap to come out from behind the bar.

"Willie," he said again, stepping down to the lounge floor.

Ennin shook his head, made sure they saw the blade catch the light from the yard. "She's dead, Mr. Maclaren."

He nodded, shifted his grip on the rifle and held it across his waist. "Okay. So what's the problem?" Ignoring Mandy's sharp look at his apparent callousness.

"She has to be buried."

Oh Christ. Jesus, Willie, please, not now, for god's sake.

A caress of cold air across his nape. He stiffened, hadn't heard the door open, but he looked anyway, and saw nothing and looked back quickly when Willie shifted his weight, shoes squeaking on the floor. The noise grated, and sparked Mandy into stepping away until a table stopped her. Her hand reached behind her to grip the back of a chair, but she didn't sit; she just stood there, watching him as he moved slowly to his left and down along the booths. When he reached the last table, he was a point on a triangle, Ken opposite him, Willie at the apex.

Ceil was on her side, facing the wall, left arm hanging behind her. He couldn't see any blood. He didn't have to; he could smell it.

A snowflake drifted, and another.

A string of pearls.

"Willie, this isn't helping."

"Stupid bastard," Havvick muttered.

Carefully, Ennin brought Ceil's hand up, rested it gently on her hip. His lower lip quivered.

The blade was steady.

"I don't know," the cook said. "I don't know what's going on."

Neil saw it then, a thin wedge of blood slipping under the dead woman. "Willie, we can't leave her here. We have to get her downstairs, with Nes."

Mandy sobbed, and swore, turned so fast she collided with the table. Swore again, loudly, and marched to the place where her coat lay on the floor. Snatched it up and held it to her chest, facing the plants, head up.

It's falling apart, Neil thought.

He set the rifle on the booth table and, with a look to keep Ken in place, walked over to the body, making a point of ignoring the way the knife tracked him. He put two fingers to the side of her neck, closed his eyes to concentrate, and found nothing. Not that he expected it, but the others expected him to check. He looked at the cook and told him again that they had to get Ceil into the cellar. Willie didn't move. Ken volunteered with a caustic "I've already got experience," but the cook stabbed him away, and Havvick threw up his hands and moved over to where Trish had dropped back onto a barstool. His arm around her shoulders, his eyelids blinking out of rhythm.

"Willie."

"Why?" Mandy asked of the ceiling. Angry, not pleading.

Neil's voice took an edge he hadn't heard in years, and didn't like hearing now. "Willie, put the knife down, now, and go open the cellar door. I'll carry her."

Ennin stared back.

Then the hell with you, Neil told him without saying a word, and eased around the body, slipped his hands under her knees and back, braced himself and lifted. Too light, he thought when she came up easily and nearly made him lose his balance; god, she's light.

Willie stayed on his knees, looking up.

"His wife, you know," Mandy said, turning around, the coat still at her breast. "She was his wife."

He saw the blood on Ceil's chest, just below the sternum, soaking into the dress, soaking into his shirt. He walked as fast as he could, Ken behind the trapdoor without having to be asked, holding it up like a shield. Pale. Jaw working as if he were chewing a fat wad of gum.

"Need help?" Strained, but steady.

"No. Thanks." He maneuvered awkwardly around the opening, wondered that the stairs seemed so suddenly narrow and deep, then cradled the woman closer, her head bobbing to his shoulder, and started down. "The rifle," he said before he disappeared.

And into the cold, the lights already switched on, the posts already casting shadows across the rough wall. Bars of a cage. He reached bottom, stumbled once, and felt a warm trickling over his stomach. Her blood. His stomach contracted, and he hurried over to the tarp, where he placed her gently on the dusty floor and stood, hands at the small of his back. Stretching his neck. Licking his lips. Looking

down at her, on her back, that gleam at her throat. Opal.
Pearl. Shaking his head quickly and lifting the tarp's edge,
averting his eyes from the body of Nester Brandt as he
moved Ceil beside him, throwing the tarp back down
when he saw them, together, and thought himself sick
when he couldn't help thinking *lovers*.

Christ.

Jesus . . .

Christ.

He made it as far as the bolted door before he had to
stop. He leaned against it, cold seeping into his shoulder,
along his arm, and wiped a hand over his face, kept the
hand over his mouth and breathed in, deeply, to smell his
own flesh and drive away the smell of Ceil Llewelyn's
blood. A burst of nausea, a swift spurt of dizziness. And for
the first time since it happened, he tried to find a reason for
Davies shooting his own wife. Right then. Not before, not
later—then. Part of it he figured was his own fault, for
leaving the gun on the counter, a truly stupidass move; part
of him told him to lay off the guilt, how was he to know
the radio man would go crazy. He couldn't have known.
Of course he couldn't. Hugh, until then, had been perfectly normal, perfectly sane, perfectly rational.

The man in black was the one they were supposed to be
worried about.

So what the hell happened?

As he started for the steps he began unfastening the
stained shirt, growing agitated when his fingers didn't work
fast enough, deftly enough, finally tearing through the last
buttons as he started up, hearing one bounce off the stone
wall, stepping into the lounge twilight and going straight
into the kitchen without meeting anyone's gaze. Straight
to the other door and straight into his office. He threw the
shirt into the waste can, looked down at his jeans and saw
the blood there as well. An arm cleared a space on the desk
with a single mindless swipe, and he sat, stripped, threw the

jeans away. Then he remembered that Davies had been given his spare clothes.

"Shit."

He punched the desktop.

"Shit!"

All falling apart.

He gripped the desk and tried to steady his breathing, tried to understand just what was going on, and only succeeded in making himself more angry. Too angry to think straight. A familiar anger so long suppressed that its revival made him gasp, but not because it was wrong. God, no. It had been wrong back then, when he had learned about the death of his father and had joined the State Police; it had been just as wrong the next time, when he had learned that the men who had gunned Mac down had been acquitted on a technicality, and he had wanted to get them. Simple revenge. No rationale necessary, or desired. He had actually taken a week's vacation to hunt them down a week after they'd been released. He had actually taken his gun along. And if he had ever found them, he knew he would have done it.

But the anger had passed.

The pride that remained finally gave way to reason.

But he had never forgotten the way he felt, both times— not just the rage, but the satisfying *sweetness* of it.

Now it had returned, and he shuddered, rubbed his shoulders hard enough to burn because it felt, this time, somehow right.

It was right, and he didn't know why.

The man in black knew.

He looked at the ceiling, unable to figure out where that thought had come from; he sure as hell didn't want to know.

But it was *sweet*.
It was *right*.
It touched his cheek and *kissed* him.

Jesus."

With an effort weak enough to make him shudder again, he ordered himself to simmer down, forget it, it was crazy, they were waiting for him out there, and here he was, sitting on his stupid rolltop desk in a pair of underpants and dark socks.

Lord.

He had to get dressed, but he'd be damned if he was going to wear those blood-drenched clothes. Besides driving him nuts, imagine the effect it would have on the others. He'd have to go to the house. No. That was out of the question. Another brilliantly stupid idea, Maclaren. In the middle of what was turning into a massacre, he was planning to go outside, practically naked, and tempt the enemy to kill again, just because he wouldn't wear bloody clothes.

He peered into the waste can, finally leaned over to fetch his jeans—they weren't so bad, not really—and pulled back sharply, clamped his arms over his stomach. He couldn't do it. He stared at the cracked plaster ceiling just as Benny Goodman returned, Krupa thumping again like a heart racing to die. He couldn't do it. Gooseflesh erupted along his arms and legs; his right heel beat back against the desk, lightly.

"All right, enough," he whispered, jumped to the floor and opened the closet, staring at the empty hooks, the hangers, looked down at himself, underwear and socks, and a sound like a laugh, like a moan, passed his lips before he grabbed a black raincoat from the last hook. The flannel lining was freezing when he put it on, oddly stiff and crinkling like wax paper when he sat on the desk again and put on his shoes.

And sat there, hands on his knees, until Mandy slammed open the door and said, "If you don't tell me who the hell he is, I'm going to scream these damn walls down."

He just looked at her.

She saw him, blinked as her gaze took in the shoes, the socks, the bare legs, the coat, and said, voice trembling, "Sweet Christ, Neil. Sweet Jesus, Mary, and Joseph, if I laugh I'm going to get hysterical. Please, God, don't let me laugh."

He got up and took her arms, squeezed until the humor fled from her eyes. And returned a second later. Desperate humor. Begging humor.

"It's all I have," he said with a shrug. He opened the door. "But I have no intention of letting you know what kind of underwear I have on."

"If it's boxer shorts," she told him, slipping under his arm into the hall, "I'll never speak to you again."

Good, he thought; good, keep it up.

In the lounge, the music low, nothing left but the drums, he said, "I have to get fresh clothes from the house," to Julia.

She looked him up and down. "What about the radio man?"

"He won't be back."

"How do you know?" Ken demanded.

"I don't," he answered, raising the bar flap, moving to the restaurant steps. "But I doubt it. At least, not before I do."

Willie was still on the floor, sitting with his back to the wall, head just below the window, knees up, carving knife hanging over one shin.

Staring at the bloody floor.

Not moving.

"Just . . ." He felt like an idiot in the raincoat, knowing they were staring at the flash of his bare legs. "Just stay away from the windows and . . . wait, okay?" A second idea. "There's a mop in the kitchen. You could, uh, clean up a little."

Trish, arms folded on the bar, head resting on her arms, said, "He'll go after you, you know."

Neil knew.

Radio man. Important man about to become more important. He'd be back for damn sure. And the first person Hugh would be after would be him. The most dangerous of the group, from Davies's point of view. The former cop. The man who supposedly knew how to shoot back. Cow boy didn't count. Despite the action earlier, Davies would consider him all talk and bluster. Neil, by his presence, was the leader. Take away the leader, the rest fall into line.

At least he hoped that's the way Davies would think whenever he stopped running. Another reason why he had to go to the house. To keep Davies away from the restaurant for a while. If he was still alive.

"Suppose," Trish called after him, "that other guy comes back?"

He didn't answer.

Ken followed, trailed by Mandy, who'd taken up her coat again.

Neil stood at the door, already shivering, sliding his hands into the sleeves to rub at his forearms. "Get the rifle," he told Ken, "and stay here, watch for me. You see Davies, lock the door and keep down. For god's sake, don't try anything, okay? No hero stuff."

Havvick nodded.

Neil wondered.

The Dorsey brothers launched a sentimental journey.

He shut his eyes, opened them, couldn't help wondering if this was how Mac had felt, reaching for the handle on the back of that truck. Had he considered the possibility that one of the men he had stopped would murder him without thinking? Cigarette smugglers. Jesus Christ, he hoped so. Otherwise, he'd died because of a dumb rookie's mistake.

And this, he thought as he put out a hand, could be one hell of a mistake, too.

Mandy reached around him, made to open the door.

"No."

"Yes."

"There is no argument here," he said firmly. "If I have to run, I know where to go. You're safer here."

"And what if you don't come back?"

"Life's a bitch," he answered. "Think of a present you can give me later."

He took a breath.

"What's he talking about?" Ken asked, suspicious, bewildered.

He opened the door.

"It's his birthday."

"No shit?"

No shit, Neil thought, and darted out to the stoop, picking his footing with care, not wanting to slip and have all that snow make the cold worse.

It couldn't be worse.

It burned his ears, froze his lungs, turned his flesh parchment brittle. Almost stopped him at the corner of the building when he asked, screaming silently, if he really knew what the hell he was doing. Across the lot, then, toward the break in the rail fence, toward the path beneath the trees much taller and much darker than he remembered them being. Sucking in a sharp breath when the snow squeezed into his shoes. Listening to the thunder of the raincoat as it crackled every step, listening to the thunder of his heart and wishing, as he slid onto the path, that he'd thought to borrow someone's gloves, someone's hat, someone's muffler.

Christ.

Half-assed all the way.

Glancing quickly toward the creek before he ducked into the trees, gasping when he thought he saw the man in black and realized it was only a fat-boled stunted oak.

Listening.

Seeing the house bob and weave in front of him, caution dictating a pause before he ran into the small clearing he laughingly called a yard, just in case someone was waiting inside. Ignoring the caution because stopping now would mean freezing to death, and if he was going to die, it sure as hell wasn't going to be out here, without his clothes on.

He slipped when he reached the porch, right foot shooting sharply to the side over a hidden patch of ice, dropping him to one knee while his hands tried desperately to shift and take the weight before something tore in his groin. A second's wait for the pain that never came, and he half-crawled to the door and opened it, stumbled over the threshold and fell inside, rolling onto his back and kicking the door shut.

Lying there.

Puffing at the low ceiling.

The warmth too much like drops of acid on his fingertips, his lips, his earlobes, in his veins.

Sitting up.

Listening.

The little house talked to itself, creaks, snaps, the rattle of a shutter when a gust of wind slapped the outside wall.

It felt . . . right; no intrusions.

Nevertheless, when he stood, he reached around the corner and turned on a living-room light and waited for his eyes to adjust, lungs taking air in quick shallow gulps.

Nothing but shadows, chairs, books, the TV.

A nod of relieved satisfaction, and he hobbled to the bedroom where he grabbed a pullover, a shirt, jeans, toed off his frozen shoes and threw them in the corner, replaced them with hiking boots whose laces dismayed him until his fingers remembered how they worked. Thinking as he dressed that maybe he ought to bring the others back here. More comfortable. Television. Radio. Beds. A fair way to spend the rest of the night, however long the rest of the night was going to be.

A grunt as he returned to the living room and stared down at the phone on a side table that wobbled whenever he breathed on it too hard.

More comfortable, he decided, and more deadly as well. Too many windows, the trees too close, and all that comfort would have them all fast asleep within the first hour, despite their fear. If the stranger didn't come for them then, Davies just might. And from the road, even in leafless winter, the house was unseen.

Damn.

Indecision and a scolding, before he picked up the receiver and listened for the dial tone, and replaced it without disappointment.

Miracles, this night, weren't part of the plan.

But he left the lamp on.

A sheepskin jacket and lined gloves from the hall closet.

Then he hurried into the kitchen and grabbed some brown paper bags from under the sink, returned to the bedroom and filled them as best he could with sweaters, socks, heavy shirts, a second pair of boots he thought might fit Mandy well enough to last her as long as Deerfield.

If they decided to try it again.

Back in the hall he willed his legs to be still for a moment, forcing himself to run inventory through the entire house, hoping he would remember that he had another weapon squirreled away. Preferably a loaded howitzer. Failing that, another gun would do just fine.

But miracles still weren't part of the plan.

Crushing the bags to his chest, he reached for the doorknob, never made it. He frowned as he turned in a slow circle that ended back at the door. Listening again. Straining. Sensing something unnervingly different now that he was about to leave. As if it weren't his house after all.

An emptiness.

He squinted.

A strangeness.

No.

A stranger.

And it was him.

He looked up in disgust, would have thumped his head smartly had he had a free hand. "Dear lord, Maclaren, you're cracking." And hurriedly, awkwardly, opened the door because even his voice didn't sound right in the house that had been his for so long.

And wasn't anymore.

He stepped out, huffed at the cold, turned and closed the door. As an afterthought, he locked it, turned again and saw him waiting, back under the trees, on the path.

Snowing. Flurries of large flakes, wet, sifting through the branches, in and out of the light that shone too brightly from the front window.

No hissing this time.

Just the snow.

Just the silence.

You know your goddamn cabins don't have any heat. I think the price you quoted me is much too high."

Neil couldn't move, and had no place to go. The door was locked, the porch was open, and Davies, even if he was a poor shot, could knock him down before he'd taken a half-dozen steps. Knock him down long enough to come up and finish the job. One way or another. On the other hand, the radio man didn't look all that steady. Coat buttoned to the neck, the muffler sloppily wrapped up to cover his chin; his shoulders jumped every once in a while, and his stance was too rigid. He wasn't quite near enough for Neil to see his face clearly, but from what looked like shadow he figured the cold made it seem as if it had been badly burned.

"I was going to try for the police, you know."

Not loud. It didn't have to be. Not at night, not in winter.

"I'm way ahead of you," Neil answered.

Davies nodded, shoulders unevenly hunched, leaning slightly forward as though he were standing into a moderate wind.

The bags crackled against Neil's chest. "So what are you going to do?"

Davies took a long stride toward the porch, and almost stumbled, batted his left hand once at the air as though driving off something that had pushed him from behind.

Frozen; he was damn near frozen.

A gloved hand wiped under his nose. "I want to come back in, Maclaren."

Neil said nothing.

"I swear to you I won't try anything. You can tie me up, chain me, whatever the hell. Just let me back inside."

"I could, but Ken'd blow your head off. And if he didn't, Mandy would. She's dead, you son of a bitch; your wife's dead."

Davies looked at the ground, snow slowly forming a lace cap over his hair. "Then let me in the house."

That voice.

It laughed abruptly, brittle and low.

"Actually, it doesn't make a difference what you say, does it? I can always break a window." Chuckling. Shaking his head at his own wit. "I just thought I'd be polite and ask."

Laughing.

He raised his head, his mouth open to take in long gulps of frigid air.

Neil didn't think, didn't plot, didn't scheme. There were no odds to determine, no *ifs* to sift through. Bags in his arms, no gun, standing in the light.

"I have a career."

Laugh.

That voice.

After a brief struggle, his right hand came out of his pocket and aimed the gun.

Neil waited.

In jerked stages as if weighted, the arm lowered to the man's side, jerked and twitched. "Career." Chuckling. "It appears, doesn't it, that I've shot myself in the foot. Metaphorically speaking."

Neil took an inch toward the post at the right of the steps.

"You know that city boy, country boy business, the things you said were bull a few hours ago?" A look at the sky, face touched with falling snow. "It isn't bull, Maclaren." Not a laugh now, or a chuckle; a tremulous note. "It's dark out there. It's goddamn dark out there." The gun hand waved. "It's never that dark in the city. Never. Not even when you die."

Neil moved again.

Davies stepped into the clearing. "Who is that man?"

"I wish I knew."

Davies snorted disbelief. "You know. I know damned well you know."

Neil denied it.

"That scruffy little man, that gambler, he knew." A puzzled shrug. "He thought he did, anyway. *I* think he did."

The gun came up again.

The voice hardened.

"I'm freezing my ass off, Maclaren. If I don't get inside soon, my throat will be gone." A violent tremor nearly knocked him off his feet. Neil moved again, within arm's reach of the post. "All those poor lonely women without their phantom midnight lover." His smile was a parody of humor. "Do you want that responsibility, Maclaren? Do you want all those women deprived? Do you want their phantom exorcised?"

If he fired, Neil figured he'd be able to duck behind the

post, give him a few seconds to rid himself of the bags and prepare a sprint to the end of the porch, over the edge, and around the house. Unless Davies got lucky.

"That man," Davies said.

Neil couldn't help it; he looked into the trees at the side of the house.

"You know him," Davies repeated. This time not a question.

"Nope."

Davies shook his head laboriously. Swayed. Made a painfully visible effort to straighten himself. The laugh, deprecating and deep. "You won't believe this, Maclaren, but when I first saw him out there, I thought it was you."

The bags began to slip; Neil tightened his arms.

"I'm cold, Maclaren, goddamnit."

Neil turned sideways, even with the post, and jerked his head toward the door. "I'm not stopping you, Hugh. You want to get warm, go on in. Shit, you've got the damn gun."

"I do," Davies answered.

He took a step forward.

"And you don't."

He fired.

Neil threw himself down and shoulder-first against the post, a shower of splinters over his head, snapping against the wall. He whirled and tensed to run, froze at the second shot because the second shot was different. He saw Davies throw up his hands and fire wildly at the sky before dropping to his face. Nothing dramatic; he simply fell. His right foot kicked snow, thudded several times, and was still.

Ken Havvick stood in the path behind him, the rifle in his hands. "You okay?"

Neil used the post to pull himself up. He couldn't speak. He only nodded, wrapping the post snugly with his right arm and watching as Kenny approached the body with caution, the muzzle aimed at Davies's head. He made a complete circle before backing away, stopping only when his heel met the porch steps.

"He's dead." He sounded as if he was going to cry. "Son of a bitch, he's dead." Keeping the rifle aimed at the radio man's head.

When Neil felt he could move without falling over, he climbed down the steps, making what he hoped were all the right noises about doing what had to be done, saving a life not only now but probably later as well, put down the rifle, Ken, and help me put him on the porch, there's no need to carry him back to the cellar.

Ken did, saying nothing.

Neil retrieved the bags when they were done and nudged Havvick with a foot, set them both back toward the restaurant not much slower than a run.

In the parking lot they paused simultaneously, first looking down at the creek, then up at the streetlamp. An exchange of glances, and they skidded to the stoop. Havvick went first and opened the door, said, "What did he mean?" as Neil went inside.

"About what?" Bags onto the counter while he watched the others rush up from the lounge.

"About knowing that guy."

"Nothing. He didn't mean anything."

"Okay," Havvick said, and Neil was too astonished to react to what was clear doubt in his voice.

Jesus Christ, he thinks I'm lying.

The door closed behind them.

Most of the cold stayed outside.

Mandy grabbed his arms and looked him over, while Trish snatched the rifle and dropped it into the nearest booth. "I thought you were dead," she said, scolding. "What happened?"

Havvick's knees buckled.

Neil grabbed him around the waist with one arm, assured a suddenly panicked Trish that no one here had been wounded, it was just a delayed reaction, and walked Ken to the first table and sat him down. Mandy stayed by the counter, emptying the bags as Neil, standing behind Ken, one hand on his shoulder, explained the delay in returning. No elaboration. He might have been taking a customer's order. He might have been listing the specials of the day. As he spoke, he glanced around the room, finally saw Julia standing down in the lounge, a stark silhouette against the back window, and signaled her to fetch some glasses and a bottle. He felt Ken shift under his grip, squeezed the shoulder once and stripped off coat and gloves, dropping them onto the neighboring table.

"You just left him there?" Mandy said as Julia stepped up into the restaurant.

He nodded.

No explanation.

He was tired of explanations, both offering and seeking. What he wanted was the glass Julia handed him, and the liquid inside; what he wanted was for dawn to pale the light glowing on the snow by the creek; what he wanted was for people to stop looking at him as though he were some kind of wizard, able to pull the world's solutions out of his voluminous goddamn sleeve.

What he wanted was to celebrate his birthday alone.

What he wanted . . . was to sleep.

He drank without bothering to lower the glass, and grimaced; it tasted like iron.

"You should have seen him, Trish," Ken said, talking to the tabletop. "He was nuts. Like a zombie."

Trish pulled a chair beside him, sat, and dropped an arm over his shoulder. Neil saw her expression as he put down the glass—the concern, the solicitude, and the way she had to work to make it work, to make her fiancé look her full in the eye and believe that she cared, that she'd been half scared to death while he'd been gone.

Good god.

"Neil?"

Julia hadn't gone.

He raised his head; it was an effort.

"The rav—the man hasn't come back, not since the van."

"He's been gone before," he said.

"It's almost three."

He laughed quickly. "You're kidding." A shake of his head. "Time flies."

Mandy took his hand and tugged at it gently.

"Time flies," he repeated, this time to himself.

She led him to a chair, turned him, made him sit.

"It wasn't like I was trying to kill him, Trish. I swear, I wasn't."

"Hush," she whispered loudly. "It's okay, Kenny. It's okay, honey."

The second Mandy walked away, Neil stood up again. "Where's Willie?"

Julia pointed to the lounge. "While you were gone, we kind of decided we were going to try for Deerfield."

He started for the steps. "Kind of?"

"It wasn't unanimous, if that's what you're asking."

He didn't give a damn. Right now, he didn't give a damn about much of anything except that somehow his restaurant, his bar, his property had been lowered into a slow-motion Hell that showed no signs of ending.

"Willie!"

Mandy intercepted him, put her hands on his chest, and he took hold of her wrists and searched her face for signs of remorse, or sorrow, or even regret that Hugh Davies was dead. There was nothing. No; a lie. There was worry. For him, he supposed, and the way he was behaving.

"Willie, damnit!"

The sweater was unbuttoned. Shadows shifted across her skin as her breasts rose and fell, as she tilted her head first one way, then the other, staring at him, trying to force all his attention on her. When he faked a reassuring smile, she gave him one in return that told him to knock it off, she wasn't born yesterday. And when he opened his mouth to call Ennin again, she stopped him with a finger.

"Trish, you think they'll arrest me?"

"Self-defense, honey, self-defense. Mr. Maclaren was there, he'll tell them."

"My father'll kill me."

"Your father's a prick."

"You know," Neil said, finally easing Mandy's hands away without releasing them, "Ken thought I was that guy."

Julia passed them, and stopped.

"Hugh?" Mandy said.

"No. You know . . . him."

He smiled at her, smiled at Julia, waited for them to laugh, and when Mandy did, and the bartender continued into the lounge without even a look, he almost told her how the house, his house, had changed. Or how he thought it had. But he didn't. If he didn't quite understand the feeling himself, he was damn sure she wouldn't. It was one of those things—you had to be there. Like the funniest joke in the world that no one else ever laughed at. You just had to be there.

A one-sided smile: "You voted not to go, right?"

She nodded. "I am a lot of things, Neil, but I'm not entirely stupid."

"Willie, where the hell are you?" He turned her in a dance that put him at the top of the steps, tendrils of a spider plant crawling over his shoulder. "Our friend out there, you think he'll try—"

"No." Her wrists slipped from his fingers. "He doesn't need to."

Ken slammed a fist on the table.

Trish fell back in her chair, scowling.

"Very cryptic," Neil said. "Remind me to ask you sometime what you're talking about."

She shrugged, rolled her shoulders, and he hated himself when his gaze was drawn to her chest, and just as quickly darted away when he swiped the plant off his shoulder. But he didn't look away fast enough not to see her lips pull slightly at the corners. Just enough. Just . . . enough.

"He's in the kitchen."

Neil looked toward the bar. Julia stood there.

"Is he okay?"

She lifted a hand—*I don't know, I guess so*—and reached behind her to turn the music down.

He threaded his way between the tables to the back window, deliberately standing well to the right of where Ceil had fallen, and looked at the gentle swells and humps where the snow had covered the rocks by the water. He considered turning off the remaining light, and instantly discarded it. Davies had been right. Without it, it would be too dark out there, and too dark in here. They had gotten used to not having the lights on; anything more now would be a shock. He dragged a finger down the glass. Funny; out there the dark was dangerous, and in here it was safe.

Or it had been. Once.

So are you an angel or what? he asked the grey and black between the trees. You on some kind of divine mission to sort out the slobs who live down here? Or was somebody lying? Did someone here actually know his name? A vendetta? Doubtful. Vendettas didn't usually include playing

cat and mouse for half the night. His gaze followed the
erratic fall of a flake he picked at random from all the others
falling more heavily now, slanting just off true as they
followed the direction of the light wind.

He heard a slap, and heard Trish begin to cry, muffled,
as if her face were covered.

He turned, pressed back against the pane, and saw them
up at the table—Kenny shaking a hand, not a fist, and the
girl slapping the air between them to keep him away.
Mandy was where he'd left her, watching the couple, too,
leaning against the railing with her arms across her stomach. In profile, she seemed taller, breasts larger, legs longer,
face more angled. Not a beautiful woman. Handsome in
the old-fashioned way. Julia had moved to the barstool by
the flap, a glass in one hand, her other hand absently pushing through her hair, over and over. By the way she faced,
she seemed to be watching him, but he had a feeling that
she couldn't see him, couldn't see anything. To test it, he
nodded to her; she didn't respond.

So, Maclaren, he thought, what more do you want?

The wind bumped against the window, neither moaning
nor keening. Just insistent.

Snow tried again to scratch its way through the glass,
neither loud nor soft. Just trying.

A scurry of drier flakes swept toward the creek, swept
over it in a bridge of fog that vanished on the other side.

An icicle began to form under the eaves.

Whit more do you want?

A laugh spurted, subsided, bubbled, retreated, the noises he made were quiet.

Mandy looked at him quizzically.

He kept his face blank.

Did you sleep with him, he wondered; were you Hugh's mistress or something? He imagined they had to have known Mandy's . . . profession, but couldn't imagine how the three of them could have been friends. Acquaintances, maybe. Something that would appeal to Davies's warped sense of humor.

Radio man.

Dead man.

Dead woman.

Startled, and a little saddened, that he was unable to find in himself what he had sought in Mandy Jones—remorse, or sympathy other than the fact that a human being was gone. No; three of them. Forever.

Nevermore.

Good god, what the hell was wrong with him tonight?

Turning sideways, shoulder now against the glass as he looked from the room to the water and woods, and back again. Letting his mind travel on its own, skittering from one image to another, none of them focused enough for him to want to examine. Listening to Trish's every so often sobbing, Julia's uncharacteristically loud drinking, and finally, an occasional ringing metallic sound from the kitchen to prove that Willie was still among the living. From room to water. Water reluctantly to room. Noting for the second or third time that night an inexplicable sensation of growing detachment, as if connections had been severed. But what they were, he didn't know; and when he tried to identify them, he decided they didn't exist.

Maybe they never had, and wasn't that a cheerful thought to herald the second half of your life, Mr. Bones?

God.

Mandy came down into the lounge. He followed her as she headed for the bar and took the stool beside Julia. And yawned.

Julia, of all things, giggled and yawned with her.

A look into the restaurant—Ken had his head down on the table, and Trish was muttering at him.

When he felt his own body gearing for a gigantic yawn of his own, he checked the snow, forced himself to watch the flakes dance around each other, leaving traces of themselves behind as his eyes began to water from the effort not to yield to the wash of weariness that flooded through him without warning.

He rubbed knuckles into his eyes. His fingers scratched rigidly through his hair until he winced when a nail produced a scratch, when the finger rubbed around the area gently as if to erase it.

God, he thought; Jesus, I'm tired.

And why not?

It was after three o'clock on the morning of his fortieth birthday.

In February.

The dead time.

Adrenaline finally too diluted to stir him, nerves exhausted from twanging from raw to numb, his mind no longer reeling but settling into stasis against a bellowing host of questions that, once answered, reproduced in greater numbers.

Why shouldn't he be tired?

Why shouldn't he get some sleep?

It might well be, in fact and in the long run, the wisest course. Sleep equaled invigoration. Rejuvenation. And once reborn, their faculties back to working on all cylinders, they would be able, at long last, to figure out a way to avoid the man outside and get hold of the police. They couldn't sleep all at once, though. Someone would have to stand guard, alert them if their unwelcome guardian made a move toward the building. And if the guy did, then what? He had already proven too elusive to shoot at with any reasonable accuracy; and they had already proven that they were too frightened to follow up on any advantage they might have gained.

What, he asked, advantage?

Name three.

He cleared his throat, looked outside and considered that streetlamp. Considered the tracks in the snow he was going to show Trish, tracks leading to the spot where the man in black had stood, the tracks leading away when he had run from their firing.

Run.

Or had walked.

Because he could explain away the fact that he hadn't found any tracks out by the creek, and why the man hadn't left tracks on this side of the water when he'd shot out two of the lights; but he couldn't explain why the tracks by the streetlamp only lasted a yard or two.

After that, there was nothing.

And there were no branches low enough, or near enough, for him to have been able to leap up, catch one, disappear into a tree.

There were footprints.

And there were none.

fairy dust

Bullshit, he thought.

raven's wings

Disgusted, tired, he pushed away from the window and stretched toward the ceiling, bent over and touched his toes, straightened and scrubbed his face and scalp vigorously.

Heard the silence.

Sudden; complete.

He snapped his fingers, and heard nothing.

He coughed, and heard nothing.

He looked over to the bar and saw Mandy and Julia talking, and heard nothing.

When he tried to move, he couldn't.

Not until he felt something at his back.

I have fallen asleep, nothing more.

A cold snake squirmed its lazy way through his stomach; a colder draft toyed with the fine hair hanging over his collar.

He couldn't move in any direction but around to the window, and his lungs hitched, the snake coiled, when he saw the man in black standing in the trees.

Nothing had changed. Not the long coat, not the flat-brimmed hat, not the black gloves. A dusting of snow across his shoulders and chest. A haze that rose from the ground to blur his outline, make him seem less like a silhouette than a phantasm growing out of the night, and tied to the night by their mutual color. Standing there. Watching. Every few seconds erased by the blowing snow, re-forming again when the wind calmed and the snow fell in straight lines. Standing there. Waiting.

Neil, without thought, was more than willing to oblige.

He sprinted across the room into the restaurant, brushing away Trish's drowsy question, grabbing up his coat and gloves and putting them on as fast as he could, vacillating for only a few seconds before grabbing the revolver, making sure it was loaded, and running back into the lounge.

"Neil!"

"Get the rifle, Julia, and load it, and watch me."

Julia started to move only when he reached the trapdoor and flung himself down the steps.

"Neil!"

Mandy's shadow in the hole as he threw back the cellar door bolt.

"Neil, for god's sake, don't leave us alone!"

"You've got Ken," he said over his shoulder at the shadow on the steps. "And Willie." He opened the door, snapped up his collar. "Don't let Julia tell you otherwise; she can shoot."

He ran out, slipping once in the snow as deep as his ankles, recovering and running on, aware that someone, maybe all of them, was standing at the window. He didn't care. He squinted hard into the snow, trying to find him, and finding him still in the same place, ran on.

Breath smoking over his shoulder.

Boots crushing the grass beneath the snow.

Keeping the gun pointed down until he reached the near bank and realized the man was gone.

It didn't stop him.

He leapt across the water, his left foot catching a rock and sliding off, bringing him to his hands and one knee, the boot barely breaking the creek's surface before he was moving again, veering around a cage of white birch, not bothering to check the ground where the man had stood.

Running into the woods.

The snow wasn't as heavy here, hissing again as it passed over branches and twigs and a few stubborn dead leaves; the wind with a voice that pushed the treetops aside but barely reached the ground; underbrush clawing for his legs, rustling over the bottom of his coat.

Hearing himself puffing.

Slowing, checking either side, spinning to be sure nothing or no one was at his back.

Leaning over as the ground began a gentle rise that would eventually become too steep to climb if he went much farther, much deeper.

Clearing his face with a sleeve.

Turning.

The restaurant reduced to a diffused white glow that turned the boles to bars that wavered at the edges and their

shadows to blunt arrows that pointed at his feet. A clump
of snow tumbling in a thick shower and splattering noise-
lessly against the ground.

Turning.

Using his left hand to grip the tip of a heavy evergreen
bough. Shading his eyes with his gun hand and peering as
deep as he could, starting when a curled strip of bark peeled
away from a branch and spiraled behind a bush. Wiping his
mouth with the crook of his elbow and moving on, not
realizing he was still holding the bough until it tugged him
back, and he released it with a curse and angry whip of his
arm.

Running a few steps, pausing, running a few steps more.

Not bothering to search for tracks.

There wouldn't be any.

Swearing at himself for not bringing the flashlight in the
office; it was getting difficult to see more than a few yards
ahead. If he kept up like this, he was going to kill himself.

He paused then at an old tree with a double trunk, the
right-hand one narrow, twisting toward the ground and up
again, a natural elbow where once in a while he came to
sit when the weather was good, legs dangling, watching
Rusty and her brood scamper overhead. He was sure the
squirrels lived up there, but he'd never climbed to find out.
He just left the peanuts behind when he went home. A
shake of his head to drive the snow from his hair, and he
wondered just what the hell he thought he was proving,
running around like an idiot in the middle of a snowstorm.

Nothing.

There was nothing to prove.

The wind rumbled.

The snow thickened.

Dark enough back here that he couldn't see all the flakes.

When his teeth began to chatter, he glanced toward the
sky and decided to head back. Nothing to prove, and while
doing it, he was going to give himself a healthy dose of

pneumonia. As if to prove that, he sneezed, coughed, sneezed again, and began walking. But he didn't stop looking. At each small tree and tall shrub, at the snow-mounds that camouflaged either bush or boulder, at the shallow depressions that weren't footprints by any stretch of desperate imagination.

When the wind stopped, the night filled the gap smoothly with the groans of sagging branches and the crunch of snow beneath his ridged soles and the labored breathing through his mouth and the grunts when a boot broke through what had looked like a solid piece of ground.

When the wind stopped, he heard the heavy stroke of wings.

He refused to look up.

Nothing flew this late at night except maybe a starving owl; but not even a starving owl would hunt in a storm.

He refused to look up.

He didn't stop moving. Faster, but not running, the footing too treacherous now that he was calm enough to think about what he was doing. Too many traps lurking beneath the snow. Too many holes for him to step in and snap or wrench an ankle. Faster, and with caution; but faster nonetheless.

The wings followed him.

A slow rippling flap. Silence. Perhaps a gliding.

He set his lips and looked straight ahead, at the faint tiny glow that told him he had traveled much farther than he'd thought, and he'd not been paying attention. But it was there, he wasn't lost, and as long as it continued to swell, stretch out, he knew it wouldn't be long before he would warm again.

Warmth; a good thing to think about.

But not good enough to prevent him from hearing the wings.

A slow rippling flap. Silence. Perhaps a gliding.

Or a landing with a faint scratching in that tree over there to his left, where a large feather-cloud drifted through the lower branches, frozen snow that ticked each time it brushed against the bark.

You're doing it again, he thought as he picked up speed; you're spooking yourself, jerk.

"Damn right," he said aloud.

Loudly.

"Damn right."

But it didn't stop the wings.

The languid flap of large wings, not the frantic pace of a sparrow.

And, at the last, it didn't prevent him from running, leaping over real and imagined obstacles, plowing through low shrubs instead of veering around them, using trees to spin him in different directions, the gun fumbled into his pocket because he couldn't shoot what he couldn't see.

And he couldn't see it, up there in the snow-slashed dark.

But he could hear it.

Neither pursuing nor following, but simply keeping pace.

Neither taunting nor threatening, yet he couldn't arrest the fear that clutched his muscles, dried his throat, widened his eyes, made his legs alternately too rigid and too rubbery; he couldn't stop jerking his head around to see what was behind him, above him, over there between those pines, a shadow floating until a trunk came between them and the shadow disappeared; he couldn't stop himself from a prayer that demanded, not beseeched.

He couldn't stop himself from calling out his relief when the restaurant began to form in the middle of the glow, and nearer, the slash of the creek through the snow.

He fell not fifty yards from the water.

A rock, a fallen limb, a slant of frozen ground—whatever it was, it was mostly ice, and he landed hard on his stomach, arms outstretched, face up and out of the snow, which let him see the cage of birch just before he struck its base. Felt the pain. Felt the blood. Felt the talons clawing at his neck.

R*aven's wings
   slowly flapping*

V acation time.

Hey, listen," Ken said, pushing into the kitchen. "You want to make up some coffee? Black. Real black. We're dropping like flies out there, man."

Willie sat at his shelf-desk in the alcove, staring at the calendar that reminded him he had a class next Wednesday at seven-thirty at Community College. It was American History. He didn't much care for history, but if he wanted to get his degree, he had to take it. So he did.

"Ennin, you hear me or what?"

Willie turned without leaving his chair. "Mr. Maclaren isn't back yet."

Havvick leaned against the butcher-block counter and shook his head. "No shit." He was tired. Willie could see that. The boy's eyes were bloodshot, and his left hand trembled so badly he finally slid it into a pocket. He squinted at the fluorescent lights set into the ceiling. Only one was lit, the one over his head. "I think . . . I think he cracked, y'know? Running off like that. Shit. I think he cracked."

Willie's eyes narrowed. He pushed the chair back and stood. "No, he's not."

The long bulb buzzed and flickered, like lightning trapped above the floor.

Ken stared at the counter, shaking his head. "The guy's got a shotgun, y'know? You can't go after a shotgun with a pistol." He sighed. "Cracked."

"No. He's not."

Willie reached into his suit jacket, touched the sheath.

Havvick punched the counter. "Son of a bitch should have done something before, damn it. He shouldn't have waited so damn long." Another sigh, more a blowing, and he turned around. "Ever since he went to the damn house, he's been . . . I don't know . . . a little weird."

The light flickered again.

"No," said Willie.

He didn't like the way the boy was talking. You talk like that and people get scared. People get scared, they do the wrong things. While Mr. Maclaren was gone, there was an obligation for him and the boy to watch out for the others. If he kept talking like that, there would only be Willie left.

Havvick rubbed his hands together. "So. Coffee?"

"He's not weird."

"Sure. Whatever you say." Havvick stepped to the stove. "Damn, this thing looks complicated. C'mon, Willie, how the hell do you make a lousy pot of coffee without blowing yourself up?"

"I'll make it." He pulled the sheath from his jacket pocket. "Go back, Mr. Havvick. I'll make it."

Ken poked at the dials, peered into one of the overhead ovens. Then he spotted the large coffee urn. "Ah!"

"I'll do it."

A tray was stacked with clean cups and saucers. Ken set them on the island counter, rattling them loudly. "So how do you turn this thing on, huh?"

Willie moved across the kitchen floor, rubber-soled shoes not making a sound. "I will do it, Mr. Havvick. It's my job."

Ken leaned over to stare at the lights and buttons at the base of the urn. "Jesus, you gotta have a degree just to make some coffee?"

"I. Will. Do. It."

"Look, Ennin, it's a little crazy out there, okay? Tell you the truth, I could use something to do. Do I push this button or what?"

"No!"

Havvick whirled at the shout, gaped at the sheath, and

at the handle of the knife, blinking when the light snapped off and on again. "Hey," he said.

"Willie?"

Julia's face in the service window. He thought she looked tired. Shadows under her eyes, and her mouth wasn't as pretty as it usually was.

He smiled at her.

She pointed. "Coffee?"

His smile broadened. "You falling asleep?"

She nodded and, as if to prove it, yawned with three fingers fluttering over her mouth.

"No problem. Mr. Havvick's giving me a hand. He's going to push the fat button there by the spigot, and you'll have it in about five, ten minutes, okay?"

"Thanks, Willie."

"No problem," he said. "No sweat." He blew her a kiss, and laughed silently when her eyes seemed to bulge, her lips sputtered, and she disappeared. Reappeared and stared at him before leaving again. Then he looked at Ken, who pressed the green button while he watched. "There's a better tray underneath. You can put the cups and saucers on it. Cream's in a server in the refrigerator."

The boy said nothing, but he did as he was told.

He was pale.

Willie looked at his hand then and shook his head; he was still holding the sheath, and the blade was halfway out. You're not thinking, he scolded as he slipped the sheath back into his jacket; if you're not thinking, you're not going to be ready when Mr. Maclaren comes back and we can go home.

"Five minutes?" the boy asked, his voice none too steady.

"Maybe ten. You can wait out there if you want."

Ken left in a hurry, and Willie chuckled. Sometimes it was hard to stay mad at nosy people who thought they knew their way around his kitchen. They weren't really dumb. They just didn't know all there was to know. How to work things. How to arrange things.

How to use things.

Like the knife.

He checked to be sure the urn was loaded, coffee and water in proper proportion, the filter clear, then returned to his desk, thinking he might be able to finish working through next week's menus and alternatives before Mr. Maclaren returned from taking care of that man.

The shoe box.

Oh lord, he thought.

The shoe box.

Oh lord, I forgot again.

He grabbed his coat down from the hook on the wall behind him, slipped into it, pulled his gloves from the pockets and hurriedly pulled them on.

Oh lord.

He rooted through an apple crate under the shelf, came up with a clean trowel, and tucked the shoe box under his arm. A glance at the urn perking away, lights all shining, cups ready to be filled, and he opened the back door, blinked at the cold, rushed outside.

Where? he wondered; where will it be?

The snowfall limited visibility, and he decided it wouldn't be prudent to go all the way down to the creek. Not with that crazy man walking around. So he reached back inside and switched on the single bulb over the outside lintel, walked straight out from the door, following his shadow to a spot just to the left of the flagstone path, right by the fence. He knelt and used the trowel to scoop away the snow until he could see the ground. Snow settled on the back of his neck. He shook himself to drive it away, then stabbed the point of the trowel into the frozen earth.

A chip came away, nothing more.

He tried again.

Oh lord, how could I've forgotten?

Again.

Despite the gloves, his hands were freezing. The trowel slipped and almost took a slice of his shin.

Oh lord.

He took out the carving knife, apologized to it for the certain damage, and stabbed at the ground.

A chip came away, nothing more.

Oh lord.

Wet flakes in his eyes, his mouth, coating his lashes until he swiped them away with a sleeve.

Oh lord.

Harder, stabbing, feeling his temper begin to unravel; faster, stabbing, thinking of the boy who had tried to steal his knives and steal his coffee and steal his machines; sweating, gasping, stabbing the ground and flinching when a pebble lashed off a cheek.

The trowel.

The carving knife.

Trembling, but not from the cold.

Sobbing when he thought he had the hole deep enough, but the box wouldn't fit, and it wasn't right that the poor creature be buried in a grave that wouldn't even hold him. Not right. He wouldn't want that to happen to him. It wasn't right.

He stabbed with the knife.

Scraped with the trowel.

Made an attempt to use his fingers and burned the tips through the gloves, hissed, scolded himself, rocked back on his heels to calm himself down.

And saw him.

Beyond the fence, on the path, not five feet away.

He saw the coat first, long and black, looked higher and saw the arm reaching so terribly slowly into the coat, higher still and saw the hat whose brim hid all the face but the nose and mouth.

"Oh."

He couldn't run; kneeling so long in the cold had robbed him of his legs.

He couldn't cry out; breathing so long in the cold had numbed his voice.

The hand moved.

Willie ignored the cramplike pain that settled in his calves and stood anyway, swayed backward, waving the knife in front of him to warn the man in black away.

A gust of wind parted the snow for a moment.

Willie's mouth sagged open.

"Oh." In relief. "Oh lord, you scared me. You know, I thought for a minute there you were—"

Julia screamed, enraged.

Startled, Willie turned as she charged headlong out of the kitchen, the cleaver in her hands. No coat. No hat. Shrieking at the man in black to leave her Willie alone.

"No!" He held out his hands, shook his head, smiling. "No, no, Julia, it's—"

She tried to dodge around him, and he didn't recognize her face, not the way it was all twisted, all flushed, but he grabbed her arm before she could do any wrong, grabbed it and flung her around in a circle, yelling at her, letting her go and gaping when she left the ground, wailing, slammed into the restaurant wall and slid to the snow.

He shook his head.

"Julia?"

He ran over to where she lay on her stomach, one leg up, knee pressed against the building. Tossing the knife aside, he dropped to the snow and rolled her over onto his thighs. "It's okay," he said. "God, I'm sorry. Are you hurt? It's okay. Look!"

He looked himself over his shoulder.

The man in black was still there, but the snow had closed in upon itself again, and it looked as if he were fading. Or backing away.

Not a sound but the wind.

In time, nothing left but the snow.

He didn't understand, but as long as Julia was all right, that she wasn't badly hurt, he supposed someone, maybe Mr. Maclaren, would explain it to him later.

"Julia, come on."

He tapped her cheek lightly.

"Julia, come on, it's cold."

He tapped her cheek.

"Is everything all right? What's going on?"

Mandy in the doorway.

He nodded. "She's all right, Miss Jones. She's just . . . all right."

He tapped her cheek.

He lifted her chin.

He saw the long clean gash the cleaver had made.

Mandy stumbled back into the building, not believing what she'd just seen.

Talons

Neil yelled soundlessly and thrashed onto his back, arms slashing the air to drive the predator off. A few seconds, no more, and he stopped, exhausted, panting heavily, cough-

ing, staring at a hand gripping a whip-thin branch stubbed
with twigs hard as thorns. He released it, and the branch
dangled there until he rolled to his knees, hands on his
thighs. A tangle of stiff weeds and offshoots at the base of
the birch cage, and after a moment he rubbed the back of
his neck self-consciously.

Groaned when an electric pain shot across his face.

He touched a palm to his forehead; it came away spotted
with swift-congealing blood.

Jesus; he shuddered, thinking how close he'd come to
putting out an eye.

Using the trunks to get him to his feet hand-over-hand
was easier conceived than achieved, but when he stood at
last and memory overrode the shocks of pain on his cheeks,
his brow, above his left eye, he put his back to the restaurant and looked into the woods.

He was alone.

He had no idea if he had been unconscious or simply
stunned; it didn't make any difference, because nothing
had changed. It was still snowing. It was still dark. He
turned carefully so not to tempt dizziness or nausea, leaned
for a second against the birch and grinned sheepishly at the
restaurant light, hoping no one had seen his less than gallant
charge. Flight, he corrected; let's not get too heroic here,
Maclaren. You were running away.

Fighting against an urge to run again, he stumbled
around the tree and headed quickly for the creek. Snow
had infiltrated every opening his clothes allowed, and he
batted uselessly at the front of his coat, at his knees when
they came up, at his hair and head. Shivering. Accidentally
brushing a finger across his chin and wincing at the pain.
He figured he must look like Frankenstein about now.

Veering around a stump.

Glancing right, glancing left, oh Jesus, seeing the man in
black just beyond the reach of the light, beside a pine
whose lower branches seemed rooted in the snow.

He slapped his coat pocket; the gun was still there.

He looked at the restaurant, frowned when he heard voices, someone yelling, saw the man again and lost control a second time. His gloved hand pulled the gun free, and his eyes narrowed against the storm as he changed direction until he was moving straight toward the pine.

No fear this time.

Just the anger, and the overwhelming *sweetness* of it, the unsettling *rightness* of it.

Walking as steadily as the snow would allow.

Firing once without bothering to aim, idly noting a flurry of debris patter through the boughs.

Slamming branches aside.

Pausing once. Firing again.

Waiting for the shotgun.

He couldn't see distinct movement, but the man began to withdraw, momentarily hidden behind the tree, then visible again as Neil shifted to his left and kept on walking.

Not thinking.

Firing a third time.

Following.

Waiting for the shotgun.

Firing a fourth time and muttering, "Bastard," when the man vanished behind another tree.

Finally allowing himself a few seconds to consider just what the hell he was doing as he stepped over a low deadfall, snapping a rotted branch in half to allow him to pass. And what the hell he was doing was being led. The restaurant was now behind him on his right; another fifteen or twenty yards and he'd be in almost total darkness. He could hear the creek, the snow, his own footsteps, and nothing more.

The man was leading him away from the others.

He was almost glad then when he pulled the trigger a

fifth time and nothing happened. He just tucked the gun back into his pocket and stopped. Stared.

The man in black was gone.

Neil shook his head; not gone. Just too far away to be seen.

He looked down then at the snow. Looked behind him, squinted, and saw his tracks.

Only his tracks.

Nothing more.

Something gnawed briefly at his stomach. He turned sharply and headed for the creek, still quickly, and still not running. "I give up," he called tonelessly as he moved. "You're not going to shoot me, so what the hell do you want?"

He didn't expect an answer; he got one anyway.

Me.

He stopped.

The man wants me.

Confused, somewhat mystified, he squinted into the woods. Lower lip pulled between his teeth, teeth pressing down until the lip slipped out. Blinking against the falling snow, lighter now, much lighter. Seeing nothing out of the ordinary. But *knowing* he was being . . . not watched, not stalked, not studied. Observed. Calmly, but not clinically. A nudge to his imagination, and he could almost see the man in black tilting his head to one side, very slightly, patiently observing him. A teacher waiting for the student to come to the conclusion he should have reached hours ago. His old commander, waiting for him to realize what he had known, somehow, the moment he had graduated into the field, and didn't recognize until virtually a decade later—that passion didn't always create the optimum future.

And in that moment, as he bit down on the inside of his cheek, drew his lips in again, the cold went away. Sound left him for the second time that night. He stood in comfort, his clarity of vision startling in its intensity . . . and suddenly the despair of an old age much closer now than youth became a trivial thing. A quirk. A passage needed to be taken because no one wants to die.

And no one, at night, really believes he'll live forever.

This, he understood suddenly, is the way it is for *him*.

He gasped.

The cold returned.

Me.

And sound.

The man wants me.

For what? To be what?

Jesus, he thought, and turned again, ran again.

To hunt.

Insane; it was absolutely insane. This isn't the stuff of the real world (as he dodged a branch that clawed tenaciously for his eyes); this had nothing to do with serving meals and paying bills and making love and sitting in front of the television set, watching all those fake cops pretend to be real (as he tripped, spun, ran again through a clearing); this had nothing to do with him.

This was insane.

And it was o so sweet as it touched his cheek and *kissed* him.

He gasped and batted the feeling away, was forced to stop at the creek to take a clean breath, staring stupidly at the creek bed, seven or eight feet across. No clever footbridge here, no convenient rocks. It was narrower up by the main building, but he couldn't bring himself to walk that far. He was cold, too cold, and he was goddamn sick and tired of playing games with shadows. Of course, if he fell in he probably wouldn't notice a damn thing anyway; every square inch of him felt frozen solid, a surprisingly not unpleasant or uncomfortable sensation. It was almost as if the cold didn't exist anymore, which was a notion he understood those who froze to death experienced.

And who asked them? he wondered; who brought them back and asked them?

A moment's irritation, so close to renewed anger that he caught his breath and held it until he had to gasp to fill his lungs.

Hunting.

Raven's wings.

Jesus," he whispered, and flexed his right leg, flexed his left, and leapt from a standing position, landing on the other side as if he'd merely taken a long stride. He didn't slip, didn't slide, didn't lose a second's worth of balance. There was a brief sense of amazement before the irritation returned, and he stalked through a sparse covering of underbrush, found himself ten yards later facing the last of his seven cabins. He could barely see it in outline in the snow, but he knew it was there because, when he turned right on the faint depression that signaled the flagstone path, he could see the other ones growing by stages out of the dark the closer they came to the bulb burning harshly over the kitchen door.

He didn't run.

He didn't bother to check the cabin doors because he knew they were all locked.

It wasn't until he was only ten feet from the fence that he realized how he'd been behaving since his last shot. Not calmly, by any means, but somehow accepting.

That did make him stop.

It made him stare at his restaurant, so picturesque in the falling snow. Serene. Postcard photograph. Welcome to Maclaren's; wish you were here and the food's not bad either.

Distant; it seemed so distant.

A glance over his shoulder; nothing there.

A glance to the creek; nothing but the haze of light and snow.

A muffled rustling.

He turned again, hand reaching for the gun before remembering it was empty.

Nothing then but voice, loud and shrill.

He hurried through the gap in the fence and realized the kitchen door was wide open, the single light over the island block counter flickering off and on.

In there? he thought, alarmed; my god, is he in there?

Cautiously he moved onto the stoop, had a foot up on the threshold when something out of place distracted him. Checking to his right he saw a body on the ground, flecked with white. Mouth partly open, he stepped through the steam of his breath and hunkered down beside Julia Sanders.

A shuddering sound, not quite a moan, as his hand passed over his lips.

The voices.

He backed off as he rose, and thumped a heel against the stoop. He didn't think about bringing her inside, and didn't speculate on the cause, or the reason for, her death. He just looked toward the cabins and asked the man in black *why?*, before stepping into the kitchen and closing the door behind him.

The warmth hurt.

It stung, then burned in pulsing waves. Across his face, the feeling that stitches were being pulled out of fresh wounds. He pressed a snow-crusted glove to a cheek and sighed at the cold, soothing this time, numbing. Listening to an argument storming through the lounge. None of it made sense; the words were unintelligible. But the tone gave him certain knowledge that the man in black wasn't here.

Nevertheless he enlisted discretion as he pushed through the EMPLOYEES ONLY door and stood at the end of the bar. The trapdoor had been closed; the interior lights were still out. A curious tension in the twilight room made him narrow his eyes, perplexed and uneasy—a feeling of imminent suffocation, an oddly acute sense of oppression. Ken stood with his back to the window, rifle in hand, halfheartedly aiming it at someone near or in the restaurant. He couldn't see Mandy.

Trish was behind the bar, by the register. "Just shoot him!" she demanded, altogether too calmly.

Havvick vacillated between obedience and defiance. "He . . . he says it was an accident."

The girl laughed bluntly. "Tell me another, okay? Didn't you see her? Jesus Christ, shoot him!"

"Why?" Neil asked flatly, and they whirled, Trish not quite swallowing a startled scream, Ken not quite able to keep the rifle from pointing at Neil's chest until he recognized the face.

"Mr. Maclaren?" It was Willie. Child-voice. Frightened.

"Neil? For god's sake, do something!" Mandy. Angry. Frightened.

He eased behind the bar, right hand trailing across its polished surface, and walked more calmly toward the corner than his nerves told him he really felt. Trish backed away from the register, uncertain, a tic snapping at the corner of her mouth; she didn't speak while he stripped off his gloves, unbuttoned and removed his coat, reached over the bar and dropped them onto a stool, a medallion of ice falling to the floor and melting. He said nothing in turn. Felt them staring puzzledly, not quite fearfully, as he groped along a shelf until he found the box of ammunition. Felt his own tension bleed off, and felt the stress in the room, like crackles of static electricity popping brightly just beyond the limits of his vision. He reloaded as Ken told him at last, and increasingly boldly, what had happened while he'd been gone. How Willie had gone outside without telling anyone, he was supposed to be making goddamn coffee, for Christ's sake, and the next thing anyone knew, Julia was dead, sliced up with one of the cook's cleavers.

Willie was slumped dejectedly on the bottom stair, legs outstretched, a carving knife in his right hand, point aiming at the floor.

Mandy was up in the restaurant, against the far wall, watching him through the spider plants.

Trish said, "Shoot him," again. Her hands were flat on the bar top, and they were trembling.

"It was an accident," Willie claimed.

"Shut up," Ken ordered.

"He's going to kill us," Trish insisted, staring at Ennin. Hands jumping. "If we tie him up, he'll just get loose and kill us anyway." Pressing down on the bar. Thumbs tapping. "We can't tie him up. We have to shoot him, the police will understand, it's just self-defense."

"I was burying the mouse," Willie said as if she hadn't spoken. He looked at Ken. Unblinking. "I had to bury the mouse because . . . I don't know. I did."

"Fucking nuts," Ken said.

"Julia was going to hurt you." Ennin turned his head, looked at Neil.

"What?"

A fast nod. "Really, she was going to hurt you. She ran out with the cleaver, my best blade she stole from the kitchen and she knew she shouldn't have done that, and I grabbed her before she reached you and threw her away before she could hurt you." He looked back at Havvick. "She hit the wall before she could stop. The blade cut her. I didn't do it on purpose. I just wanted to get her away."

Trish opened her mouth to protest, to argue, to order, and Neil grabbed her shoulder. Hard. "One more time," he warned, deceptively low, "and you won't say it again."

"Hey!" Ken snapped.

She glared at him, furious, then scurried out from behind the bar to stand beside Havvick. Beside, and slightly behind, squeezed between him and the window, hands clasped and up against her chest. Ken didn't look at her, but he nodded as if to tell her she had done the right thing.

"Put the rifle down," Neil said, moving sideways toward the open flap. "Willie, put down the knife."

No one moved.

Swiveling the last stool around until he could sit and still face them, he eased up onto the leather seat and placed the revolver on the bar, rested a forearm, fingers tented over the butt. "Please," he said, more like a command. A look to Mandy; she hadn't moved. "Now. Both of you, please. Before someone else gets hurt."

Havvick snorted.

Sighing, Willie let the knife drop between his legs. It didn't topple; it rested against his right calf.

"Ken?"

After a moment's proof that he didn't have to do it, Ken placed the rifle on the table in front of him, stock toward him, barrel pointing at Ennin.

Neil nodded.

But the room didn't feel any more comfortable. Though the feeling of suffocation had dissipated, the tension somewhat lessened, the oppression remained. He had to snap away the temptation to go outside again, just to breathe.

Falling apart.

His eyes widened imperceptibly.

. . . falling apart.

He looked down at the floor, at his boots heeled around the brass ring near the bottom of the stool.

I'll be damned.

For the first time in a long time, there was a flash of satisfaction. Ironic, considering the circumstances, but it was a question at last answered.

"Well?" Ken demanded.

Then a small voice, forcibly calm, before he could answer: "Where were you, Neil? All this time, where were you?"

He looked at them all in turn without raising his head, then raised his head and leaned back. His hand didn't leave the gun. He made sure he could be able to see outside while, at the same time, keeping Willie in sight.

"Chasing him."

Havvick nodded, a hand waving in the air. "Right. And I don't suppose you've got his scalp to prove it?"

"I didn't say I caught him. I said I chased him."

Ken turned away in disgust, nudging Trish to one side. "Goddamn loser, man." He waved at the backyard. "All that time, and you couldn't even catch him."

"We heard shots," Trish said.

"I fired," Neil admitted. "Three or four times."

He waited; Havvick didn't bother to respond.

"If you were chasing him," the small voice said, Mandy's voice still behind the plants, moving closer, "how could you be over by the cabins?"

"I was, just a minute ago. I followed him down the creek, gave up when it was obvious I'd freeze to death before I even got close, so I crossed over and came up the path."

"He didn't shoot?"

"Nope. It was all me."

Should I tell them, he thought; should I tell them why I think he wants me alive?

No; they wouldn't believe it anyway, and to be honest, I'm not so sure I believe it myself.

"So you weren't there—"

"I already said."

"Oh no," Willie protested; a single shake of his head. "I saw you, Mr. Maclaren, honest. You were right there, right in front of me. Julia . . . she came out yelling, she wanted to keep you away from me because you were going to hurt me." He sniffed, picked up the end of his tie and twisted it around his fingers. "I saw you pulling out the

shotgun. You were there. You were going to shoot me."
He looked up, face twisted suddenly to stone. "Goddamnit, she's dead because you were going to *shoot* me!"

Neil shifted uneasily, less because of Ennin's abrupt
harsh anger than at the flicker of doubt he saw cross Havvick's face, the glance the cow boy gave to his fiancée.

"Look," he said, "this is getting us—"

Willie leaned forward, almost rose. "Vacation time is
over, Mr. Maclaren," he said. "I know what I saw."

There was no arguing with him, and no time to search
for an explanation. He just gave the cook a look, and
looked at the others. "The idea," he said, a lecturer's tone,
"is to make us fight each other."

"But he was there!" Willie insisted, not giving up, twisting around to plead his case to Mandy Jones.

"All he has to do is hang around long enough, keep us
confined—or make us believe we're confined—and let us
do the fighting for him." He sneezed. He pulled a handkerchief from his pocket and blew his nose. "He was
keeping me away."

"Sure." Ken faced him, settling on the narrow wainscoting sill, knowing it was too narrow and bracing himself
with feet and hands on knees so he wouldn't have to move,
spoil the pose. "And while he's at it, he's got fourteen tons
of bulletproof clothing on so we can't hurt him, and he can
still outrun you." A nod. "Sure."

"He was," Willie muttered sullenly. "He was."

"Are you saying we could have gone home any time we
wanted?" Trish said, incredulous. "Are you saying he
wouldn't have stopped us if we'd tried to leave?"

"Oh Christ," Ken said, sighing loudly. "He already did,
Trish. Christ, use your head."

"Oh."

"Yeah. Oh."

She put both hands to her head, fingers buried in her
hair. "But . . ."

Neil waited.

Ken rapped the pane with a knuckle, marking time, marking his impatience.

"But he killed Mr. Brandt," she said quickly, before Havvick could stop her. "And he can't know that we'll hurt each other. He can't know that, not for sure. What if we didn't?" Her hands fell to her sides, grasped her legs. "What if we just sat around and waited for someone to come help?"

A response was unnecessary.

He saw it in the way her expression required some kind of reason, and discovered something else she had already forgotten—the empty road, the dead telephones, the way the man in black moved from one place to another unseen and unheard. The tracks; it always came back to the tracks.

She tried to laugh, coughed, tried again and glared at Ken, who only shrugged his disdain for her half-baked theories, spoken and implied. An angry step toward him became a march through the tables until, halfway across the floor, she stopped and stared at Willie.

The cook looked up at her, suspicious.

"It couldn't have been him," she said quietly, pointing at Neil. "He wasn't wearing a black coat."

"I saw him" was all Willie would say.

"No." But gently.

"Aw, Christ," Havvick said.

"You were," Willie said to Neil. "And you made me hurt her." He started to rise, lost his balance, sat again. "You were there, and you made me hurt her."

"No." Trish smiled. "No."

"I saw!"

Her expression said, *poor little fella, you're crazy and you don't even know it, what a sap.*

Her voice said, "Willie, don't be silly."

Lower lip trembled, nostrils flared, feet scraped on the floor as Ennin lunged to his feet, the carving knife thrust toward Trish Avery's stomach. She backpedaled with a startled gasp, while Ken snatched up the rifle and put it to his shoulder.

Neil fired once, at the ceiling.

They froze.

"See what I mean?" he said, and put the gun back down.

I want to know why," Mandy asked, coming away from the corner to the top of the stairs.

"Psycho," Havvick offered solemnly. "Guy gets his kicks watching other people go nuts."

"Oh god," whispered Trish. "Oh god, oh god."

Then, out of nowhere: "My lord, look at your face!"

She stood in front of him before he realized she had moved, took the side of his jaw with a firm finger and turned his head toward the feeble backyard glow. A sympathetic inhalation. The hand dropped away, and he managed a halfhearted shrug, told her it wouldn't kill him, just some scratches from an unexpected meeting with a stubborn tree. It looked worse than it was. Her eyes told him, as they examined his brow, that there were things up there a little bit more than mere scratches.

The carving knife was on the table, and Willie was at his side in a hurry, looking, frowning, making Neil swing between wanting to giggle at their seriousness and wanting to smack their faces off their heads.

"Miss Avery," the cook said over his shoulder, "where's the first-aid kit? From when you were fixing him up."

"It's okay," Neil insisted irritably.

Willie ignored him.

"I think it was put back behind the bar," she answered.

And Ken said, "It doesn't make any difference. You're not going to touch him."

They looked.

He had the rifle.

Without thinking, Neil started to move, checked himself and didn't even bother thinking about picking up his gun.

Havvick, a shadowy silhouette, said nothing, but Mandy and Willie each took a stool anyway, perching wordlessly on the edge while Trish slipped into a chair and clasped her hands on the table, tossed the hair from her eyes. She looked as if she wanted to approve, but didn't yet understand where her boyfriend was heading, and if, when he got there, it would have been worth the trip.

"Pay attention," Ken said. "I got it figured."

A low rumbling became a roar as snow loosened on the roof and sent an avalanche over the eaves.

The temperature rose a few degrees as the storm wound down, just a few drifting flakes, and a mist gathered over the surface of the creek, unmoved by the wind that stalked the tops of the trees.

Mandy crossed her arms under her breasts, leaned back and dared him to convince her.

Neil wondered what universe the kid was living in, if he had heard a single word since Neil had returned. But by his stance, he knew that cow boy was both confident and frightened. A move in the wrong direction would put a bullet in his head.

He felt it then himself—an almost subliminal vibration of fear that settled below his waist, made him tense his groin and swallow.

Not cop-frightened, not the fear that someone might without warning turn into a bad guy.

Another fear.

He didn't know what it was yet, but it made his mouth go dry, and he had to swallow several times more to keep himself from choking, from retching.

Pay attention.

There are two answers, Havvick told them, shifting as if he wanted to pace and didn't dare, looking for a moment as if he wanted to apologize, and didn't dare.

The first one is easy, the one they had started with. There are two guys out there. Like Neil said earlier, the

Holgate brothers, dividing the action between them. One works the north side of the road, the other works the creek and woods. Same coats, same hats, bulletproof vests like he'd said before, and with the snow and the dark, even a pair of dissimilar brothers like Curt and Bally could be made to seem alike by people too frightened to take a good look. The idea is money. Sooner or later, someone is going to offer money, or a demand will be made. Not all that hard, since Havvick himself wasn't exactly living off food stamps, and the radio man was probably richer than they thought. All the Holgates have to do is wait. Sooner or later. Bound to happen. Which is why the old fart was killed—he really had recognized one of the brothers. They didn't count on the rest. But it's no skin off their backs, as long as they get what they want. And when they get it, they disappear. No one can prove it was them, now or later.

"And you're in on it," he said to Neil.

Who coughed, laughed, couldn't stop laughing even when Havvick jabbed the barrel toward him, making sure he could see the kid's finger on the trigger.

What you got, Havvick said to the others, is a guy used to be a cop, now runs a two-bit bar and restaurant, for god's sake. No money in that. He isn't old, but his pension sure isn't going to buy him anything decent in Florida or wherever it is old farts go when they're waiting around to die.

"You're out of your mind," Mandy said sadly.

"So tell me," Ken countered, "why he isn't dead? He goes out there three times, and that guy doesn't shoot at him once. Brandt goes once and gets his head blown off."

"Don't be—"

"He has a gun, right? He uses it, and the rifle, and doesn't hit the guy once." His smile was cold, matched the draft snaking through the lounge. "Nobody is that bad a shot. I was with him, remember? On the road?" Easing back to the window. "Think, okay? He sits around, he does something, he sits around, he does something else. Like . . . like he's waiting for a signal. Like he already knows what's going to happen next."

Neil couldn't understand why they were listening to this drivel without going for his throat. He couldn't understand it. He supposed, he hoped, it was because they were tired. So tired their brains weren't functioning properly. It had to be. He kept his fingers tented over the revolver. "You didn't hit him, either," he reminded him.

"Maybe I didn't, maybe I did," Ken answered. "Just because there wasn't blood on the ground doesn't mean I didn't."

No, Neil thought; it wasn't falling apart, it was exploding.

Trish yawned.

"And," Ken said with deafening soft finality, "Willie saw him."

"I did," Ennin agreed, almost apologetically. Almost, but not quite. "I'm not wrong. I saw him. He made me hurt Julia."

Neil couldn't believe it, couldn't credit what he'd heard. Willie Ennin taking sides against him. Mandy Jones suddenly, ominously, silent. "So what are you going to do? Wait for the cops to show up and turn me over to them? Tell them I'm the one who made you shoot Hugh Davies in the back?"

Uncertainty lowered Havvick's shoulder, lowered the rifle, though not all the way.

"I don't know," he said, "because there's the other thing."

Jesus.

Dear Jesus, make him stop, give me strength.

"That he's not real."

Pay attention.

Mandy hopped off the stool, ignoring Ken's backward movement and the raising of the rifle as she threw up her hands. "You *are* out of your mind," she declared.

"Somehow," Havvick said, distaste all too clear, "I'm not all that shook by what a hooker has to say."

When she gaped, turned and took an angry pace toward Neil, Ken's laugh turned her around again. "Julia told me, okay? Don't get all bent out of shape."

Trish stared. "Really?"

"Not real," Willie said, half to himself. He swiveled his seat around, leaned his elbows on the bar. Shook his head. "Has to be real, Mr. Havvick. He killed people."

Mandy's cheeks flushed, but Neil couldn't look at her, not now. Havvick was spiraling slowly out of control, the same loss he'd felt himself, out there in the woods.

"Tracks," Ken said simply, and looked right at Neil. "You showed me where he stood, remember? After the sonofabitch torched my van? I saw what you saw, you know. You think I'm stupid or something, but I saw it. He didn't leave any tracks."

"Kenny, stop it," Trish interrupted, a mild scolding. "We already went over that."

"Enough firepower to stop a bull, and he . . . went away."

"Kenny!"

"Oh Christ, get real," Mandy said acidly. She looked at

Neil. "It's bad enough, that other thing about some idiotic money scheme of yours, but this is . . . this is insane."

"It's his father," Ken said.

Mandy laughed.

A second, two, and Trish laughed as well.

Willie giggled.

A cloak of ice settled over Neil's shoulders, a great wrestling with his will to keep him from shouting, from reaching for the gun, from appealing to Mandy not to believe this damn fool. He took his time sliding off the stool, a provocative sideshow of stretching arms and rolling shoulders, using the momentary distraction to pull the revolver close to the padded lip of the bar. When he faced Havvick again, he took a deep breath to rein his temper and made sure the kid knew it. Felt it.

His lips parted.

Closed.

Parted again: "I don't believe in ghosts."

"Kenny, please."

"It's simple, Neil. Your old man is pissed. You went after the guys who killed him, and you didn't get them. You chickened out. You fucked up. And then you went and quit. So he comes back, right? He wants you, not us. That's why you're not dead. He wants you real slow."

Willie spun again. "I—"

Ken cautioned him with the rifle. "Brandt says he thinks he knows who the guy looks like, right? You say the guy's Neil. Or looks like Neil, right?" Then he smiled, *so figure it out for yourself,* and said, "I don't believe in ghosts either, but it looks like I have to, don't I." His voice caught. He cleared his throat. "I don't want to."

"Kenny, stop it!"

Neil heard it, then—the opening notes of a hysterical song, each one just a little higher than the one before it.

"We're in here, doing things we don't even dream about."

It wouldn't be long before the notes blended to a scream.

"Julia was right. About the raven, I mean."

He braced himself, not knowing if the kid would shoot now, shoot later after his tirade, shoot at all.

"And it's all your fucking fault!"

Trish put a restraining hand on Ken's hip, and he slapped it away, scowling. Trembling. Checking the yard, shaking his head.

Neil leaned a hip against the bar, the gap just behind him. "Ken, I hope to hell you can hear yourself. Because you're scaring more than Trish here." His tongue felt dry, throat lined with pebbles. "What about the Holgates?"

Ken's head began to tremble, evidence of great effort. "Shut up," he said. The rifle's barrel wavered. "It's all your fault."

"The Holgates makes more sense than ghosts, you know."

"Shut. Up."

Neil did.

He sensed rather than saw the finger tighten around the trigger.

Mandy stepped away slowly, one leg crossing over the other, watching Ken steadily while she brushed by Ennin, watching Neil as she backed around the corner and finally stopped. "So what do you want him to do?" she asked calmly.

Out of the line of fire, Neil thought; a very practical woman.

"Don't," Ken snapped at her. "Don't talk to me like I'm him." He nodded sharply at Willie. "You can think I'm crazy or not, I don't give a shit, who the hell cares about a fucking whore anyway, but don't . . . don't talk to me like that."

She was rigid. Not breathing.

Neil could see it on her lips, straining: *cow boy*.

Trish started to get up. "Kenneth, that's enough."

Without looking, he backhanded her across the mouth, knuckles slamming her down and over the chair to the floor. Not looking when she cried out, not looking when she couldn't get herself untangled from the spindle legs, not looking the least bit contrite.

He looked terrified.

"You," he said to Neil, "are going back outside."

Neil shook his head.

"You're going outside," Havvick repeated. "Let him do what he wants, that's not our problem anymore. Let him do what he wants, get him the hell off our backs." He started to move between the tables, changed his mind suddenly and moved back to the window. "Just get out, Neil." He used the rifle as a pointer. "Get out."

"If," Mandy said, "that man didn't kill him before, all that time, why should he do it now?"

Havvick whirled on her. "You on his fucking side?" he shouted. "You his goddamn birthday present or something, that why you came way the hell out here?"

Trish whimpered, pushing herself frantically on her buttocks until she came up against a booth.

Mandy shook her head in an eloquent display of disgust.

Havvick fired.

Trish screamed.

Neil grabbed the revolver, ducked and whirled around through the bar's gap, paused as he slapped through the swinging door and saw Mandy standing there, a hand flat against her chest, the only sign she was alive her tongue darting out, in, out again to wet her lips.

She wasn't even blinking.

Then he was gone as Havvick snapped his head around, all the noise erupting behind him, standing in the dark hallway and telling himself the nightmare couldn't possibly get any worse before shoving into the kitchen—his office was a dead end, in more ways than one—listening for pursuit, keeping the long butcher-block counter between him and the other door.

Waiting for the next shot.

His left hand in a hard fist while he tried to decide what the hell to do next.

In the snow was out of the question for now, his coat was back in the lounge; in here, on the other hand, he was pretty well trapped and there was no place else to go.

He heard Mandy yelling.

If it came to it, if he was in fact forced out of the building, he could probably make it to one of the cabins. It wasn't perfect, but it would be safer than trying to go somewhere else. Not the house; that would be the first place cow boy would look.

He heard Trish yelling.

And not the road. The man in black was out there, working his own intention. Whatever that was.

A glass broke.

you know

Something, maybe a chair, turned over.

He didn't hear Willie, and that made him wonder.

Then a shadow filled the service window, and he dropped below the counter, pressed his back against it, cursing silently when Havvick fired without taking aim, drilling a gouge from the center of the wood, splinters in the air, the sound too loud, putting him inside a large toneless bell. Above his head, the pots and utensils swayed.

And the fluorescent bulb still flickered.

"Son of a bitch!" Havvick yelled.

Another chair toppling; another glass breaking.

"Just keep her the hell away from me, Trish," Ken ordered. Quieter after that, trying to be reasonable. "C'mon, Neil, don't be stupid. Get the hell out."

Trish and Mandy, fighting?

Where was Willie?

Neil crawled to his left to the end of the island counter, the kitchen door directly opposite. Frost around the edges of the panes. He couldn't see out; the glass was a mirror that showed him the room behind him. Flickering as the light did. He wasn't there; his reflection wasn't there.

"Ken," he said, twisting around to sit again.

Cow boy didn't fire.

"Ken."

"Please, Neil. Please get out."

Flickering.

Neil looked across the room, started when he saw someone staring at him, relaxed when he realized it was only his reflection in the convex face of the oven's gleaming enamel front panels. Distorted. Not really human at all. For his own peace of mind he raised a hand to it, saw it shimmer, and smiled.

"Neil, for Christ's sake."

"Ken," he said, looking up at the ceiling.

"Neil, damn it, if I come in there, you're gonna shoot me."

He grinned. "Nah. I'm gonna bake you a cake." He sobered instantly. "Kenny, it's not my father. The rest may be right, but he is not my father."

There was silence.

Buzzing in the light.

Then: "He wants you."

Surprising himself, Neil gave him the truth. "I know."

Silence again.

The whisper of a wind sliding across the window by Willie's desk, the door.

"Who . . . who is he?"

Neil almost said *I don't know.*

Instead: "No tricks?"

No hesitation: "No tricks."

Pay attention.

Watch the news, Ken, read the papers, and listen to them, the people, the way they talk when the cops are done inside a house, or an apartment, or a store, it doesn't make any difference where the hell they are. The blood's always there. And the bodies. Sometimes just a couple; sometimes too damn many for the bags they brought with them, for the ambulances waiting at the curb. And sometimes, not always, there's a survivor, you've seen what they look like, and he swears on his mother's grave while they're hauling him away that he doesn't remember what happened, or that he lost his temper, or that he was drunk, or he was on drugs, or maybe he just didn't do it, you gotta believe me, it was someone else, not me, I wouldn't do something like that. Listen to the neighbors. Such a quiet kid, man, woman, girl. He helped my little girl across the street every day. She always found time to baby-sit when I had to work an extra shift. There must be some mistake, he wouldn't do anything terrible like that. He went to church.

Almost always it's at night.

Almost always, the neighborhood didn't hear a thing, if there was anyone around to hear.

Almost always, the one who's left, if there's anyone left, that is, he's put away for a long time, people picking at his mind, trying to learn, trying to find out what's going on in his head. Maybe he says something to them. You hear that maybe he says things got weird, time stopped or the world stopped or everything just stopped and things got weird. Maybe he says the Devil made him do it.

Maybe he did.

It doesn't matter. They don't listen.

A nice boy.

He goes to church.

A nice family; they laughed all the time.

Nice bunch of people. Not perfect. Who the hell is? They must've been on dope or something, go figure.

Listen to them, Ken, because later, hardly ever on the same day, you hear that sometimes, once in a great while, these people the cops or neighbors found, they actually killed each other, and sometimes it was just one, just two.

Ordinary people.

Nice folks.

They go to church.

They don't go to church.

What difference does it make?

They're dead.

Pay attention.

Once in a while it isn't drugs or liquor or tempers at all. Once in a while it's him.

It was quiet in the kitchen, in the lounge.

A listening kind of quiet.

Small sounds from the building, hardly any noise at all, an adjusting against the wind, a faucet dripping slowly, the creak of a chair as someone shifted in it.

Small sounds.

Not loud as Neil waited for Ken to laugh, to call him nuts, to try to shoot him through the counter walls. He wasn't sure himself; it had all come to him as he spoke, and as he glanced out the door window to the black-ice early morning. Thinking as fast as he could.

If that's true, then who is he, Mr. Maclaren? What does he do? Why does he do it?"

Small sounds.

People stirring.

I don't know who he is, Ken. I swear to God, I don't know."

Then what the *hell* is he?"

Fairy dust
raven's wings

A hunter."

Suddenly weary, he sagged, head lowered, staring blindly at his legs.

Urgent whispering in the other room.

He didn't know, couldn't tell, if what he had said was the perfect truth. Parts might be wrong. But not all of it. He had seen too much now, watched the man in black too long, not to believe, though not without shrieking denials back there where some light still clung to his mind. But that wasn't important, that place where the light dwelled. It was a false light. The light that made masks out of people's faces.

It was the other part that mattered.

The part that wasn't screaming that convinced him he was right.

And he knew, when the whispering stopped, that they believed it too.

The clearing of a throat: "Neil, you gotta go out there, man. If you stay here, we're gonna die, and shit, I don't want to die, y'know?"

Tell me about it, Neil thought.

Tell me about it.

"Ken, listen. If we figure out who he is . . . what he is—I mean, what sort of creature he is, not a real man—maybe we can figure out a way to take care of him."

Havvick snorted. "You believe that?"

"I believe he's not natural, if that's what you're asking."

His eyes closed.

He held his breath.

Please.

"No," Ken said, talking to someone else. "He's in there, behind that wood thing."

"Mr. Maclaren?" It was Trish. She sounded pained, but he couldn't tell if it was physical or emotional. "Mr. Maclaren?"

The ceiling light buzzed.

Snapped.

Went out.

"Shit," said Havvick.

Not truly dark. A faint glow from the other room, from the yard, caught in highlights on the hanging pots, on the stainless steel. A glow from the tiny bulbs on the urn Willie forgot to shut off. It didn't take long for vision to adjust.

But it was dark enough.

Vague outlines only; nothing more than that, and through most of the room, much less.

"Mr. Maclaren, if you go out there, and you know he's not going to hurt you, not if he hasn't before, if you go out there, Kenny'll give you money. All you want."

Hell.

Oh hell.

"That'll send him away, I know it will."

Neil closed his eyes again, opened them and ordered himself to pay attention. Not to the girl. To the room, the things around him. There must be something, some way, that he just wasn't seeing.

"Mr. Maclaren?"

He laid the gun against his chest. Gripped it, regripped it. It was possible, just possible, that a shot in their direction would scare them, make them run. If not, Ken would fire back, but in the dark he'd fire wildly, and rapidly; he was too scared to think or aim straight. And once the rifle was empty, Neil would be able to leap up and . . . do what? Rush them? Take them prisoner?

"Mr. Maclaren, if you don't do it, you know we're going to have to hurt you, or kill you. We're going to have to throw you out anyway, dead or not, to show him there's no reason to stay here anymore."

He exhaled loudly; it wasn't a sigh.

Happy birthday to me, he sang silently to himself; happy birthday to me.

Well, Mac, it looks like I screwed up again.

But the man in black wasn't his father.

"Mr. Maclaren?"

A hinge creaked softly, and he looked right, looked left, testing for imagination and knowing it wasn't. One of them had come in, using the dark, using the voice. He held the gun tighter and looked for something that would assure him he'd be able to use it on people he knew. Hurt first, dead if they had to, she had said; that's what they wanted, but they didn't want to die. If he hadn't been the target, he would have laughed.

Slowly he shifted, peered around the island to the EM-PLOYEES ONLY door, and he mouthed an oath because there wasn't enough light to see by. He thought he could make out its outline, but he couldn't be sure. And if he stared at it long enough, things would be moving there that weren't there at all. He blinked. Nothing moving there, nothing but air between him and the wall. He eased up onto his heels, hunkered, and turned toward the hallway door, hidden around the counter's other corner.

Listened.

Heard nothing.

A creak from above; something shifting on the roof. Then a muted rumbling as more snow cascaded over the eaves.

Whispering in the lounge.

Why the hell, he wondered, did he call it a lounge? It was a bar, for crying out loud; just a small country bar.

The scrape of a sole on the tile floor.

God, he thought; please, God, no.

Hushed: "Mr. Maclaren?"

He made his way to the far end of the counter, put his back against it, ran his fingers over the gun, feeling the metal, smelling the cold of it, maybe smelling the powder of already expended ammunition. Breathing through his mouth to lessen the sound. Close to grunting when he finally turned the gun around to use the butt as a club.

Hushed: "Please?"

If he said anything, they'd know where he was; if he tried to open one of the doors on the island's face, they'd hear it.

They knew where he was anyway.

Except for whoever was crawling across the floor. Behind the butcher-block island; yes. But not precisely where. In the middle, at one of the corners. A hell of a chance to take; after all, he had a gun, he was the quarry, he was cornered. He didn't think it was Ken, he liked the rifle too much, he'd still be at the service window, hoping for a shot.

Willie.

And his carving knife.

A hell of a chance.

Nes would have been proud, and he wished he knew on which side the gambler would have placed his money.

Neil!"

It was Mandy.

"Neil, watch—"

The arm came in a blur around the corner, white arm and silver blade, the point slamming deep into the counter door, taking part of Neil's upper arm with it. He yelled at the pain, grabbed the wrist before the knife could be pulled out of the soft wood, shifted and yanked and dragged Willie around to the floor on his back.

Havvick fired.

Sparks off the oven top.

Ennin moaned and kicked, thrashed his free arm ineffectually, couldn't escape because Neil had planted a knee in his stomach, a hand around his throat. White suit and no light, it was like fighting a man with no head. He pressed down and heard the cook gag, felt the struggle cease almost immediately. A groan.

"Go *on!*" Trish said.

"Like hell," Ken answered.

Neil leaned down and close, to be sure the cook could see his face. Brought the revolver up to be sure he could see that too.

Willie stared at him.

No vacations in those eyes.

Anger; betrayal.

Neil drew back his lips against the fire in his arm, shook

his head *it wasn't me, you damn fool* and released the throat, reached around and tugged the blade from the counter door. Another look, a command, *you're not going to hurt me,* drawing the hammer back for emphasis, put his full weight on the knee still in Willie's stomach and withdrew it just as fast. Ennin rolled immediately onto his side, curled, retched loudly.

"Ken, either put the rifle down or get the hell out of my place."

No answer.

"Damnit, Havvick, I'm not kidding around."

No answer.

Willie moaned, didn't move.

Neil kept his back to the kitchen island as he sidled around the corner, straining to see if someone else had entered the room during the brief struggle. He could see the hallway door. A look to his right and he could see the rectangular service window, no shadows there, no rifle.

He smelled blood.

He couldn't feel it.

Pushing away from the counter at the count of five, not really able to run because his legs were still too stiff from crouching, trying to keep his feet from touching the floor, making noise, pushing through the door and freezing low in case Havvick had the brains to put a bullet through the lounge door.

Willie moaned, loudly.

There was a shot.

Neil flinched, cocked his head when Trish screamed a begging, and pushed hurriedly through into the other room, half bent over, ready to drop, squinting against the outside light. Then rising slowly.

The room appeared empty until he heard quiet sobs around the corner. Staying behind the bar, he moved forward, revolver back in a firing grip.

"It has two," he heard Mandy say, bloodless, cold. "Breathe or sneeze and it goes in your ear."

"Please," Trish begged, weeping.

He reached the register and saw them, wasn't sure exactly what he saw until Mandy looked at him. And didn't smile.

Ken was still at the service window, facing him, cheek pressed hard against the shelf, rifle on the floor at his feet. Mandy stood behind him, holding a small gun, a tiny gun, at the back of his ear. Trish had moved to the far end, hands in a struggling mime of despair at her waist, her chest, across her face, back to her waist.

"Please," she pleaded.

Mandy's hair was atangle. A large welt blotched her right cheek, and her dress was torn raggedly from hem near to hip up her right leg. When he showed her the revolver, she jabbed the derringer cruelly into Havvick's skull, a warning or retaliation that ignored his yelp, and moved away, past Neil, not speaking, looking straight ahead. A bruise between her eyes, neckline torn to expose most of her breasts. At the open flap she paused and dropped the gun on the bar, then reached out to the metal rack and pulled down her coat. Put it on. And stood there, facing the far wall. Stroking the fur collar under her chin.

"Don't," Neil said calmly when Ken tried to rise.

"Oh please, Mr. Maclaren," Trish said, rushing forward, putting a hand on the small of Kenny's back. "Please don't."

Face streaked with tears and makeup; despite her voice, the ratcheting catch of her sobs, she looked like a woman suffering too many damning years.

Ken just stared at him.

Willie, faintly, moaned.

Trish leaned over Ken's back, not touching, protecting, but she stuttered too much to be able to beg again.

"For Christ's sake," Havvick said, looking up at her without turning his head. "Jesus, knock it off. He's not going to go shoot me."

She asked him with a hand waving weakly.

Neil shook his head.

A backward step, and she scrubbed at her cheeks with the backs of her hands. One by one. Wiping them on her hip.

"Stand up," Neil said.

"Told you," Ken said to Trish, straightening, brushing his palms down the front of his shirt.

Neil shifted his weapon to his left hand and extended his arm, aimed the gun at Havvick's mouth. "Maybe," he said, "I lied."

Ken's astonishment lasted barely long enough for the word before he began to blink rapidly, breathe in shallow gulps, the muscles at the side of his neck straining. "Look, Neil—"

"This is *my* place. I don't give a sweet damn what you think will stop our outside friend, but you're not going to chase me out of *my* place."

"Look—"

"I am." Arm steady, the gun an extension of his fingers, nothing more. "And what I see, you don't want to know."

sweetness

Neil blinked.

Indignation narrowed Havvick's eyes, thinned his lips as he stared at the mouth of the gun and tried to think of something else to say. Something to fight back with that wouldn't pull the trigger.

He failed.

"Sit."

Trish instantly skittered around the bar to drop onto a stool, hand still in motion; Ken reached down for the rifle and changed his mind with a sickly smile when the gun followed him without wavering, following him back up and around to a seat beside the girl, staring at the bottles or maybe, Neil thought, at his reflection and seeing . . . what?

His injured arm burned.

He looked right, down at the bar, up to Mandy's face. "That's your protection?" Amused disbelief.

"They're usually close enough that I don't need a cannon."

Makes sense, he thought.

"You're all right?"

She shook her head; she nodded; she shrugged and settled the coat over her chest. When she dropped her hand, it parted slightly, and she shrugged again. "I'll live" was all she said.

With no place to sit, he leaned against the register to take some weight from his legs, and tried to see what damage had been done to his arm. The shirt was torn, but he couldn't see the flesh. The wound was there; he could feel it. Grimaced when he flexed to see if the blade had gone into muscle and doubted it. What made him uneasy, however, was the blood. He couldn't feel it, and it should have been running down his arm, dripping from his fingertips. It was no minor scratch. Willie had slashed rather than stabbed him as he'd pulled away. Had the cook been closer to the corner, had his reach been a bit longer, the knife would have gone straight into his chest. The image made him queasy. He coughed, and brought his hand up, felt the queasiness again when he saw the blood drying on his palm, in the cracks of his knuckles.

It was, almost comically, reassuring.

"I'll get the kit," Mandy offered.

"Stay put," he told her gently, noting how Ken tensed at her voice and Trish leaned away without leaving the stool. "I want everybody calm for a change, okay?" He arched his spine away from the register for temporary comfort, settled back. "Willie?"

No answer.

"Willie, you all right?"

A muffled groan, and he assumed the answer was yes.

"Come out when you're ready. Nobody's going to hurt you. It's over."

Another groan.

He squeezed the bridge of his nose, rubbed his eyes, and wasn't surprised to find traces of grit there. Now that he wasn't running, hiding, trying not to get killed, he was more tired than ever, and more than ever needed not to be. A point of colored light by the bottles brought with it the temptation to crank up the big bands again, give the room a semblance of normality, perhaps a shield against the menace prowling the woods, in the snow.

Damn.

He looked outside quickly.

No one there.

The snow had stopped falling.

"Pay attention," he said.

A twist of pain made him grunt.

Mandy was out of her seat and behind the bar before he could stop her. She rooted around the lower shelf until she located the first-aid kit and thumbed it open, the lid cracking against the bar top, too much like a shot.

Sorry, she mouthed.

A pair of scissors in one hand, the other resting on his shoulder, she began to cut away his sleeve.

"Assuming what I said before is right," he said to Ken, to Trish, "it's pretty obvious that the weapons we've got here aren't going to do us much good."

"No shit," Havvick muttered, but without acid.

"And unless you just happen to have some holy water or a cross in your purse, Trish, I can't even begin to think what we can use."

The sleeve fell away.

Cool air against his skin.

"What about me?" Mandy muttered, picking up a bottle of Merthiolate.

He smiled.

She grinned.

"Then what are we going to do?" Trish asked. She sounded numb. Too much in too short a time that seemed like a lifetime. If there was any fight left, it would have a struggle breaking loose.

His chin stabbed upward as Mandy liberally applied the disinfectant, and he sucked in air, held his breath until the burning dulled.

"Sorry," she muttered. Automatic. She didn't feel a thing.

"Yeah."

"Look, we know what he's up to, right?" Ken's hands were on their sides on the bar top, looking as if they needed to grab something more than simply air. "So why don't we just take the guns, the knives, whatever, and lock them away someplace. You gotta have a safe, right? We lock them in there, we can't kill each other anymore."

"Then?" Trish said.

"Dawn's only a couple of hours away. We wait. When the sun's up, he goes away and we get the hell out of here."

"What if he doesn't go?"

Ken's disgust closed his hands. "Those . . . those times, Neil, you talked about. You know."

He nodded. "Far as I know, it's pretty much always at night, yes."

He stiffened yet again when Mandy positioned a pad over the wound and began to wrap it in gauze.

Ken looked at Trish, *see? stop asking stupid questions,* and brushed a sleeve under his nose. "No sweat. Besides," he reminded her, oddly calmly, "it isn't us he's after, right?"

She looked doubtful, and perplexed, and he rolled his eyes as he looked away, turning the stool slightly so he could see the snow and creek outside. "Christ," he whispered. "Christ."

"Is he right?" Mandy said, sealing the gauze with a strip of surgical tape.

Neil couldn't do anything else but nod.

"But . . ." She stepped away with a pat to his arm and frowned. "I thought he was after you."

He was, but at the moment Neil didn't know why, didn't know what he had done. The only thing he knew, what he didn't speak aloud for fear of setting Havvick off again, was that the man in black didn't want him dead. Not yet.

A thought: maybe never.

By degrees of light and shadow Ken's head turned around.

"If, like you said, he's a hunter . . ."

Neil watched him. Cruelty in the eyes, sly cruelty born of triumph.

". . . he wants a trophy."

"Like Nester and the raven," Trish blurted, brightening, gasping at her inappropriate reaction and lowering her head, averting her face.

A smile on Ken's face. Or at least a pulling movement of his lips. Neil wasn't sure which.

"You."

Neil couldn't breathe. His lungs worked, his mouth was open, but he still couldn't breathe.

Half a smile remained as Havvick casually left his seat, nodded to himself as he looked out the window, and strolled, actually strolled down to the end of the bar.

"Neil," Mandy said softly, urgently.

"Tell me something, cop," Ken said, stepping around to the opening, looking along the bar's length, looking down at the floor. At the rifle. Equidistant between them. "In those stories, was there ever anyone missing?"

"Don't," Neil said. No details required.

"You know what I mean." A step forward. "What do they call it, someone unaccounted for?"

"Don't."

The air shimmered.

Maclaren's vanished.

A dusty street, scattering pedestrians, horses rearing, wagons fleeing.

draw, you no good son of a bitch.

Bootheels. Spurs. Dust devils. Wind.

draw

Step.

"I used to think all those TV shows, those stupid movies, they were bullshit, Neil. Monsters and ghosts, vampires. Stuff like that's for suckers. You can't see it, touch it, feel it, it isn't real."

Step.

"Kenny?"

"Quiet, honey."

Step.

"It's amazing what you can learn when you don't want to die."

Neil raised the gun. Slowly.

Ken hesitated, but the smile didn't. Lopsided. Just this side of a sneer, this side of a dare.

"But I ain't gonna be like those other guys, man." He stabbed a thumb toward Trish. "We're not ending up in some funny farm someplace, and we're not going to jail. Soon as your buddy gets his trophy, leaves us alone, I ain't saying a goddamn word. Trish and I, we spent the whole night in bed. Neil Maclaren? Never heard of him."

"Don't," Neil said.

"The truce is over," Ken Havvick said.

Don't, Neil thought, prayed, begged, commanded, as Havvick winked boldly at his girl and reached down for the rifle.

Mandy picked up the derringer, cocked the second hammer.

It wasn't enough.

Havvick smiled.

you aren't going to shoot me

The kitchen light flared on.

Ken jerked upright, startled at the glared intrusion, scowled at the service window and suddenly threw up his hands as Willie Ennin launched himself through from the other side, screamed hoarsely when the serrated carving knife penetrated the hollow at the base of his throat.

He fell with Willie atop him, arms and legs thrashing blindly, while Neil backed away instinctively, half poised to run, yet unable not to watch the futile struggle on the floor, unable to believe it when Trish screamed as Ken screamed, and scrambled over the bar, fell to her knees and grabbed for Willie's hair, grabbed for his arm, finally climbed-fell over them both and landed on her rump, snatched up the rifle, shrieked as she put it against Willie's temple.

And pulled the trigger.

On her knees before the retort, the explosion, had faded, on her knees and facing Neil. Sweater dark-stained, hair over her eyes, rifle held tightly against her waist and aimed at his heart. Haggard. Panting. Wide-eyed with rage.

"I don't know if it's still loaded," she said hoarsely.

There was no reluctance involved; Neil lowered his gun.

She looked down then as he did, to the blood spilling between her knees over the floor.

She gagged.

Mandy swayed as if to move, and he slowly, very slowly, gestured her to stay exactly where she was.

Trish spat, spat again, rocked back to her heels, spittle clinging to her chin, rocked awkwardly to her feet and came toward him.

"Trish," he said.

She stabbed the rifle at him like a bayonet, and he gave way without argument. Backing up, using his left hand, his gun hand, to guide him along the bar to the gap. Mandy was already through and edging toward the center of the room. Her hands were empty; he didn't know where she had put the derringer. But it was just a glimpse. Maybe he'd missed it. At the moment he had to concentrate on Trish Avery, on her lips forming soundless words, on the unsteady aim of the rifle, on the way she followed him, drunkenly, until he thumped against a chair, skirted it and its table, and watched as she pulled her coat from the stool where someone had dropped it before. Obeying when she signaled again to put the revolver in his pocket. Thinking he ought to say something to her, try to draw her gently out of the shock that had made her a robot, try to make her understand that . . . that it was self-defense that murdered

Willie. Or it wasn't really her. Or it wasn't really any of them and that going out now was too dangerous to consider.

He said nothing.

And he didn't try to stop her when she stepped up into the restaurant and finally released one hand long enough to wave him and Mandy into the nearest chairs.

Jesus, he thought.

At the door she hesitated.

When she turned around, she had no face, and she had no face when she put the rifle on the display counter and pulled on her mittens, settled her beret and fussed it into a position she liked. She glanced around as if checking to be sure she hadn't forgotten anything, then opened the door.

"Kenny," she called, "I'll see you tomorrow night."

The door stayed open when she left.

When he was sure, really sure, she wasn't coming back, he hurried up out of the lounge. Not running. A cautious stride. Forsaking the door for the time being to kneel into the last booth on the right and part the drapes. Mandy took the other side, fumbled with the stiff material and finally, with a curse, yanked the drawstring to free the window.

"Oh god," she said.

He was there.

Trish was already at the parking-lot opening in the fence, trudging determinedly through the snow, hands in her pockets, head down, following the tracks of the van, then walking around the vehicle itself. Out of sight for a few seconds that made Neil want to scream. Back in view in the middle of the road, not looking behind, to either side, kicking once to send a plume of white to precede her, one caught by the wind and blown back in her face.

She walked westward.

He was there.

She walked westward.
And was gone.

And he was there.

Neil swung his legs around until he was sitting, watched as Mandy did the same, and for his money, she was altogether too damn calm. He didn't look out the window. He didn't have to. Just as he knew he didn't have to chase after Trish. She would walk on, not stopping, talking to herself, until she either dropped or the sun came up. Going after her would be futile. Either way she was lost.

He frowned.

He shook himself, head and shoulders, provoking a guarded questioning look from across the table, but he waved her off, a left-hand shrug, and tried instead to put what he felt into words:

"I think . . . I think he's done."

As simple as that.

he's done, Mandy, you're safe, I'm not going to hurt you

She glanced out, looked at him, and there was a symphony there of infinite sadness and equally infinite regret, not of things as they might have been had things been different, but of things as they were.

No.

As they would be, when it was over, truly over.

"If he's done," she said, "why won't he go away?"

He had an answer that was no answer at all and so kept his silence. A touch of his finger to her wrist, cool skin, soft skin, and strength beneath it all, before he slid out of the booth and walked over to close the door. As he did he realized he hadn't really felt the cold; it was the hanging plants in what wind had slipped inside to touch them, and a fluttering of napkins on the tables.

He didn't look across the road.

"I'm it," he said to himself, and said it again when she

approached him. "Ken was right. I'm it. That's why he's still here."

His nose wrinkled then, a scowl as he realized that what he smelled was blood and the emptying of dead men's bowels. He forced himself to swallow, to take a breath through his mouth as he remembered all the dying.

"Are you all right?"

"Not a bit," he answered, smiling wryly. A move away from the door, out of the man in black's line of sight. A deep breath. A shake of his head. Once; just once. And a sigh.

She looked around him to the door, then into his face. "I think," she said, "this is the part where you rip off all my clothes, I rip off all yours, and we make passionate love on one of these tables." She parted the coat and examined her dress. "You don't have a hell of a lot of ripping to do."

He wanted to laugh. He wanted it badly.

She let the coat fall together.

He pulled the gun from his pocket, ignored her surprise, and made sure he still had something left in there to shoot with. That it wouldn't do him any good didn't faze him; it was, at the last, just something to do. Before he went outside.

"You can't," she said, grabbing his arm.

"If we stay in here . . . if *I* stay in here, the night will never end. Trophy, remember? I don't think he's the kind of guy who leaves the hunt without one."

The hand fell away. "I don't believe this. You're really going out there? Of your own free will?"

"Free has nothing to do with it, Mandy."

When she grinned, he blinked.

"That's the first time tonight you've called me by name."

Other times, other places.

No, he thought to her; *this* is when I rip off all your clothes.

He kissed her.

She held him.

He kissed her again and eased her away.

Then he turned around and picked up the rifle, checked with a wish and prayer, swallowed when he saw one bullet left, and tucked it under his left arm. He could have tried running, he supposed; left Mandy here and gone into the woods, up the hill or along the creek, but each time he pictured himself slinking through the trees, dodging boulders and deadfalls and sinkholes and burrows, he felt an odd sort of shame. Not a twinge of machismo, but a sense of things just not being right. If being a trophy was inevitable, he wasn't about to show the hunter his back.

Running was something he'd been doing for too damn long.

He approached the door, felt his knees weaken.

Dumb; this was dumb.

"Maclaren?"

"If you can stand being in here with them," he said, looking over his shoulder toward the bar, "you'll be all right until sunup."

"Oh, no, I'm not staying," she said. "No way in hell."

"But you can't go with me, you know that."

She raised an eyebrow. "You ever think maybe I'm the trophy he wants?"

He did laugh then. "Not for a minute."

"Me neither." She buttoned the coat, took her gloves from the pockets and pulled them on. Turned the collar up. Stroked the fur. Checked her feet, and he saw that she still hadn't taken off the boots. "I can't stay here, Neil."

She was right.

He knew she was right.

He opened the door and let her out, looked back and scowled when he realized that this wasn't his place anymore. It was different. He'd felt it before, felt it strongly now. *He* wasn't here anymore, and that made it a place owned by a stranger. As he closed the door behind him, habit testing the lock, he remembered a similar feeling hours ago, about the house.

A frown.

Something here wasn't right.

Somewhere back there he had missed something vital.

But when Mandy took his arm and they stepped down to the parking lot, he shook the misgivings away. And deliberately refused to look at the road, at the streetlamp. Instead he watched the snow, the tracks there of their flight, twisting around to follow them to where the van had been parked, a barb caught in his throat when he saw Nes's bicycle propped against the building. He swallowed; the barb was gone.

Across the snow-covered gravel, and a glance down the slope to the creek.

The mist had risen to a fog.

Temperature's going up, he thought, and inhaled deeply as a test, and realized that it wasn't nearly as cold now as it had been. Warm enough, in fact, to birth fog in the trees around his house, drifting it slowly toward him. Pale fog. Winter fog. Swirling lazily away from their legs as they walked up the slope to the road, closing lazily behind them. Knee-high now, and later, it would be waist-high, head-high, finally high enough to qualify as a true morning cover.

Later.

Not now.

H e was there.

She stopped at the log covered again with snow, and told him with a shake of her head that she wasn't going any farther.

"You'll be okay," he said.

"Yeah. I always am."

An awkward moment until she kissed him, quickly, tenderly, leaned away and said, "There's nothing on your face."

The blackened van a derelict ship.

He passed it without a touch, took a breath and stepped into the middle of the road.

The rifle was awkward, the gun too damn heavy, but the night had to end sometime, and it might as well be now.

When the fear hit him, a bludgeon between his shoulders, he stumbled, stopped and told himself that the dream could end any time now, any time it wanted, don't go on on his account; and when the wind began to blow, and didn't touch the rising fog, he told himself that he'd probably be in the papers a day or two from now, and his picture on television, and Maclaren's Food and Lodging would be a nine-day wonder for the idly curious and all the closet ghouls; when he looked back and couldn't see Mandy

Jones, it took most of him, almost all of him, to remember how she looked.

I'm not going.

The hell with you, I'm not going.

The hunter didn't move.

The wind took the snow and added it to the fog.

Neil raised the gun, cocked the hammer, and said, "I'm not going," as he fired.

The hunter didn't move.

I hit him.

Missed him.

He moved closer, feeling anger replace the fear, frustration replace the terror, firing at every step and wincing at every shot, swearing at the man in black, who didn't move an inch.

When the gun was empty, he threw it aside and took the rifle in both hands.

One bullet.

Useless.

But he wasn't going to run.

And he wasn't going to fire until he could see that goddamn face.

Why us?" he asked then, loudly, staring at the space beneath the hunter's hat.

The answer in the silence was too obvious to ignore—because they were there, nothing more.

Why me?" escaped before he could haul it back.

The answer.

In the silence.

He knew then what was wrong, what hadn't been right since the beginning, and for a moment the terror returned, the denials, the urge to flee. All of which subsided as soon as the man in black disappeared.

He was there, as always, just beyond the streetlamp light; and he was gone.

Neil stared at the place, looked side to side up the road, his face working until he understood that the trees were clearer now. Not as dark. More distinct.

Even as the fog and wind brought him to the shoulder and down into the shallow ditch, he felt the sun begin to rise.

He shook his head, and wiped his face, and dropped the rifle in the snow.

He climbed out of the ditch and held on to the streetlamp pole as he looked down at the ground where the man in black had stood. At the duster, and the hat, lying side by side in the snow.

He felt the grin before it started. Jesus Christ, what did I do? Felt the laugh before it came. What the hell did I do? Felt the wind for just a short time before he felt the wind die.

"Goddamnit, what the hell did I do?"

He circled the discarded clothing warily, looked deep into the woods, checked the branches overhead, looked back across the road. Crouched down and touched the cloth, poked at it with a finger, straightened and poked at it with a toe.

"Mandy!"

What the hell did I do?

And why the hell, he thought as he grabbed the coat up in anger, couldn't I have done it before, before all those people died?

He fingered the material, couldn't identify it, coarse and soft at the same time, light and heavy, warm and cool.

Why, he wondered, holding the coat in one hand, did Nes have to die? Julia? The others?

Because, he thought, they did.

Despite what Ken had thought, and Ceil, the man in black had no hidden agenda, no subtle secret motive. He wasn't an avenging angel and he wasn't a demon after souls and minds.

He was a hunter.

That's what he did.

"Jesus," he whispered.

A quick wind, a gust, and he shivered, started, nearly dropped the duster when he realized with a quick groan that he wasn't wearing a coat.

A look to the place where he had seen Mandy last, sliding into the snow's bleak fog.

She had known.

there's nothing on your face

A look to the place where his home was, his business was, where Rusty the poor thing would have to find someone else to feed her come spring.

He flexed his arm; there was no pain.

"Oh no," he denied, but he didn't drop the coat. "Oh no, this isn't . . . oh no."

He picked up the hat, turned it around, peered inside.

The wind whispered, stirred the fog.

He put the hat on, wished he had a mirror, wished he could see himself acting like a fool.

It fit.

He almost smiled.

He shook the snow off the duster and slipped one arm into a sleeve, paused and looked at Maclaren's one more time.

Slipped the other arm in and settled the coat around his shoulders.

It fit.

It was perfect.

He reached inside and found the shotgun's stock, drew back his hand and found it gloved in leather.

Mandy, he thought, will laugh at him, the Holgates will think he had finally lost his mind, and Jesus, what the hell would Mac think, if he could see his son now.

He didn't know.

But it was right, the last of the night.

It was right, and it was sweet.

And when it kissed his cheek, he closed his eyes and sighed.

The wind blew.

Snow fell on his shoulders and sparkled in the predawn light.

F*airy dust*

One last look behind; and he couldn't find his tracks.
As he walked into the woods, he pulled the hat low,
sniffed, and rolled his shoulders slowly.

R*aven's wings*

And wondered where he'd show up next.
Not that it mattered.
He'd be there soon enough.
And soon enough they all would know.